Educated at a co-educational Quaker boarding school, Rebecca Shaw went on to qualify as a teacher of deaf children. After her marriage, she spent the ensuing years enjoying bringing up her family. The departure of the last of her four children to university has given her the time and opportunity to write.

If you want to learn more about Rebecca Shaw and her novels, visit her website at: www.rebeccashaw.co.uk

LOVE IN THE COUNTRY

When Seb moves to Barleybridge the last
thing on his mind is romance. Eager to
embrace the new life of a country vet and
make a good impression, he's almost forgotten his ex-girlfriend Carly as he contends
with a menagerie of diverse clients, all with
their own expectations. The alpacas with TB
and the need to destroy an injured pony, in
front of his heartbroken young owner, become
part of Seb's steep learning curve. The course
of his work leads Seb to a friendship with the
upper class Jilly and rather more than that
with Maggie, whose family owns the alpacas.
But when a surprise meeting in the Practice
turns his head and touches his heart — he
knows that these dalliances are just youthful
romps.

REBECCA SHAW

LOVE IN THE COUNTRY

Complete and Unabridged

CHARNWOOD
Leicester

First published in Great Britain in 2009 by
Orion Books, an imprint of
The Orion Publishing Group Ltd.
London

First Large Print Edition
published 2009
by arrangement with
The Orion Publishing Group Ltd.
London

The moral right of the author has been asserted

British Library CIP Data

Shaw, Rebecca, *1931 –*
    Love in the country. - - (Barleybridge novels)
    1. Barleybridge (England: Imaginary place)- -Fiction.
    2. Veterinarians- -England- -Dorset- -Fiction.
    3. Country life- -England- -Dorset- -Fiction.
    4. Large type books.
    I. Title II. Series
    823.9'14–dc22

ISBN 978–1–84782–923–8

Published by
F. A. Thorpe (Publishing)
Anstey, Leicestershire

Set by Words & Graphics Ltd.
Anstey, Leicestershire
Printed and bound in Great Britain by
T. J. International Ltd., Padstow, Cornwall

This book is printed on acid-free paper

List of Characters at Barleybridge Veterinary Hospital

Mungo Price   Orthopaedic Surgeon and Senior Partner

Colin Walker   Partner — large and small animal

Daniel Franklin Brown Partner — large animal

Scott Spencer   Partner — large animal

Virginia Havelock   Large animal vet

Valentine Dedic   Small animal vet

Rhodri Hughes   Small animal vet

Sebastian Partridge   Large and small animal vet

NURSING STAFF

Sarah Cockroft (Sarah One)

Sarah MacMillan (Sarah Two)

Bunty Bird

RECEPTIONISTS

Joy Bastable (Practice Manager)

Lesley Jennings

Dodi Pilgrim

Annette Smith

Miriam Price   Mungo's wife

Duncan Bastable   Joy's husband

Letty Walker   Colin's wife

Rose Franklin Brown	Dan's wife
Zoe Spencer	Scott's wife
Megan Hughes	Rhodri's wife
Nina Dedic	Valentine's wife
Dicky Bird	Bunty's husband

THE BARLEYBRIDGE PRACTICE

BEULAH BANK MOOR

ASKEW NEWTON

LORD ASKEW'S

BEULAH BANK TOP

NEWTON NEW ROAD

BRIDGE LANE

BARLEYBRIDGE P

RIVER FARM

RIVER CHESS

BRIDGE END FARM

BARLEYBRID

BRIDGE FARM

BRIDGE LANE

WOOTTON

WOOTTON CAUSEWAY FARM

LOWER KIRKSTALL

WOOTTON CAUSEWAY TROUT FARM

CHESHAM CRISPY CHICKEN CO.

KIRKSTALL HILL

1

Seb checked his watch. Ten minutes to eight. He was in good time for the first day of his new job. It was two years since he first qualified, yet he still felt a thrill.

A strong draught told him the rear door to the animal hospital had been opened and into the reception area came Joy Bastable the practice manager.

'Seb! You're here. You've found your way. Well, of course, you must have, and to prove it you're standing in front of me!' She put down her bag on the reception desk and turned to study him. What a lovely chap he was. Not handsome in the modern manner, but sweet and kind like her Duncan. Very like Duncan, in fact. 'Look! Here's your name-plate. This morning you'll be in this last consulting room here, newly built just in time for you to use. It slots in here. Look.' She held up the name-plate for him to see. It read: '*Sebastian J. Partridge* B.Vet.Med., M.R.C.V.S.' Seb almost burst with pride.

'You put it in,' Joyce said. 'It moves with you, you see, to whichever consulting room you're in.'

Seb dropped it into place and stood back to admire it. This was his reward. Despite his family's opposition he'd stuck to his guns, determined to be a vet and not the farmer the rest of them assumed he would be. Living on that isolated family farm for the rest of his life?

Absolutely not. His dad had been bitterly disappointed, but Seb couldn't help himself. He knew his brother was neither physically nor mentally capable of making a success of the farm, but a lifetime incarcerated there with nothing but bleak hills for company . . . well, he couldn't. So here he was, ready to begin.

The emptiness of the reception area was disturbed by another blast of air and down the passage from the back door came a tall man with brown hair lightened by the sun. He wore a bush hat, an open-necked khaki shirt with pockets and epaulettes, and suede Timberland boots. Round his neck was a gold chain with a thick wedding ring threaded onto it.

Joy introduced him. 'This is Scott.'

The said Scott held out his hand. 'How do you do. I'm farm animal, not small.'

The accent gave him away. 'You're Australian?' asked Seb.

'I am. Australian by birth but English by inclination. Welcome to the practice. Best place on earth to be working. He looks as though he might turn out quite well, doesn't he, Joy?' Scott grinned broadly and play-punched Seb on his shoulder.

Joy looked Seb up and down. 'Indeed he might.'

'Is my list ready?' Scott asked.

'Of course. Busy day. But that's what you like. How's the baby doing?'

'Very well indeed. Three children keep Zoe very busy so it's a good thing the baby's better behaved than the last one was.'

2

'Well, Zoe deserved it to be so.'

'She's a glutton for punishment; she's decided four would be a good idea.'

'Heaven help us!'

'That's what I said.' Scott smiled.

Suddenly there was an influx of staff arriving. Scott collected his list and left to begin his busy day. The introductions flustered Seb, and he got names and faces all mixed up. Then a woman arrived in their midst, with dark curly hair and a generous smile, her hand outstretched in welcome. 'I'm Miriam Price, Mungo's wife,' she said. 'I've got a pot of coffee waiting in the flat upstairs; come up and have a cup before your day begins. I shan't keep him long, Joy.' She tucked his hand into the crook of her arm and led him down the passage. 'Mungo's just finishing breakfast.'

They climbed the stairs to the Prices' beautiful welcoming kitchen, and he felt immediately at home. Mungo was reading the paper and looked at him over the top of his reading glasses. 'Morning, Seb. Welcome to Barleybridge Veterinary Hospital.' He reached a hand round the edge of the paper and shook Seb's vigorously.

Miriam asked, 'Black? Milk? Sugar?'

'Milk and sugar, please.'

'I've a full list of clients this morning, Seb, so drink up and I'll go down with you and show you the ropes before I begin.'

'Thank you.' Seb, remembering an incident that had occurred when he'd come for his second interview, recalled Mungo's explosive temper and was grateful for his warm welcome.

3

Miriam anxiously enquired, 'Flat all right? I made sure the boiler was on in good time. Are you pleased with it?'

'Yes, it's lovely. Thank you.'

'Anything you need, just let me know. I look after the flat, you see.'

'There's nothing I can think of at the moment. I hadn't expected two bedrooms; it feels luxurious.'

Mungo rattled his paper and Seb took the hint and drank his coffee right to the bottom. 'Ready when you are, Mr Price.'

Mungo stood up, folded his newspaper and headed for the stairs. 'You're lucky to arrive when the building work is finished. It's been hectic here this year, but finally it's done and now we've to earn the money to pay for it all. Ah! I see your name-plate is up already.'

The scene in the waiting room was transformed. The empty chairs were filled with clients holding cages housing gerbils or hamsters or birds, cats in baskets and dogs on leads. There was a general air of anxiety and activity to which, Seb realized, he *belonged*.

A consulting room door opened and a voice called out, 'Lucky Campbell'. It was immediately followed by a sharp click of the heels and a nod of the head. The client got to her feet and said, 'Good morning, Mr Dedic.'

'That's Valentine Dedic,' said Mungo. 'Don't be fooled by the clicking and bowing; it may look amusing but never under-estimate him. He's the sharpest knife in the drawer. Remember that.'

Mungo ran through the equipment in the

state-of-the-art consulting room which was to be Seb's for the morning. Seb's head whirled with detail and he desperately hoped he would remember it all.

'Right. Time I wasn't here,' Mungo finished. 'Immaculate scrubs at all times. Only the best for our clients, with the highest standards of diagnosis, of course. Absolute integrity. No free consultations, much as some of them would like to get away with one. We have expenses and are not a charity. But do not over-charge. If clients feel that's what you've done they'll be resentful and it doesn't do the client-vet relationship any good at all. Here in this folder is our list of statutory charges. Ask for advice whenever. You're bound to need it at first and no one minds helping you out. Must go. Have a good morning.'

Seb took a deep breath, put on his scrubs, hung his stethoscope round his neck and looked at his list. So this was where it all began. The very first real step up in his career. This was the start of a new life, leaving behind, he hoped, the horrors of his first two years in practice, where he'd been marginalised and made to feel useless. Here he could prove just how good he was.

His first patient was a canary called Nellie. Problem? Removal of band. It all appeared too easy for words.

He opened his door and called out, 'Nellie Smithson.' A huge man got to his feet with the canary apparently in the cardboard box in his large fist.

Seb held out his hand. 'I'm Seb Partridge. I'm new.'

'Student, are yer?'

'No, qualified but new to this practice. Can I see the bird?'

'This 'ere is Nellie. Good name for a canary, don't you think? Have to hope she'll sing well, else I shall look silly.'

Seb had to acknowledge he didn't know why.

Seemingly surprised by Seb's ignorance, Mr Smithson said, 'You know — Dame Nellie Melba, the famous Australian singer from way back. This 'ere canary, I bought her yesterday. Took a right fancy to her, but I don't like this band round her leg. She's not fully grown, I'm told, and I'm frightened her leg might grow more and the band be too tight. You can hardly move it as it is now. See what you think.'

He withdrew Nellie from the cardboard box with the greatest of gentleness despite his large hands and thick fingers. She was a vivid yellow, with every feather well groomed and aligned.

'She's a great specimen.' Seb tried moving the band on her leg and agreed that it was already tight. 'Best off, I think. Would you like me to do it for you?'

'That's what I've come for, to have it cut off.'

It was the work of a moment to snip off the band. Seb held it out for Mr Smithson. 'Want to take it? Keepsake?'

'No, thanks. That's it, then.'

'Where did you get her from?'

'Chap down the market. He included the cage, too.'

Seb took the opportunity to examine her while she lay so quietly in his hand. While he was

6

looking at her feet he asked, 'The perches in the cage, are they covered with sandpaper?'

'Yes, they are. Gives the bird a better grip, he said.'

'Will you take my advice? All they're going to do is make her feet very tender and sore. She needs smooth perches. Imagine if you had sandpaper lining your shoes. You wouldn't get far, would you?' Seb said this as gently as he could so as not to give offence. With Nellie resting on her back on the palm of his hand, her head held securely between his finger and thumb, Seb held her feet out for inspection. 'Look, they're becoming inflamed already.'

Mr Smithson was appalled. 'They are. They are. Well, young man, you do know your stuff. I shall be back with my Nellie should a problem arise. Thanks for telling me. I'm straight back down the market to give that chap a piece of my mind. Now, how much do I owe?'

'They'll deal with that at the reception desk, Mr Smithson.'

'Right. Thank you very much.'

Seb glanced at his statutory charge list and tapped the price into his computer.

Next was a dog for its annual booster. Well, that was easy enough, except Rex bit him good and hard and the client almost collapsed with apologies.

'That's fine, Mrs Evans, I've kept my tetanus up to date so — '

'Are you inferring my Rex has rabies?' She hunched her shoulders defensively.

'No, of course not, but every vet has to keep

7

their tetanus up to date. One never knows.' He smiled sweetly at her and that did the trick.

She beamed back at him. 'Of course, it's only sensible. You'll go far, Mr Partridge. I shall ask for you next time.'

For one brief moment Seb thought she was going to kiss him, and he blushed. She noticed the blush and smiled at him, gave him a wave and left. Another satisfied customer, thought Seb. In fact, that morning he had a legion of happy customers and felt well pleased with his first morning's work. In the afternoon he assisted Valentine with three operations and was complimented on his intuitive help.

'You've a good instinct for surgery, Seb, congratulations.'

'Thank you. I always enjoyed surgery at college.'

'Why don't you ask Mungo if you can watch his last operation this afternoon; it's very complicated and interesting.'

'Would he mind?'

'He likes enthusiasm. Try him and see. It's a badly smashed jaw.'

'I will then.'

Seb found Mungo in the orthopaedic operating theatre, newly built along with the extra consulting rooms and the increased accommodation for intensive care.

'Of course. Come in,' he said in reply to Seb's request.

Mungo didn't speak again except to ask Bunty the nurse for instruments or mutter furiously about the owner who'd given this dog such a savage beating that his jaw was broken in three places. Most vets would have suggested the dog be put to sleep but Mungo, despite knowing he most likely wouldn't get paid for his efforts, with his exceptional skills and his intense compassion for animals in pain, was willing to operate.

After two hours' intense concentration he straightened his back with a great sigh. 'Bunty, thanks for your help. It's worked out better than I'd hoped. Take care of him. Enjoyed that, Seb, did you?'

'I most certainly did. Thank you for letting me watch.'

'Perhaps next time you might like to help?'

'That would be a privilege.' Seb helped Bunty lift the dog onto the trolley and wheeled it into the intensive-care room for her.

As Bunty settled the dog in a cage with a drip and a fleece over him to keep him warm, she asked, 'You do realise you've just been watching a genius at work?' Seb detected a note of passionate devotion in her voice but he was tactful enough to ignore it.

'Of course I do.'

'I've worked for him for ten years and he gets better all the time. People come from miles around, you know. He doesn't turn up his nose at mongrels or moggies; if they need his help they're all the same to him. A scruffy mongrel gets the same attention as a top show dog. We've a mongrel in next Monday from eighty miles away, coming on the recommendation of a grateful client of ours. I wouldn't change my job for anything. I've told Dicky he needn't think when he retires from the police that we're moving away because I couldn't. Not a single mile.' Bunty gave him a trembling smile that Seb put down to fatigue, but he felt a mite of pity for poor Dicky.

He'd been lent an aged Land Rover belonging to the practice until a permanent vehicle was available, but the fact didn't diminish his high spirits; he'd had such a spectacular day nothing could dishearten him. What finally put the icing on the cake was Scott saying, 'I've got a call-out — want to come?'

'Yes, please, I'd love to.'

'It's not far. A sow in trouble. Owners are Francesca and Cecil Goodwood, and a more peculiarly matched pair it would be hard to find. Lovely people, though. Come on, be sharp. They ring up and expect me there within five minutes.'

Scott paused to put his head round Joy's office door. 'Joy, I'm taking the mobile scanner, OK? I'll bring it back before I go home.'

The moment Francesca Goodwood saw Seb, she beamed at him. 'Well, young man. Seb, you say? I hope you know how lucky you are to be watching Scott at work. His veterinary skills are top of the shop and if you do as well as him you'll do all right, believe me. You look a grand chap to me. This way. Cecil's brought Constantia in to give her a bit more comfort; she's in the farrowing stall in the barn — more room for you, you see. She's a favourite of his.'

'Cecil?'

'Yes, Scott, like I said, believe it or not, Cecil is in there with her now.'

10

The barn was mainly used for storing the straw used for the pigs' bedding but Cecil had organised some bales to form a compact area for housing Constantia and the three piglets she'd managed to give birth to before her trouble started.

'Evening, Cecil. I can see why you've taken a fancy to her. I've no doubt she's a winner.' Scott was instantly on his knees examining Constantia. 'Fancy name, lovely sow. My stethoscope, Seb. Thanks.'

Seb watched while Scott examined Constantia, and to him there was something rather disturbing about Scott's careful examination. It felt rather over the top.

Eventually Scott sat back on his haunches. 'Have you any other sows just pigged?'

'Why?' Cecil asked, looking panicked for the first time.

'I'm not happy about her, things appear very wrong. I was thinking of handing her three piglets over to another sow, just in case.'

Francesca choked on her words. 'Just in case what?'

'How long has she been at this?'

'Well, we didn't notice until about an hour ago that she'd started, by then she already had the three, so we don't really know.'

Cecil began to shake. 'Not my Constantia, not her.'

'First litter?'

Francesca nodded.

Scott slowly shook his head. 'She's completely stopped having contractions.'

11

'Can't you give her something out of that magic bag of yours? You've always worked the miracle before.' By this time Francesca was kneeling in the straw beside Scott, a trembling hand resting on his shoulder.

'I'll give her some oxytocin but we'll use the scanner first and see just exactly what's going on in there. Hopefully the injection will start up the contractions again. She's definitely got more piglets inside — a good number, I should say.'

Cecil rubbed a hand across his eyes. 'Well, let's get on with it then. No point in hanging about.'

'I agree.'

Fascinated, Seb watched the screen. The piglets were lying head to tail in the womb. But at the same time he could feel Scott's anxiety.

'I'll have to reach inside and get out the first one. Here, look down this side — it's big and it's stuck fast. That's what's holding everything up, I think.'

Scott stripped off and put on his calving gown. He rolled up the sleeves as far as he could and, almost lying down on the barn floor, reached inside. The other three stood breathless, waiting for a result. It seemed an age until Scott grunted his satisfaction and managed to release the piglet. Out it popped and Scott gave it to Francesca to clean up and get it breathing.

'It's a whopper! An absolute whopper! Never seen one as big.' Cecil was beside himself with joy. 'He's a Goliath, he is. My God! No wonder she was having problems.'

The oxytocin gradually began to have an effect

12

on the sow's contractions, and slowly but surely the rest of the litter made their appearance. The piglets burst into life with astonishing swiftness and were searching for their mother's teats in no time at all. Seb was full of admiration for Scott; there was no sentimental tosh, simply the drive to get the matter dealt with and have a successful conclusion. Whereas Seb could have wept tears of joy as each piglet appeared. They were such jolly little things with lovely curly tails and sweet little faces.

'Just look at them! Aren't they all wonderful? Well done!' He stopped his tears and took a tight grip on himself as Scott spoke to Francesca.

'There we are. Thirteen safe and sound. They all look as though they'll thrive.'

Cecil fetched a bucket of hot water, a bar of soap and a clean towel. 'There we are. Thanks very much — she'd have died without you.'

'All part of the service.'

Cecil pulled up a box and sat on it to watch the litter. 'It's grand, is this. Thirteen. Good old Constantia.'

★ ★ ★

As Scott revved up his Land Rover, Seb said, 'Why was one of them so very big?'

'It happens. Frankly, I think we got there just in time. She was beginning to flag, and with a piglet that size I'm not surprised. Been in labour a lot longer than they realised, I think. Newborn piglets are pretty mobile virtually immediately, but those first three little beggars were stronger

13

on their feet than I would have expected.'

Scott dropped Seb off at the practice, returned the scanner and left Seb to make his way home in his old Land Rover.

On his way back to the flat Seb took a wrong turning and spotted a fish and chip shop with a queue of customers inside. He decided to pick up his supper, but he was the sixth in the queue and had a while to wait.

Someone roared in shouting, 'Three plaice and chips a.s.a.p.! Who's driving that old Land Rover outside? Eh?'

Seb put up his hand. 'Me.'

'You the new vet, then?'

Seb nodded.

'Thought so.'

Seb smiled. 'I'm Seb Partridge, and you are?'

'I'm Phil Parsons, Applegate Farm. Pleased to meet you.' He offered his hand to Seb and shook his vigorously. 'You'll have some good times there. They're a great bunch.'

'Thanks. I'm sure I will.'

'That other vet in the High Street packed up two weeks ago. Miserable beggar, he was. I don't wonder he lost all his business to your practice. No wonder at all.' There followed an in-depth discussion about which animals each of the customers had taken to the Barleybridge practice at some time or another, and suddenly, all over again, Seb felt he belonged. There was an outbreak of hand-shaking and back-slapping for Seb, followed by free fish and chips. He held out his money but it was sturdily refused.

'By heck!' said Phil Parsons. 'You're favoured.

Take 'em while you can, it won't happen again.'

The whole queue dissolved into laughter.

Someone else shouted, 'Don't miss out on your salt and vinegar! Put plenty on, them's free, and they'll taste even better than normal. You're favoured, you are.'

The man behind the counter took their teasing in his stride. 'You lot can shut up. You're all here because I sell the best fish and chips for miles, and well you know it.' The till rang and the fish and chips were served sizzling and crisp as fast as he was able.

Seb left to a chorus of 'goodnights', greatly moved by the enthusiasm of the queue. So this was what being a vet in a country market town meant; people knew you and, not only that, accepted you immediately.

Seb watched TV while he ate his supper. Kindly provided by the practice, the set wasn't very up to date, but it was satisfactory. This then was the life he had always longed to live, and the time spent observing Mungo Price repairing that dog's jaw had been absolutely fascinating. He was obviously a very skilled surgeon and fired Seb into wondering if he too could reach that level of skill.

He'd always enjoyed surgery when he was at college but at his first practice he hadn't had the opportunity to observe that level of expertise. If serious orthopaedic work was needed then it was given to a referral practice and Seb had never had the chance to watch. Three breaks in the jaw, but with clever drilling and pinning it had been restored to almost perfect condition.

In fact, come to think of it, he'd never been trusted with anything that required diagnosis or research or the use of his brain. He'd always been given the routine stuff, like boosters and nail clipping, and he'd become thoroughly disillusioned about his veterinary prospects. For two years he'd laboured on, then one bright shining morning he'd seen the light, as his mother would have said, and decided to find a new job. He'd even got a flat, too. At the other practice he'd found his own accommodation and it had been grotty, cold and depressing. But here! Seb glanced round the flat, admiring the comfortable terracotta-coloured sofa, the light cream walls, the luxurious sheepskin hearth rug and the black stove glowing behind the glass doors and throwing out enough heat to warm his flat and the next-door flat, too. He'd have to turn it to low.

For over an hour Seb dozed, relaxed and happy. The TV programme had changed twice by the time he woke and he had to smile at himself. One day at work and he was so tired he'd fallen asleep like an old man. The phone rang. That would be his mother he was sure, but it wasn't. It was Dan, one of the farm vets he'd spoken to at lunchtime, ringing to see if he'd come round to their house for a drink.

'I'd be delighted.'

'Scott's coming and Ginny and Gab. It'll give you a chance to get to know them.'

'Lovely. Where exactly do you live?'

'The address is Rose Cottage, appropriate as my wife is called Rose, and we live down Newton

New Road, it's — '

'Don't worry, I have a map.'

'It's called New Road but it's ancient, about two hundred years older than most of the roads round here.'

Seb had to laugh. 'Right, I'll be there. Won't be long.'

Sometimes Seb had difficulty with small talk and though he was glad to be invited, that nervous edge which always beset him when meeting new people manifested itself. But he needn't have worried because he was welcomed like a long-lost brother.

Rose, with her American accent, embraced and kissed him as though she'd known him all his life, and that broke the ice for him. Ginny shook hands rather more formally but Gab, her husband, shook his hand vigorously, clapping him on the back and saying, 'Welcome, Seb, to the Barleybridge Veterinary Hospital. I can tell you'll fit in brilliantly.' He was only too obviously an outdoors man; weather-beaten with the air of a farmer about him. A very good-looking son of the soil, Seb thought.

'Ginny and I own Bridge End Farm,' Gab continued. 'Been there two years now and we're really beginning to turn it round. In a very poor way when we bought it, but with Ginny's veterinary skills and my farming experience it's going from strength to strength. Not to be confused with Bridge Farm, which my father owns; they're very close. But you're not farming, are you?'

'I only have experience with small animals but

17

I am intrigued by farm animal work.'

Ginny interrupted. 'Don't believe a word he says. I happen to know he spent a blissful couple of hours watching Mungo at work this afternoon. Seb's much more interested in surgery.'

'Surgery?' Scott looked appalled. 'Surgery? Oh, my God! Surgery? Mungo's minute, detailed orthopaedic work? Heavens above. In the open air, in a field or a barn — now that's *real* surgery.'

Seb, a little taken aback by Scott's remarks, hesitated for a moment and then replied, 'Yes, I love it. You should have seen — '

'Stop this minute! Dan, get the man a drink immediately; his need is greater than mine.'

They all settled down in comfortable chairs around a blazing fire in the huge inglenook fireplace. Genuine horse brasses lined up on the brickwork and brass fire irons shone as though they'd been polished that very day. With a good drink in his hand, Seb began to relax.

Above the noise of everyone's voices the wail of a very young baby floated downstairs. Rose sprang to her feet. 'That's James. Sorry. Feed-time. Anybody mind if I feed him down here? Otherwise I shall miss all the fun.'

They all agreed she mustn't miss the fun and Rose returned down the stairs carrying a baby so like Dan there was no doubting who his father was.

Seb had to say so and Rose replied that Serena was like her and the two boys like Dan — 'Thank goodness.' She laughed at Dan, who

18

grinned back, and settled down like an earth mother to feed the baby. No one minded, no one was embarrassed, and the conversation flowed as before until someone mentioned the Hunt, which would be leaving from Barleybridge town square the very next day.

Seb had reservations about hunting, so he held back from any comment until he had a chance to see how everyone else felt.

Gab only too obviously approved, Scott kind of half-approved, and Ginny was so against it that Seb was surprised the other vets were still speaking to her.

'Well, Seb, where do you stand with hunting?' Ginny asked.

So Seb had to declare, 'The Hunt at home goes over our farm fields. I've grown up with it, accepted it, and although I have never hunted myself I cannot say I disapprove; it's all part of country life to me. When I see our chickens dead because the fox has been past on his nightly inspection and discovered that the chickens have not been locked up for the night, and they're slaughtered right to the last one, then I think the fewer foxes there are the better.'

'That's not the fox's fault; it's your fault for forgetting to lock them up,' Ginny protested loudly.

Seb spoke up in defence of the chickens. 'If the fox took just enough food for itself, then I suppose it wouldn't appear so cruel, but slaughtering them all needlessly is . . . well, not fair.'

An explosion of opinions flooded the room

and baby James took fright.

Dan said, 'Remember the baby!'

The argument, now far too fierce to be called a discussion, continued, but Seb kept silent and didn't join in again. As the new man of the party he decided that was more diplomatic. Eventually, at half past eleven they decided to agree to differ and they all dispersed.

As Seb was getting into his Land Rover Dan came to speak to him. 'Stick to your own opinions, Seb, it's your right. They all get worked up about it. They forget the number of times the Hunt goes out and never even sees a fox. Goodnight. Thanks for coming. You should do well. If surgery is your passion you couldn't have a better teacher than Mungo.'

'That's right. Thanks for inviting me. Sorry I stirred things up, but that's how it strikes me.'

'Well, at least the death is quick with the hounds whereas shooting them can leave them dying in agony for days. Goodnight.'

2

Full to the brim with enthusiasm, Seb got to the practice even earlier the next day, but it gave him a chance to talk to Scott, who invited him to visit a couple of farms with him that afternoon if he was free. 'I'll be here at lunchtime because Zoe's lunching with Rose and exchanging baby talk so we'll see if you're free. I'll mention it to Joy.'

'Thanks, that'll be great.'

'You'll love it here when you get settled in. Lovely staff, great clients. Wonderful place to live. Wouldn't be anywhere else in the world.'

'Don't you miss the sun and the wide open spaces?'

'And the flies and the boiling heat and the thousands of sheep to shear and the million miles to see a neighbour? No, I do not. A quiet trundle down to the Fox and Grapes, a pleasant chat over a pint with country people is much, much better. Right?'

Seb laughed. He had thought Australia would be too captivating to leave, but apparently not.

His first client that morning was Miranda Costello. He flicked through the on-screen notes and saw that Valentine had added 'difficult client' to them. A rabbit named Lettice was the patient.

'Lettice Costello, please.' The dazzling Mrs Costello rose to her feet and sailed forthwith into his consulting room. Musk! That was it, she was wearing musk perfume and he didn't like it. Still, she was a client and smiling broadly at him.

'Why is it that all the vets who work here are good-looking?' she said. 'There's Valentine, there's Scott, there's that Rhodri with the Welsh accent, and now you.' She put her head on one side and looked up at him beguilingly.

'I'm Seb Partridge. This is my second day at the practice. What can I do for you, Mrs Costello?'

She patted his forearm. 'Miranda to everyone who knows me.'

'What seems to be the problem?'

Miranda's eyes welled with tears. Two large ones spilled down her rouged cheeks. She sniffed loudly. 'Sorry. It's Lettice, you see. In my bones I know there's something wrong with her. What, I don't know, but there is. I've tried to ignore it, pretend it isn't there, but it's no good. Yesterday I had to face up to it. Now if it's too much for you I'll see Valentine instead; he'll know what to do.'

'Let me try first, Mrs . . . ' She wagged a finger at him. ' . . . Miranda. I kept rabbits when I was a boy at home. Come to think of it, I kept almost every pet you could name. I might have known I would turn out to be a vet. You get her out.'

Seb placed Lettice on the examination table. 'What is it you had to face yesterday, exactly? Tell me in your own words. Take your time.'

A pathetic smile flickered at the corners of Miranda Costello's mouth; she was so grateful for his understanding. 'At first, like two or three

22

weeks ago, I thought she must be pregnant, though I couldn't see how. I only have girl rabbits, but then you never know. I was so excited. Baby rabbits! Would I be able to part with them? Should I keep them all?' She paused to gain control of her voice. 'But I realise now the swelling is bigger, and she'd have had the babies by now, and . . . she's almost stopped . . . eating, and things are not working their way out at the other end, if you get my meaning.' A long, heartfelt sob halted any further conversation.

Seb knew precisely what the matter was the moment he examined her. The lump was monstrous and beyond veterinary care. 'Are you brave, Miranda?' he asked.

His answer was a nod. 'You mean you need me to be brave now?'

Seb nodded, too. 'You love her, I know, and so we must decide what to do. You see she's probably in pain, and we can't have that, can we?'

Miranda shook her head.

'We've got to take the pain away, haven't we?'

'You mean you could operate?' A gleam of hope shone in Miranda's eyes.

'No, I'm afraid not.'

'You mean she's too old?'

'How old do you think she is?'

'I don't know. So she's not pregnant?'

'No, it's a swelling that shouldn't be there and it must be causing her pain right now. If you like I'll get a second opinion from one of the other vets. Would you like me to do that?'

'It's not that I don't trust you, because I do, but . . . yes, seeing as you're new. Yes, I would.'

'Hold her. I'll get someone.'

Rhodri had a short gap in his appointments and was about to sink his teeth into a tempting sandwich Megan had made him for his lunch, even though there were three more hours to go before his lunch-hour.

Carefully wrapping his sandwich up to keep it fresh Rhodri followed Seb and greeted Miranda like a long-lost friend, shaking her hand and patting her forearm. 'Miranda! Long time no see. How are you?'

Bravely Miranda smiled at him. 'Not too good today.'

'I expect not. Seb says you'd like a second opinion on Lettice?'

Miranda nodded.

Rhodi took over at the examination table and gently examined Lettice, his face grim. 'I'm sorry, Mrs Costello, but . . . Seb is absolutely right. I'm afraid it's all too late. Lettice is in pain and the very kindest gift you can give her at this moment is to have Seb put her to sleep and out of her misery. It's a massive growth and will only get worse. The pain will become indescribable; in fact, it is at that level now, I should imagine. Poor old thing.' Rhodri gently scratched Lettice behind her ear.

'I see. I'd be doing her a kindness, you mean?'

Rhodri nodded. 'I'll leave you to it.'

After he'd gone Miranda said, 'Same thing happened to my mother. She never told us she had a lump and when she couldn't stand it any longer she admitted it and we had to watch her die filled to the brim with morphine and still she had pain. At least I can put Lettice out of her agony before she gets even worse.'

Seb watched the decision being made and regretted he had it to do, but do it he must. 'Believe me, it's for the best. She'll know nothing about it. Nothing at all. You sit down there in the chair and we'll put her on your knee and you can cuddle her while I get the injection ready and then she'll fall quietly to sleep.'

'For ever!' Miranda gave a strangled sob, which struck Seb right to his heart. But he gently laid Lettice on Miranda's knee and turned away to prepare the injection.

Lettice was given enough cuddles to last her for weeks as Miranda stroked and stroked her from head to toe, whispering sweet nothings to her with tears pouring down her face.

Lettice fell asleep for ever within seconds and Seb left Miranda to cuddle her a while longer.

'Now shall you take her home, or would you like me to dispose of her for you?'

Seb knew instantly he should have phrased that better, but Miranda didn't appear to notice how clumsy he'd been.

'I have a graveyard for my pets, in a quiet corner of my garden. Did I say garden? More like a tip but there's loads of wildlife. I'll take her.' Completely forgetting she'd brought Lettice in one of her cat baskets, Miranda stood up and shuffled out into the waiting room with Lettice in her arms before Seb could stop her, so every anxious pet-owner witnessed the departure of

Lettice, who was so obviously dead it brought a gasp of horror from them. Seb followed her out with the cat basket but too late to prevent the clients from being shocked.

Silence fell in the waiting room. Dodie Pilgrim the senior receptionist almost collapsed at the sight of a dead rabbit being carried through reception. Miranda came to a halt and declared loudly to anyone who cared to listen, 'This is Lettice, out of her pain and gone to the rabbit heaven in the sky where all the carrots are juicy and fresh, the grass as green as green, and the burrows warm and cosy.'

This highly romantic picture of a bunny heaven left not a dry eye in the waiting room. Hankies came out and were swiftly put to use, loud sniffs were heard, and there was an outbreak of patting and stroking of the animals awaiting their turn.

Seb raced outside with the cat basket, saw Miranda safely installed in her van and waved her off. He returned feeling drained by his experience of putting a beloved animal down in front of its owner, only to find himself, when he went back in, facing the stern, beckoning finger of Dodie Pilgrim. She nodded her head in the direction of the back office and Seb followed her, puzzled as to why she needed to speak to him.

Between clenched teeth Dodie said, 'Dead animals go out through the back. It's a wonder our clients haven't collapsed *en masse* with the horror of what happened just now. You remember that, right? Dead — out the back, no messing. Alive — out the front. OK?' She emphasised her point by prodding his chest vigorously with a very sharp finger.

When lunchtime came Seb wondered whether he should eat his sandwich and drink his tea somewhere other than the staffroom because he couldn't face the wrath of Dodie Pilgrim. Someone had mentioned her a couple of times when he came for his second interview but he hadn't imagined that she could be so . . . well . . . vicious. He felt so depressed about Lettice he went to sit outside on the bench by the back door to eat, all alone, looking up at the cold, unwelcoming foothills of Beulah Bank Top. Was that snow he saw on the top-most peaks? Surely not. His spirits plummeted even further.

The back door opened and Dodie came out. Seb stood up. 'Sit down, boy.' She joined him on the bench, a vast mug of steaming coffee in her hand. 'She also left without paying. Cardinal sin, that.'

'I'd forgotten that. The last place I was at sent out monthly accounts. I just didn't think.'

'Obviously.'

'It seems so thoughtless to ask for money in those circumstances.'

'It isn't. They know it and expect to pay. Chasing unpaid accounts takes up too much time and the bad debts that arise . . . You see, when you've been here a while your earnings will cover your salary and allow us to make a profit to pay for the upkeep of this place, but at the moment, with no clients of your own yet, you don't earn your salary. Understand?' She turned her head to smile at him.

'I understand. It won't happen again.'

'Good boy. The clients you dealt with yesterday were mightily impressed, especially that canary man. Keep it like that and you'll do all right.'

'Thanks.'

Dodie disappeared inside, leaving Seb to finish his now almost cold tea and reflect on life. But his mood lifted when he remembered he was going to a couple of farms with Scott after lunch.

★ ★ ★

'We're going to Applegate Farm first,' Scott said. 'Don't be surprised by anything, right? The Parsons are excellent clients, every bill paid on time, but inclined to be hysterical. You'll see what I mean when you get there. Got your wellingtons?'

'Yes.'

'Good. Believe me, you'll need them.'

'But it hasn't rained for days; it can't be muddy.'

'Believe me, you'll need 'em,' Scott repeated.

They pulled into the farm lane. Phil was in the yard looking out for them. He gave Seb a nod, remembering him from the fish and chip shop the previous night, but was obviously too anxious to say anything. Scott expected to be seeing the goats, or more likely one of the cows, but no, Phil headed straight for the house.

'What's this, Phil? I thought I was seeing a cow.'

'It's Little Scott.'

'Your boots off, Seb.' They both kicked off their boots and left them in the yard.

Seb had something of a surprise when he was introduced to Blossom. Having seen Phil he had not anticipated that Blossom would be so . . . well . . . so glamorous.

'Oo-o-h!' murmured Blossom. 'You must be Seb. Phil said he'd met you buying your fish and chips. Why, you remind me of Scott when he first came to the practice. Just lovely. Believe me, lovely.'

Scott, anxious to know why he'd been called out, said, 'Why are we here?'

Blossom whispered, 'It's Little Scott; she's swelling up and we don't know why.'

'Swelling up?'

'Yes, she's in the basket by the fire.' She waved a vague finger towards the fireplace and then got out a tissue from the pocket of her skirt.

'But you should have brought her in; this is a small animal job. Seb, step forward.'

Seb pulled the cat's basket further into the light.

'Well,' he said eventually, 'it's my honest opinion that Little Scott is about to give birth.'

'Give birth!' Phil and Blossom said together.

'She can't be!' added Blossom. 'She isn't that kind of a cat.'

'I would suggest she is. Look, she's straining.'

Scott was down on his knees immediately. 'My God! She is.'

Blossom went to the door and shrieked, 'Hamish!' three times. Young Hamish, who'd lived with the Parsons for years, arrived in a

29

rush. Blossom, almost incoherent with delight, told him what was happening. His reply was that he'd told her a while ago Little Scott had been up to some hanky-panky with the tom from the caravan site so there was no wonder.

'But I didn't believe you. She's never bothered about male cats, ever.'

'Bit late now. She must have done.'

Phil slumped down into his fireside chair. 'Kittens. Would you believe it? Is she all right, Scott?'

'Seb thinks so and that's good enough for me. We can spare half an hour and then we've got to go. Clients to see, work to be done.'

Seb glanced up at him. 'I could always stay, if you like. Get back on the bus or something. You could see the other clients. Whoops! There's one coming.'

'There is!' The farm kitchen filled with silence as the tiny kitten was squeezed out onto the blanket. The kitten was the image of its mother. Immediately Little Scott began cleaning the kitten's face, then started on its body.

In no time at all another one began to arrive, head first, and this time it was jet-black with white paws.

'It is the tom from the caravan park, like I said. He's black with white legs. It is him. I said so.' Hamish clapped Scott on his shoulder. 'I was right.'

There appeared to be a lull in the arrival of the kittens and Scott decided he had to go. 'Take care of her, Seb, she's my namesake. I'll ring in an hour and find out what's happening.'

Disappointed, Blossom said, 'Can't you stay a bit longer?'

'Sorry, but Seb knows what he's doing. Stick at it, Little Scott.'

Another hour and a highly charged Seb, now quite beyond himself with satisfaction and delight, declared this was the last one. It was the smallest of the four of them and didn't begin to breathe immediately. Seb cleared its mouth and nostrils himself and gave it a quick shake to shock it into breathing. Anxiously they all watched and waited, and eventually Seb's rough treatment worked. He gave the kitten to Little Scott and they sat back to admire the afternoon's handiwork.

'Well, I never,' said Blossom. 'I didn't imagine . . . did you, Phil?'

'Never occurred to me. But you were right, weren't you, Hamish? She's a right little devil, aren't you, Little Scott?'

'I'll give her a drop of warm milk and brandy, eh? Just to perk her up a bit.' After she'd administered the brandy Blossom said, 'I'd like to keep the gingery one.'

Hamish declared he liked the black one with white feet, while Phil decided he liked the ones that were like twins, with tabby and ginger markings. 'Shall we keep them all? Just this once and then we'll get Seb here to spay her. What do you say, Blossom?'

'I agree. I mean we've no farm cats at all now, we lost them all when they got that peculiar virus thing, and Little Scott is a house cat really, so let's indulge ourselves. Thank you, Seb. Now look, Hamish can drive you back to the practice. Never mind about catching the bus; it only comes once in a blue moon. I'm sure there's things you should be doing. Thank you so much for what you've done. Sometime we might have an emergency and you'll come and you can see the kittens while you're here. God bless, Seb. They're gorgeous. Really gorgeous.'

Seb was grateful for the lift but after three minutes of his journey back to the practice he wished himself anywhere but where he was. Hamish was the most unpredictable, mad driver he'd ever met. It was when Hamish went through a second red light that Seb realised his end might well have come and he didn't take a breath from then on all the way back until they finally came to a juddering halt in the car park with the most tremendous screech of brakes and gears.

In a feeble voice Seb asked Hamish how long it had been since he took his test.

Hamish turned to stare at him and said, 'Well, don't let on, please, no one knows, but I've never taken one. Most of us don't bother round here, but you'd never know that I'd had no lessons, now would you? Just learned on the tractor and that.'

'Oh! I see. Well, thanks for the lift. I shall keep your secret, promise.' He clambered out, shook his trembling legs into life, and marched as best he could towards the back door, to be met by Dodie, who'd been watching from the laundry room. She stood in the open doorway, grinning at him.

Very solicitously she asked, 'Cup of tea?'

Seb nodded.

'He's notorious for being a bad driver, I'm amazed you accepted a lift.'

'I didn't know. Anyway, it would have been churlish to refuse and one does have to consider client relationships.'

'You're being pompous, Seb. Go and sit down and I'll bring you a cuppa; you look as though you need it.'

Seb nodded and make a vow that never would be accept a lift from Hamish ever again, not if he wanted to live. He had a feeling that Dodie had added something alcoholic to the tea in his mug, but he didn't protest.

★   ★   ★

The following day was one of those mysteriously quiet ones which occur from time to time for no apparent reason. It was especially quiet for Seb who as yet had no real client list of his own. Scott had a rather interesting farm call to make, however, and suggested that maybe it could be of value to him.

They drove right through Barleybridge main square, but as they approached they met a traffic jam caused by the Barley-bridge Hunt. 'Blast,' said Scott. 'I forgot. Just our luck. We're stuck good and proper. Impossible to turn round and go the other way. Oh, well, there we are. Get out if you like, Seb, and have a look round.'

'OK, I will.'

The pavements were thronging with people

waiting for the off. The centre of the square, cleared of traffic, was jammed with horses and their riders. There was an air of excitement which reminded Seb of his childhood when he too had gone down to see off the Hunt. The hounds were milling about and the strong smell of the pack filled his nostrils. There must have been twenty-five or thirty of them, all at the peak of fitness, lean, eager, completely silent and full of anticipation. He found himself being sniffed in the vain hope he might have titbits in his pockets. The Master of Hounds and the whipper-in in their red jackets were keeping them under control without the need to use their whips. Seb noticed two hounds had escaped their notice and were running about between the horses. A crowd of riders wearing black jackets had just come swirling down the road to join the others and created something of a flurry as space was so limited.

One horse, a magnificent, well-bred creature, was spooked by the two loose hounds that had wandered away from the main pack. The woman rider had difficulty controlling her mount as it tossed its head and spun about, with the hounds springing out of its way as best they could. Suddenly it reared and when its front hooves came down it knocked one of the hounds to the ground. Someone shouted, 'Jilly!' Another rider called out, 'The hound!'

The whipper-in made his way across, growling, 'Bracken!'

Seb instinctively went forward to see if he could help. 'I'm a vet. Can I do anything for him? I'm from the Barleybridge Veterinary Hospital.'

Bracken was shaking himself, apparently prepared to carry on as though nothing had happened.

'I see. Well, you could examine him, if you please.'

'Certainly.'

'Bracken! Stay!'

It was a serious pleasure for Seb to examine the hound. He was so alert, so in the prime of life, so full of energy, without an ounce of excess fat on him that Seb's delight in handling him knew no bounds. His ribcage was unharmed, and there appeared to be no sign of pain when he felt down his legs, nor when he put pressure on Bracken's vertebra.

Seb looked up at the whipper-in. 'I'm pretty sure there's no harm done, but keep an eye out just in case.'

'Thanks for that.'

Jilly looked down at him from the back of her horse and thanked him. She was haughty with a very clipped accent, one of those strong horsey women, fearless in any situation, and possibly older than she appeared. 'All right, is he? Good. I'm Jilly Askew, niece of the Master. Do you hunt?' She leant down and offered to shake hands.

Seb shook his head.

'Do you ride?'

Seb shook his head again.

'I was going to offer you a ride on the estate, but there we are. I'm here for another two weeks. You're . . . ?'

'Seb Partridge.'

'Quaint name. Nice to have met you. See you again sometime.' She touched the brim of her hat with her riding crop and joined the mêlée of riders.

In moments the decision was taken that the Hunt should leave. The Hunt Master made a speech thanking the public for turning out to see them off and for their contributions to Hunt funds. Then the Master of Hounds raised his horn to his lips. Every single hound gave itself to the sound and set off at speed behind him, followed by the stream of riders in their stocks and black coats and caps, and suddenly the clatter of horses' hooves on tarmac was a distant memory, the excitement left the square and in an instant life was back to normal; the traffic flowed, the pedestrians wandered away and Seb got back into Scott's car.

'That was brilliant. There's such an atmosphere, it's unbelievable. Someone called Jilly lost control of her horse and — '

'That would be Jilly Askew, Lord Askew's niece. He's Master of the Hunt, I think. Very big chap, white hair, red face?'

Seb nodded.

'Jilly's a well-known rider, always comes for the Hunt. What had she to say for herself? Something bullish no doubt.'

'Nothing, really, except she seemed to dismiss me when I said I didn't ride. It was the hound her horse stood on that was worrying, but I examined him and he appeared fine.'

'It happens.' Scott checked the traffic and

pulled away. 'Best not let Ginny know what you did; she'll probably have you hanged, drawn and quartered for having anything at all to do with the Hunt.'

Seb had to laugh. Had he known that before the week was out Jilly Askew would be asking him to go out for a drink with her, and that he was soon to meet the love of his life, he might not have been so carefree.

3

'Ready, Seb?' It was Scott waiting to take him home to supper.

They called in first at the Fox and Grapes for a drink to give Zoe time to feed the baby and get the other two to bed. 'Well, not so much Oscar to bed now he's seven and quite presentable to people with no children,' Scot explained, 'but certainly young Jake and baby Amelia. You see, Seb, I adore them but then they are mine and I can quite understand that people without children could find them a complete pain.'

'I like children very much indeed.'

'Oh, well. Maybe it wouldn't have been a bad idea then, but us being here for a while does give Zoe some space. You know, I never cease to be amazed at how well she has adapted to being a mother; she's just brilliant, patient, well organised and contemplating a fourth one, would you believe. What are you having, Seb?'

'I'll have half a pint of Wobbly Boot.'

They settled themselves by the huge open fire that had welcomed travellers for more years than any architectural historian could count.

'I enjoyed going round the farms this afternoon with you,' Seb said. 'It's interesting meeting the farmers; they're all so different.'

'Indeed they are. But if you're interested in surgery you couldn't have a better teacher than Mungo. He is superb. I've nothing but admiration for him, but it's not for me. I enjoy the hustle and bustle of the farmyard, the lambing, the calving, the equine. Small animals leave me cold.'

'Good thing we're not all the same, then. This beer's a bit strong.'

'Never tried it. Never heard of it even. Must be new.'

'I've had it before but this seems extra strong.'

'Empty stomach, perhaps.'

'Could be. How long have you worked in England, then?'

'Lost count. Came, went back home and then came back again. Me and Zoe got together, married and had babies. Best thing I ever did marrying Zoe. Never thought I'd say that. Independent, playing the field, that was me. But having babies — wow! That's another brilliant occupation. By the look on your face you don't agree.'

Seb hid his feelings. 'I'm too young yet. I'm thinking about my career rather more than marriage.'

'Quite right, too. Just what you should be doing.' Scott looked into the distance and added, 'There's plenty of lovely girls round here. You'll be spoilt for choice.' He checked his watch. 'Let's be off. Ginny and Gab are coming, and Valentine, too, so we can't be late or Zoe's plans will go into melt-down.'

★   ★   ★

A closer look at Valentine and Seb could recognise blatant charm riding high, and when

Gab arrived with Ginny he recollected what he'd noticed the previous day, the rugged attraction of a son of the soil.

As they walked through to the dining room Seb caught sight of himself in a mirror and didn't see any of that in his own demeanour, rather the opposite: he came across as mild, self-effacing and scholarly, and was very depressed.

They had an uproarious meal. Stories were exchanged, with lots of laughter and teasing, and Seb loved it all. At home on his family's hill farm, the pressure of making a profit no matter how small overlaid their jollity, and mealtimes were inclined to be dour but this . . . this was how meals should be, and he laughed as loud as anyone. Then Scott's mobile rang and Zoe looked at him, waiting to hear his reply.

After a short conversation he clipped his phone shut. 'Call out. Lord Askew's champion Guernsey cow, the one he's won all the prizes with. Must go. You know what's he's like, leaving it all too late . . . '

Ginny stood up. 'Let's all go.'

'All of us?'

Zoe said, 'I can't because of the children. You all go; I'll clear up.'

Gab offered to help Zoe with the dishes. Scott agreed it would be a kindness to Zoe if Gab stayed behind.

So out into the cold frosty night went Seb, Scott, Valentine and Ginny. Scott's new Land Rover made short work of the journey and at that time of night the traffic was minimal.

They roared into the beautiful Georgian courtyard where the stables were, and then through the archway to the cow byres. They jumped out. Valentine had never been there before and was mightily impressed. 'This is beautiful,' he said. 'The cows are kept in here? I can't believe it. There are people living in worse conditions back home. This is luxurious.'

Too late Ginny remembered she was still forbidden to come to the premises after the débâcle with Lady Mary's eventer, so she kept to the back of the group, hoping she wouldn't be noticed.

Scott shouted, 'Keiran! Scott Spencer here. Keiran! You rang.'

Keiran popped his head out of a door. 'My God! What's this? A gaggle of vets? Come in. It's Guinevere. I've put her on her own. She's in a right mess. Aborting. No doubt at all.'

Scott led the way in. There was plenty of room for all of them. One brief inspection was all Scott needed.

'You're right,' he said to Keiran. 'What's brought this about, then?'

Keiran shrugged. 'No idea. She's been straining for hours, I just bloody hope it isn't catching because if the others start, his lordship, the old — ' Keiran, alerted by a footstep he knew only too well, quickly touched his cap. 'Good evening, my lord. See . . . they've brought the big guns with 'em, so we should be OK.'

Lord Askew came in and closed the door carefully. He briefly nodded to them all, too preoccupied by anxiety to bother speaking to them. He looked directly at Scott. 'She's my best ever. Past showing now but she's having perfectly splendid calves, aren't you, Guinevere old girl? And her milk yield is amazing. Well, is it all too late? Eh?'

''Fraid so, my lord. I should have been called earlier.' He refrained from adding 'as usual'.

Lord Askew looked discomfited. Then he noticed Ginny and went on the attack. 'That woman . . . what is she doing here? I forbade you — '

Scott intervened. 'We happened to be at a party together and she came along for the ride. No offence meant, just coincidence. But she'll sit in the car, if you prefer, sir. I'm the vet on duty.' Lord Askew dismissed the idea, all too anxious to see his prize cow attended to.

Scott stripped off and put on his calving gown and trousers. 'Seb, you give me a hand. She won't bring this one without help. Ropes, Seb. I brought them in.' He turned to Lord Askew. 'I'm afraid the calf may already be dead.'

Lord Askew stamped his wellingtons. 'Blast it. Surely not.'

Scott nodded. 'I'm fairly sure. But I'll get it out and we'll see. We may manage to revive it. After all, it's almost due, so it's not that early.'

Though it felt too cold in the byre to be stripping off, Seb took off his jacket and pullover, hung them on a convenient hook and rolled up his shirt-sleeves to await Scott's instructions.

'The calf's too big for her, but it is the right way round and what you've got to do is slip this

42

loop of rope round the front legs.' Scott handed over the rope. 'Earn your keep, there's a good chap.'

Seb, rapidly recalling his days at college, did as instructed and managed to get the rope tied round the calf's feet with reasonable speed.

'That's it, well done.'

At a signal from Scott, they began the slow steady pull to withdraw the calf from the uterus.

'He's in a good position. Steady now, Seb, use her straining to our advantage . . . that's it, slow and steady when she strains.'

Lord Askew shuffled about anxiously. 'Take care of her; she's the priority. If the calf's dead, so be it, though it's damned annoying.' He scowled at Keiran, stood on Ginny's foot by mistake and didn't apologise, eyed Valentine with suspicion, clamped a cigarette in his teeth and lit it, then swore like a trooper.

But Scott and Seb were making progress. The feet were showing and the nose of the calf had momentarily appeared and then disappeared just as quickly, then reappeared as Seb and Scott used another contraction to its best advantage.

'We're nearly there!' Scott said through clenched teeth.

Lord Askew shouted, 'Come on, you two, put your shoulders to it. Keiran, I don't know why you asked these sods to turn out, you could have done this on your own.' He half bit through his cigarette in his excitement and had to spit bits of it out on to the floor, almost starting a fire in the straw which he stamped out with his big boots.

Seb caught the calf as it slid slowly out and

laid it gently on the floor.

Almost hysterically Scott yelled, '*Rub* it. Get some straw and *rub* it. Clean the mucus away. Don't pussyfoot about, just do it, work at it, *go on! Hurry up!*' He grabbed a big handful of straw himself and rubbed the calf's ribcage vigorously, but it wasn't breathing. 'The mucus! Clear its passages; you've not done it right. Go on. *Do it!*'

Satisfied that the mucus had now been cleared, Scott picked up the calf by its legs and swung it about in an attempt to shock it into breathing. Finally his method worked. The calf snuffled and coughed and they could see its narrow ribcage beginning to move rhythmically.

Lord Askew was beside himself. 'Brilliant! The little beggar's going to live! Look at him. Just look at him. A bull calf, and does he look good! He most certainly does. My God he does. He'll be a winner, just wait and see.'

They all watched in silence as Guinevere nuzzled him comfortingly and the calf, worn out with his exertions, met his mother for the first time and began to learn how proud she was of him.

'You're a beauty, young man. You're a beauty!' Lord Askew bent to stroke him. 'I'll call you Arthur. Appropriate, don't you think?'

They were all fascinated by the bonding of mother and calf.

Keiran squatted down and finished cleaning Arthur with another generous handful of straw. 'He's a beauty indeed, m'lord,' he said softly. 'What a privilege to look after him. What a privilege. You're right that he's a champion in the making.'

Even Valentine, who'd never had the slightest interest in tending farm animals, preferring the cleaner and more antiseptic care of small animals, found it in his heart to be moved by the beauty of the calf. 'He's one of the best, isn't he, my lord?'

'Come on, all of you. Scott and this new boy can clean up, and we'll all go to drink a toast to Arthur in my study. Champagne all round.'

Keiran, knowing his place in the scheme of things, didn't follow them out to the house, but stayed in the byre admiring Guinevere's calf, thinking of the show-ring triumphs he would surely bring to the house of Askew.

★ ★ ★

Seb felt completely out of place in Lord Askew's study. For more than two hundred years it had been the hub of the vast Askew estate and it breathed money and status. The beautifully panelled walls, the stag heads mounted on the walls and the oil paintings of champion hunters, hounds and lap dogs made it a very masculine room. In the centre stood an enormously impressive desk from which, for generations, Lord Askew's ancestors had overseen the vast estate.

The butler had already brought the champagne from his pantry into the study along with sparkling cut-glass champagne flutes, and was busy opening the magnum as they arrived in the study.

Lord Askew proposed the toast. 'To Guinevere's calf Arthur Askew. To him good health and many championships. Arthur!'

When the second glass had been served Ginny began to study the oil paintings. Mellowed by the champagne his lordship went to stand beside her to talk about the horses. She discussed the pictures with some considerable knowledge and he began to warm to her, having at first imagined she was merely examining them to impress him.

Scott, remembering Zoe, decided it was time to head for home. He cleared his throat and said, 'I'm on call. Do you mind if we leave now?' Valentine and Seb were only too glad to be leaving but Ginny, finding herself making headway with Lord Askew, was reluctant.

'Must we?' she said.

Scott said, 'Yes, we must. Thank you for your hospitality, Lord Askew.'

'Thank you for saving Arthur. Greatly appreciated.' He shook hands with Scott and the four of them took their leave.

Standing together by Scott's Land Rover, the idea was mooted that they'd all go to Seb's flat, Scott and Ginny to reminisce about the time when they lived in it and Valentine to see it for the first time.

So they went to Zoe and Scott's, picked up their cars, and drove to the practice flat, leaving Scott at home with Zoe.

Seb put his key in the flat door and pushed it open. 'Wine — red or white — or beer?'

'Beer! Beer!'

So Seb got out the only glasses he had and

began pouring the beer.

'I say, you've struck lucky, Seb, you've got a new sofa!' This was Ginny taking her chance to examine the flat. 'The one I had was lumpy and like concrete all at the same time. I do believe this is brand-new! It's certainly not Miriam's old one — that was silvery grey. Lucky you. Has the tap been sorted in the bathroom? I had it looked at twice but the damn thing wouldn't stop dripping.'

'No dripping tap now.'

'Ooo, who's teacher's pet, then?' She swung round to examine the rest of the living room. 'And a new bookcase! I don't believe this! When I lived here the bookcase leaned over to one side and one night it collapsed.'

They were all laughing at Seb's red face, and Gab made matters worse by noticing that the hearth rug was very superior compared to the one Ginny and he had rolled about on. Then Seb's face went even redder.

'Give the fellow a chance,' Valentine said. 'He's not been here a week yet, time enough for romance. Leave him be.'

They spent another half an hour joking and teasing, and then Ginny said, 'Time we went. Night, Seb. So glad you're working at the practice, you're a refreshing change from the one whose place you've taken. Arthur Hetherington! God! Was he a misfit! Grumpy old man he was, except he wasn't old, but he was grumpy and lazy to boot. And I'm being polite!'

Seb went to bed that night both exhausted and exhilarated by the kindness of his new

47

colleagues. They all worked so well together despite being very different kinds of people. He hoped it would always be like that. He couldn't bear arguing and back-biting; he'd had enough of that where he'd worked before.

★ ★ ★

Seb worked hard the next morning. The canary man, Mr Smithson, was one of his clients. He'd been so taken with Seb's apparent understanding of the needs of canaries that he'd been out and bought all the necessary wire netting, the requisite shed and the lengths of wood, and, with the help of a carpenter friend, had made an aviary to accommodate some more canaries. His intention this morning was to ask Seb to visit his home and check his amateur construction before he painted it.

Flattered by the confidence Mr Smithson had in him Seb agreed to fit the visit in during his lunch-hour.

'It's not far, I'll gladly come. You must have worked fast to get it up by now.'

'My mate had measurements taken and wood cut while I was still thinking about it. I've left him finishing the last of the wire netting. It's turned out bigger than I expected, but let's face it, it'll make life sweeter for them, won't it? We haven't got as far as nesting boxes yet. See you about . . . ?'

'A quarter to one?'

'Great. I don't mind paying. It's my big new hobby, you see, and I'm determined to do it right. See yer then.' Mr Smithson scurried out.

When his last client had left Seb went to have a word with Valentine. 'I'm free to assist with those spays this afternoon, but I'm just popping out first to see a client. Won't be long.'

'Who?'

'Joe Smithson.'

Valentine grinned. 'A year ago he decided to breed gerbils but his wife said they were like rats and refused to allow it, said she wasn't having her conservatory over-run with any damned gerbils. He was bitterly disappointed. What is it this time?'

Seb smiled. 'Canaries. He's building an aviary for them and wants me to inspect its suitability. So maybe they'll fare better.'

★ ★ ★

Mrs Smithson welcomed him with open arms. 'So glad you've come to see the avairy. Joe's that thrilled with it. I've made ham and mustard rolls for lunch — will you have one? Joe and his pal are having a beer with theirs.'

'Not for me when I'm working, thank you. Just the roll, please.'

'A mug of tea?'

Seb agreed that would be welcome. 'Shall I go through?'

'You'd better; he's been clock-watching since half past.'

The avairy, even in its unpainted state and without perches, looked excellent. Joe appeared to be getting into breeding in a big way.

'Why, it's excellent,' Seb said. 'You'll have to advertise — made-to-measure aviaries. It's wonderful. Well thought-out. What about perches?'

'Them's coming next.' Joe pointed to lengths of dowelling waiting to be sawn. 'It's OK, then? I need to be sure.' He was filled to the brim with satisfaction, was Joe. 'I'm searching out a better class of breeder for my initial stock, and when they're all installed I'll give you a ring.'

They settled down on three old chairs outside the conservatory with a weather-worn table in front of them loaded with beer, tea and bread rolls bulging with ham and mustard. Despite the cold Seb enjoyed his lunch, eaten as it was with such companionable men. They talked canaries the whole time; even the carpenter friend had a contribution to make.

Seb finished his roll, drank his mug of hot tea and got to his feet. 'Must go, I'm assisting at three operations this afternoon so can't be late.'

'On canaries?' asked Joe.

'No, cats.'

'Well, I must say you're versatile you vets. Fur as well as feathers. I admire it in a chap so young.'

'Thank you. Will you thank Mrs Smithson for the lunch? I'll go out by the back gate. Be seeing you soon, I'm sure.'

'Thanks for coming. Wait till it's finished and it's full of the little blighters.'

Seb glanced at the pair of them as he closed the back gate and smiled to himself; he was looking at complete happiness and it gave his heart a tremendous lift.

But what he faced when he returned to the practice annihilated his satisfaction.

'Seb!' It was Dodie holding the reception desk phone. 'For you. Jilly Askew.'

'Who?' Seb mouthed silently.

Dodie clapped her hand over the receiver and said, 'Jilly Askew. Here, take it!' And she stood, openly listening to his conversation.

'Good afternoon, Miss Askew,' Seb said politely. 'How can I help?'

'You can't, Seb. This is a social call. I'm asking you out for a drink. I'm the one you spoke to at the meet, remember? Are you free tonight?'

'Yes, I am.'

'Good. I'll be in The George about nine. Would that be convenient?'

'That would be delightful. I shall look forward to seeing you. Is your horse OK after the little contretemps with the hound?'

'Oh! Yes, thanks. Absolutely fine. See you about nine then. Bye!'

Seb handed the receiver back to Dodie. He felt a little shell-shocked.

Dodie couldn't resist saying something. 'Well, that's a turn-up for the books. I heard you'd seen off the Hunt and examined one of the hounds.'

'Yes. I wish I'd said I was on call.'

'I could always create an emergency and then you couldn't go. How about it?'

'It was so unexpected. What does she want from me? Someone like her?'

'I daren't enquire!' Dodie was bursting to laugh but for Seb's sake she managed to contain herself. Indeed, he was quite right — what did someone like Jilly Askew want with Seb? 'Where are you meeting her?'

'At The George.'

'In that case, smart casual.'

'But — '

'Jacket and smart trousers.'

'I haven't got anything smart. Nothing. What the blazes shall I do?'

'It's the man she's after, not the clothes. Just do your best.' Dodie had to retire to her office. She closed the door and began to laugh as discreetly as she could. Poor Seb. He was like a lamb to the slaughter. Fortunately for him he'd no idea about her reputation, but ought she to warn him? Perhaps she should.

Seb was still standing in reception gazing into space when she re-emerged. 'Seb, I feel I ought to say something. About Jilly Askew. Are you listening to me?'

Seb nodded.

'She's well known as a hunter of men, to put it bluntly. Bit past her sell-by date, you know.'

'Ah! Right.'

'So be warned.'

'Yes, of course. I see.'

'And Valentine's about to start.'

'Start what?'

'Operating. Spaying, you know. You promised to help?'

'Ah! Yes. I did.'

'Go on, then, get cracking.'

Valentine was just about to begin his first spay. 'Here you are, then. Get gowned up and you start the first one. Everything all right at Joe

Smithson's? No problems, were there? You seem very agitated.'

Seb didn't reply. He put on a gown, a pair of plastic gloves and went to the operating table. Sarah Cockroft was assisting. Seb acknowledged her with a nod and made to pick up a scalpel.

'Just a minute! You're shaking, you can't operate like that. What's the matter?'

'Sorry, I'll be all right in a mo.'

'No, you won't. I'll do this. You can do the second one once you've calmed down.'

By the time the second spay began Seb was under control and did an excellent job in Valentine's estimation.

'That is good, very good,' he said. 'Couldn't have done better myself and I don't give praise lightly.'

Out of the blue, Seb said, 'Do you know Jilly Askew?'

Sarah snorted her amusement.

Valentine looked Seb straight in the eye. 'Why?'

'She's rung up and asked me out for a drink. At The George.'

Sarah's jaw dropped. 'Asked *you* out for a *drink?*'

Valentine, realising that Seb was still at the starting gate as far as women were concerned, said, 'How's this come about?'

'By chance. Scott and I got held up by the Hunt in the main square and I got out to see it, and her horse panicked and booted one of the hounds so I volunteered to check it over.'

Sarah muttered, 'You never did!'

'Well, why not? Animal with a problem. What does a vet do? Nothing?'

Sarah declared, 'But the Hunt . . . it's taboo.'

'Is it?' Seb looked at Valentine for confirmation.

'In the circumstances I agree you could do no other, but as a general rule this practice doesn't agree with hunting.'

'*Everyone* disagrees?'

'Scott, Ginny, Colin . . . Dan and Rhodri could go either way. Mungo, if it meant more money in the coffers, would have us as the official Hunt vets. So there you are.'

'And you?'

'Just don't care. There's for and against, believe me. Is that what your shaking hands were about? Jilly Askew?'

Seb laughed at himself. 'I can't think why she's asked me, I really can't. We barely exchanged more than a dozen words.'

Valentine grinned. 'Never mind, it'll be good experience for you.' He began the third spay on a lovely seven-month-old cat, with long brownish gingery fur. 'Isn't she a lovely cat? Not pedigree but somehow from way back a pedigree has emerged in her genes. The owner is a dear old client of mine, a Mrs Bookbinder. She adores her dog and now she's taken to cats as well. Wealthy, too.' He looked up at Seb. 'You'd do well to cultivate *her*.' Valentine gave him an amused wink and Seb had to laugh.

'That's how you keep your clients, is it, by flirting with them?'

Scalpel in hand, Valentine paused for a

moment. 'That's more like it; Jilly's only asked you out for a drink, nothing more, so enjoy, dear boy, enjoy!'

So that night Seb showered, put on his very best clothes and sauntered out to meet Jilly Askew, with Valentine's advice ringing in his ears.

4

Jilly was waiting for him in the bar looking so much more relaxed than when he spoke to her at the Hunt. Her thick black hair was styled into a sharp bob level with her ear-lobes, her skin sparkled with good health and she was full of *joie de vivre*. In fact, Jilly was a very different person from the one he'd seen mounted on that magnificent horse.

'Good evening, Seb.'

'Good evening, Jilly. I almost didn't recognise you. That sounds very impolite but . . . it's true.'

'I know. On a horse I change my character. I'll get the drinks. What's your favourite?'

'Allow me.'

'No. I invited you, therefore . . . '

Seb gave in graciously. 'Just this once, then. A whisky and water for me.'

'Right. Hate whisky myself.' She bounded off to the bar and he could see by the way the barman greeted her that she was someone who carried a lot of social weight at The George.

'Here we are.' Jilly sat down, placed her vermouth and lemonade on a mat, crossed her long, slender legs and said, 'I'm not the horsey type at all. I ride because the family expect it of me, but I dislike it. Every single one of them rides, including my aunt, daily in some cases, but if I never saw a horse again it wouldn't trouble me.'

'I see. Why not admit it?'

'If you knew the Askew family you'd know what I meant.'

Seb raised an eyebrow.

'The pressure is unbearable. You're dismissed as a complete outsider if you don't ride. Have you always wanted to be a vet?'

'For as long as I can remember. My parents own a farm in the Yorkshire Dales and fully expected me to follow on, but I couldn't. The urge to be a vet was too powerful and though I knew it would upset them I followed my own star. They've got used to the idea at last, thank goodness, but it was very dodgy at the time.'

'You'd laugh if I told you what I want to do.'

'No, I wouldn't.'

'It's so outrageous that if I mention it in the family they fall off their chairs laughing.'

'Try me. I won't laugh.'

Jilly took a deep breath. 'Promise?'

'Promise.'

'I went to Oxford, like all self-respecting Askews do, got a first in medieval history, and have made no use of it since, no use at all.'

'You mean you don't work?'

Jilly agreed she didn't. 'Good thing I have family money otherwise I couldn't survive as a paid-up member of the unemployed.'

'So what do you want to do that's causing your family to fall off their chairs?'

'Teach history in a secondary school. I'd like to be of value in this world.'

'What does your uncle think about that?'

'He's kindly disposed to the idea actually.'

'If that's what you want to do, do it.'

'But Lord Askew's sons and that bitch Lady Mary are so scathing about it.'

'Have you done your postgraduate diploma?'

'No. They'd think I'd gone stark staring mad if I did.'

'Then show them you mean business.' Seb reached across and patted her hand. 'Go for it.'

Jilly blushed with delight. 'You really think I should?'

'Of course. Why not? I'm a great believer in people doing exactly what fires them up, whatever the obstacles.'

'You wouldn't laugh at me, then?'

'Absolutely not.'

Jilly squeezed his hand and immediately they became friends. Seb guessed she was about ten years older than himself but that didn't appear to matter. She didn't seem ten years older with her bright, up-to-the-minute designer clothes and that fabulous black hair, and her slender figure. Her face hadn't a single wrinkle and her large, dark-blue eyes were full of passion and vitality.

'Do you know, I might do it, I just might. You speak from experience — can you say you're convinced you did the right thing, despite your parents' disappointment?'

'I couldn't be happier.'

'Really?'

'Living on the farm would have been all right, but being a vet makes every day . . . well, it makes every day spectacular.'

Seb felt her relief when he said that. How come she was so unsure of herself when she belonged to such a prestigious family and had money and standing in society?

'My turn to buy the drinks. Same again?' he asked.

'Yes, please.'

The bar was filling up now and Seb had to wait to be served. He glanced across at Jilly and saw a man was talking to her, he looked like one of those upper-crust people he was inclined to despise. But he'd moved on by the time Seb had been served with their drinks.

The rest of the evening was filled with the kind of conversation held by people who are endeavouring to get to know as much as possible about each other, and by the time they were parting company because it was getting late, Seb found himself feeling great attraction towards Jilly. She was so different from the woman on horseback he'd first met — softer, more kindly and much more understanding than he could possibly have imagined.

'Are you free on Friday night?' he found himself saying. 'We could have dinner this time?'

'That would be great. Thanks. And thanks for coming this evening. It's a real pleasure to speak with someone who doesn't live and breathe horses!'

* * *

The following day Dodie made a point of telling Seb they'd had an emergency appointment. 'Will you see her as your first client? It's a dog.'

The client came into his consulting room

59

without her dog, and she was in a dither. 'My dog is out in the car. I've scalded him. Not on purpose, of course, but I have and he's, well, he's . . . ' She burst into tears.

'Look, bring him in and I'll take a look at him, see what we can do.'

'He got under my feet and I got cross with him and then I tripped and . . . the kettle . . . it had just boiled . . . it spilled all over his head and I . . . '

'What breed is he?'

'A dog. Oh! I mean, he's a Welsh terrier.'

'In that case, I can carry him in. Come with me. You are . . . ?'

'Delia Loveday. He's terrified. I can't persuade him to get out.'

Seb took her out by the back door and discovered the dog cowering in the back of her estate car. The moment he put his hand on the rear door the dog bared its teeth and growled exceedingly loudly, then hurtled round and round the car, barking threateningly.

'What's his name?'

'Dai.'

'Right. Dai, Dai.'

Dai growled, showing his fangs so close to the window that it steamed up.

'My word! He's very upset. Doesn't appear to have damaged his eyes, though, so that's a plus. What's his favourite treat?'

Delia Loveday hesitated and then admitted that a piece of Mars Bar was what he liked the most.

'Mars Bar. Right. I don't suppose you have one on you?'

'Here, in my pocket.' The Mars Bar was in a plastic bag already cut in small pieces ready for any emergency. 'I always have some with me when we go out, just in case.'

'Just in case?'

'Well, you see, he can be difficult to handle. Bites, you know, if he doesn't want to do what I say.'

'Bites? But you're his owner.'

'I know. But he does. I have to be careful.'

Seb kept his opinion to himself. 'You open the window at the front just a tiny bit, then shut the door again quick. I'll hold a piece of Mars Bar close up to the gap so he gets the smell of it. Where's his leash?'

'In my other pocket, here.'

'Right. Operation Dai. Now . . . you be ready with the leash. While he's occupied munching the Mars Bar I'll get it clipped on to his collar the moment I open the door.'

'It won't work, he's too sharp.'

'We'll try.'

They did Operation Dai three times, and each time he got the treat but they didn't succeed in getting the leash clipped on.

The back door crashed open and out came Dodie Pilgrim. 'I've been watching this . . . *pantomime* from the staffroom window. Give me the leash. And you can put that Mars Bar away. Mars Bar, indeed. Whatever next? He's a dog not a person. What's his name?'

Humiliated, Seb said, 'Dai. Mind, he's scalded his head, it'll be very sore. That's why he's so frightened.'

'Right! Watch!' In a voice more suited to Trooping the Colour, Dodie said firmly, 'Dai! Come!' She then opened the rear door and said it again, in a tone that brooked no nonsense. Dai hesitated for a moment and then squeezed between the front seats and patiently stood in front of Dodie allowing her to clip on his leash, with not a single fang in sight, nor even a murmur of a growl. 'Come, Dai!' Dodie said bracingly. A slight tug on his collar and Dai jumped down on to the tarmac.

'In!' Dodie opened the back door and marched Dai into Seb's consulting room. She picked him up and stood him on the examination table, then gently cuffed him under his chin saying, 'There, that wasn't too bad, was it?' To his owner she said, 'All he needs is firm handling,' and marched out.

The moment Dai realised he'd been out-manoeuvred by Dodie Pilgrim he submitted to Seb's examination. Treating him with the greatest respect when he saw the scald on his head and ears, Seb gently studied the extent of the damage.

'When it first happened what did you do?'

'I poured jugs of cold water over it to take the heat out, like I would have done for the children. That's why he's still damp. Did I do wrong?'

'No, in the circumstances you did the right thing. Because his fur is thick on his head I think he's escaped the worst. There's no sign of blistering, but it's red and obviously very tender. I suggest you remember not to pat or stroke his head, because that really will hurt. Let's keep a close eye on him and if things begin to look worse, then bring him in and I'll reconsider treatment. I'm a great believer in leaving scalds alone, no greasy creams, just nature. It's very red now, but that will begin to fade. I will, however, give him an injection for the pain and shock.'

Dai gracefully accepted the injection without any opposition and looked at Seb as though thanking him. This was noticed by Mrs Loveday. 'He's taken to you, I can see. We used to go to the vet nearer home, but they got thoroughly unpleasant with him because of his bad temper and I had to stop going about two years ago. He'd never have let them near him with a needle, not like he's just done with you.'

'Has he not had his boosters, then?'

Mrs Loveday shook her head.

'I won't do it today, he's had quite enough of an upset already. Bring him in when you're ready and we'll do them then. Here, Dai.' Seb brought out a box of dog biscuits from a cupboard and gave him two. 'They'll be better for his teeth than Mars Bar.'

Seb smiled so sweetly at Mrs Loveday that she didn't take offence. She smiled back. 'Thank you so much. I do appreciate him liking you, and you liking him. I'll make an appointment for next week or earlier if his scald isn't looking good. I don't know your name.'

'I'm Sebastian Partridge. Be seeing you.'

'Mr Partridge. I'll remember that. Thank you very much.'

With no clients of his own to see Seb went to help Valentine, who had a full list.

Valentine went to his door and called out, 'Kiki Beaumont,' accompanied by his familiar heel-clicking and bowing.

Apparently the cat and the owner shared the same name because as she charged into the consulting room she called out, 'Hi! Remember me? Kiki? And how is Valentine? Gorgeous as usual? Oh! Who's this? You're new, aren't you?' She came to an abrupt halt in front of Seb and looked up at him, bright-eyed and intrigued. 'Oh! I say! This place does seem to attract the most gorgeous men. I assume you're qualified?'

'Indeed.'

'Are you going to deal with my darling Kiki, then?'

Valentine agreed he could and stood back to watch the performance.

'If you'll allow me.' Seb checked what needed to be done by bringing up on the screen the notes on her last visit. 'Right. If you'd like to get her out of the carrying basket . . . '

Out of the basket came a Persian cat more splendid than Seb had ever seen. She was pure white, almost dazzlingly white, and every single square inch of her extremely long fur was beautifully combed.

He couldn't find words to express his delight. 'Why! She looks beautiful. You must spend hours brushing and combing. Hours and hours. She's magnificent.'

Kiki, the owner, glowed with pleasure. She clasped her hands together under her chin. 'She is beautiful, isn't she? She's an indoor cat. I don't let her out. She sleeps on my bed, and we lead a wonderful life together. If anything happened to her . . . well . . . I daren't even think about it.' She shuddered at the thought.

'Hold her, I'm ready.'

But Kiki asked for Valentine to hold her cat. 'I can't look, you see.'

'That's fine. Valentine?'

So Val held her, and Kiki the cat behaved beautifully and was back in her basket in a moment.

'Thank you. By the way, I'm having a cocktail party next week. Could you come? Help you get to know people in Barleybridge, wouldn't it? I've loads of friends; they'll all love you.'

Behind her back Valentine was slowly shaking his head. Seb took the hint. Searching frantically for a reasonable excuse he invented a girlfriend.

'I'm terribly sorry but my girlfriend is in hospital having an operation this morning and . . . well, she'll need looking after when she gets out. Perhaps another time.'

He felt a complete fraud, but it had to be done. Kiki showed only mild disappointment, almost as though she expected a refusal, and floated out, leaving Seb feeling uncomfortable at the easy way he'd invented his lie.

'Why did you shake your head?' he asked Valentine.

'My dear Seb, you'd probably find yourself the only person at the party, or she'd have completely forgotten all about the invitation and gone out. It happened to Rhodri and to Graham, a vet before your time. She invites me often but I always say I'm on call. Your excuse was marvellous, though. How did things go with Jilly Askew, by the way?'

'Ah! OK. She's quite different when not sitting on a horse. Really quite different.'

'Do I detect a hint of further drinks?'

'Well, yes. Actually. Yes, you do.' He almost told Valentine about her ambition but decided against it. After all, it was her secret.

But by lunchtime it was all round the practice that he'd been seen drinking with Jilly Askew because Scott's Zoe had been attending a meeting at The George and had seen the two of them sitting talking in the bar.

Ginny pulled his leg mercilessly in the staffroom. 'So you've become part of the Hunt brigade, have you? We'll be having to pay to speak to you soon. You should know we have nothing whatsoever to do with it as a practice.'

Seb was riled by her attitude. 'Just because I have a drink with someone it doesn't mean I approve of everything they do.'

'Whoops! You're cross with me. Dear, dear. Sorry. We attend Lord Askew's horses and his farm animals, but we have nothing to do with the Hunt and you should remember that.'

Dan, angered by Ginny's attack on poor innocent Seb, reminded her she had been barred from the Askew estate. 'Is this a case of sour grapes, I ask myself, Ginny?'

The wind taken out of her sails, Ginny backtracked. 'It's better he knows where we all stand, Dan.'

'Speak for yourself. If the Hunt decided to have a new vet I'd be the first to agree to us being chosen. Not that it's likely. Harvey Johnson-Munt is well entrenched there, but the money involved would transform the practice profits.'

'Over my dead body.' Ginny was red in the face with anger. 'It's cruel and barbaric and needs to be stopped.'

'Well, it hasn't stopped and in any case they follow an artificial trail now so there's no question of fox hunting as it used to be.'

'Until by chance they come across a fox. The essence of the Hunt is there just the same, and I for one won't tolerate it.'

Mungo walked in, sensed the charged atmosphere and asked Dan what the matter was.

'Just a clash of opinions, Mungo. Storm in a teacup.'

'Don't you believe him,' said Ginny. 'It's more than that.'

Mungo looked at everyone and no one volunteered a reply so Ginny spoke up and went straight for the jugular.

'Hypothetical question, Mungo: if the Hunt veterinary post became vacant for whatever reason, would you take it on if invited?'

Without a moment's hesitation Mungo said, 'Yes.'

Stuned silence prevailed until Ginny said bluntly, 'In that case I'd resign.'

Mungo remembered the times when he'd wished she would and replied, 'So be it. You're not a partner and while I take into consideration all my staff's wishes, such a huge opportunity cannot be turned down, believe me.'

'I see. So my opinions count for nothing.'

'For God's sake, Ginny, you wouldn't be tearing the foxes to pieces yourself, now would you? Simply attending to the good health of the animals involved. I don't want to hear anything more about your principles, nor anyone else's. As you said, it's all hypothetical. Just came to say we're having an Open Day. We haven't had one for three years and it's time we did. It'll be the last Saturday in November. Everyone on parade, OK? By the way, you'll be pleased to hear that Kate Howard is starting on Monday so we shall have plenty of veterinary expertise available . . . should we ever be invited to be the Hunt vet.' He glared at them all, then escaped as quickly as possible, leaving behind a staffroom heaving with unspoken thoughts.

Dan, determined to lighten the atmosphere, turned the conversation to Kate. 'Kate! A vet at last! Wonderful! You haven't met her, have you, Seb?'

'No. I've heard about her, though.'

'She's great. We all love Kate, don't we, Ginny?'

Ginny, still tight-lipped, muttered, 'Yes,' and left the staffroom.

'Bit younger than you but don't imagine she'll be wet behind the ears. Sharpest knife in the box, is our Kate. Prize-winner, don't you know!'

'Help!'

'No need for you to worry. You're bright enough as it is, and doing so well already.'

'Thanks.'

'If you've a quiet day come with me on my rounds, Seb. OK?'

'Thanks, though I am just beginning to get busy.'

'Good. It takes time.'

Seb, horrified by Ginny's blunt attack on his drink with Jilly, had been on the verge of telling them what she was really like, but held back just in time. He wasn't the kind of person to enjoy controversy but if he wanted to see Jilly then see her he would. He was looking forward to that meal on Friday. But he realised that the veterinary world was a small one, and trying to conceal one's social life would be a waste of time. So maybe he'd have to put up with being taunted by Ginny. Did he care? No, he did not.

5

On the day of his second date with Jilly Askew, Seb had been given a routine job to do on an old dog called Chuck. His breath smelt apallingly, caused by his teeth being coated in tartar and food debris. Bunty had taken upon herself the task of assisting him, and pointed out a back tooth which was breaking up with decay.

'That must be painful. Bits have fallen off it,' she said.

'You're right! What a mess for the poor old chap. Why don't people take more care of their animals?'

'Well, Seb, in this particular case, the owner is an almost blind old man who is devoted to poor Chuck and relies on him for companionship.'

Seb felt embarrassed. 'Sorry, Bunty, I didn't know. I'll remove the tooth.'

'No, you won't. Not till I've asked the owner. If more has to be done than first mentioned then we have to get permission, although it's not often refused. I'll be a minute or two. He takes ages to answer the phone.'

Seb carried on taking the tartar from Chuck's teeth, thankful that Bunty knew the rules.

She came back in after a while. 'That's fine by him. He's worried sick. I feel so sorry for him. He manages with the minimum of help, but he does have a neighbour who takes the dog out every day so that's a blessing. Finished?'

'Just got the tooth to remove. What do you think? They were bad.'

'Look, you've missed a bit, down here by the gum on the small teeth at the front.'

'So I have. Let's hope it improves his breath; it was disgusting.'

Valentine was called in to see what he thought after they'd done the extraction, and liked what he saw. 'You're very good, you know, despite not being allowed to spread your wings at your last practice, Seb. Excellent job. Thanks. Why don't you ask Mungo if you can watch him do an operation after lunch on a cat involved in a road accident? Sounds a really complicated job. That is, if you've nothing else on at the moment.'

Seb's mind was immediately seized by the idea and he sacrificed his half-day. By closely studying the X-rays Seb could see what a difficult operation it would be. His practical approach to life made him ask Mungo if in fact it would be kinder to put the cat to sleep.

'Yes, I suppose so, in a way,' Mungo replied, 'but she's only a year old with lots of life still left to live and I *know* I can do it. The owners are willing to pay for my time, and if the result gives her years of enjoyable life then . . . '

'But it is a bad break. Let's face it, the thigh bone is in *pieces*. Maybe you won't be able to make it right.' The moment he'd finished speaking he could have bitten his tongue out, and he got the broadside he deserved.

Mungo's face grew pinched with annoyance. 'I have years of experience in this field. Sometimes I do have to say that what you've suggested is the

71

right thing to do, but not this time and don't ever, *ever* question my judgement again.' Mungo gave Seb a tight smile, which went some way to softening his criticism but not entirely, and Seb vowed never to doubt Mungo ever again.

By the end of the afternoon Seb decided that Mungo was right to have confidence in his own ability, because what had been a shambles of shattered bone, nerves and muscle was patiently sorted out, pinned and braced so wonderfully well that Seb was left in awe. A final X-ray of the completed operation showed a thigh beautifully aligned; only time would eventually prove whether or not the cat would have full use of its leg, but Seb was so impressed he just knew she would.

Bunty, with adoration on every inch of her face, wheeled the cat away to intensive care. Mungo called out after her, 'Someone to stay the night, please. Check every two hours.'

'I'll organise it.'

'Thanks, Bunty.' Mungo turned to Seb. 'She's an excellent nurse — efficient, conscientious, dedicated. Where would we be without them?'

'We wouldn't. Thank you for letting me watch. I've learned a lot.'

'Good.' Mungo stretched and yawned. 'That's me for the day. Be seeing you, Seb. You appear to have made a good start. Dodie keeps singing your praises. We've someone rung in who's got a herd of alpacas, and is not awfully pleased with their current vet. Would you be interested?'

'I've no experience but I can always learn.'

'That's the way. I understand from the

veterinary grapevine that they have used about four different vets in the area and we're their last hope, so it sounds as though they might be difficult clients.' Mungo walked away looking drained and so too was Seb. It was the level of concentration needed and the meticulous exactness of the work over a long period of time that was exhausting. Never the less, he'd thoroughly enjoyed his afternoon.

* * *

When Mungo had gone up to the flat, exhausted and longing for Miriam's warming presence, he found she was out and so too was Perkins. He stood at the window from which he could see Beulah Bank Top and thought he could see her coming down from the top. It *was* Miriam. He watched her striding home and shockingly for a second he could also see the shadows of their two children either side of her. If they'd lived they'd have been . . . what? . . . ten and eleven. Would one of them have wanted to be a vet? More than likely. The screaming pain of their deaths within six months of each other roared through him again. He turned hastily away from the window and went to put the kettle on to make tea for him and Miriam. He hardly ever got the chance to do things for Miriam; she was always doing the caring.

When he heard Perkins pushing the flat door open with his nose, he filled up the teapot, added it to the tray and carried it into the sitting room. Perkins followed closely and sat down bolt upright waiting for a biscuit.

'Perkins! No,' said Mungo.

Perkins' ears drooped and he looked exceedingly sad as only he could. Miriam came in.

'Tea, darling?'

'Oh! That's wonderful. Good outcome?'

Mungo nodded. 'Took a while. In fact, I've only just finished. But yes, I think we're going to be all right. Seb's a good chap. Going to be very good, actually. I'm glad you persuaded me to take him on.'

'Well, he's different from the rest. None of that overt sexual charm like the others. In a way . . . he reminds me of Duncan.'

'Joy's Duncan?'

'Yes. He could almost be his son. Maybe that's why Joy is so taken with him. He's got that quiet I-need-mothering look just like Duncan.'

'Here, sit down.' He dropped a kiss on her forehead as she helped herself to a biscuit. 'He's astute where operating is concerned, very methodical and precise. Good attributes. Time will tell.'

Mungo couldn't withstand Perkins' pleading eyes any longer and dropped, accidentally on purpose, a corner of biscuit in front of his paws. It was swiftly gobbled up but not so swift Miriam didn't notice. 'Mungo! If you had to exercise him every day you wouldn't be giving in like that. He knows it's no good looking at me for biscuits.'

'He deserves some treats at fourteen. He's not so sprightly as he was, you know.'

'Actually, you're right. He isn't. He's glad to turn for home sooner than before.'

Perkins knew he was being talked about. His ears drooped again and he began to look guilty of he knew not what.

Mungo ruffled his ears. 'Never mind, old boy, it happens to all of us.'

Miriam protested. 'Don't say that. I don't want him to die.' Her eyes filled with tears.

'Darling, he will, you know. It's inevitable and you'd better face up to it. Now rather than later.' He made it sound as though he'd faced up to it himself but in fact he hadn't. Not his Perkins. Not the dog who'd given them comfort when . . . 'We'll get another one.'

'Another dog will never replace Perkins.' The tears welled in her eyes again. 'I love him so.'

'Come and sit on my knee.' So she did and they comforted each other, one remembering the miles Perkins walked with her when she couldn't bear being in the house with her memories another minute, the other what a stout companion Perkins had always been to him.

'In any case, Mungo, we couldn't have a puppy in a flat. Perkins only manages because I take him out a lot, but he's old in dog terms. A puppy would go mad in here.' She stood up and went to look out of the window, suddenly desolate, her soul meandering without purpose in some distant wilderness. With a devastatingly sad tone in her voice she said softly, 'Sometimes, you know, like today, the two of them . . . they're with me when I'm out with Perkins, like they used to be. You remember?'

Mungo stiffened. The shock was almost too much, that they both had been aware of them at the same time. It was more than flesh and blood could stand. Mungo felt her isolation and went to stand beside her with an arm round her waist. Frantically searching for something to say to lift the gloom they both felt he came up with, 'It's been ages since we had a dinner party here in this flat. How about it?'

'For the staff, you mean?'

'Yes. Not the lay staff, just the others. How many would there be?' he counted on his fingers. 'Rhodri and Maggie, Dan and Rose, Valentine, Seb, Colin and Letty, Scott and Zoe, Ginny and Gab. There'd be fourteen of us.'

Not at all inspired by Mungo's enthusiasm Miriam replied, 'Too many in this flat. We haven't even got enough chairs. Nor plates. And what about Joy and Duncan?'

'We could always bring some chairs up from the waiting room.'

Miriam shook her head.

Perkins got up and went to sit beside her, leaning his body against her legs to let her know he was there for her.

Mungo, not knowing what to say next, muttered, 'Got to go check on my cat. I won't be a minute.'

He stood in the intensive-care room contemplating the cat. She was coming round, stirring a little, puzzled, trying to make sense of her surroundings.

'Now, Kitty, how's things?'

But how were things for him? More so, how were things for his Miriam? He had no answer to that.

Bunty burst in. 'Is she all right? When I saw you coming in here I thought the worst?'

'She's doing fine.'

'I couldn't bear it if she died. She's such a lovely cat, not an ounce of nastiness in her, not even when she's in awful pain.'

'She's young and healthy, should be fine, though it was a long operation. Do her owners know?'

'Of course. First thing I do. Sarah Cockroft's volunteered to sleep in. We can rely on her.'

'Yes, of course. We're lucky, you know, having those two girls. They're so reliable.'

Longing for recognition, Bunty asked, 'And me?'

'And you. Goes without saying. Thanks.' Mungo patted Bunty's arm in appreciation as he left.

Mungo went to sit in his office for a while leaving Bunty glowing with his approval. Suddenly he leapt to his feet and dashed upstairs to the flat.

'Miriam! Let's have it at The George! How about it? Celebrating the real conclusion of our extension now the building work is finished. Eh!'

Not wishing to disappoint him Miriam turned from the window with a smile. 'What a good idea. yes, that will be lovely. A really posh do. No skimping. Posh frocks. Smart suits. Something we can all look forward to.'

'Excellent! Love me?' He swung her round and kissed her.

'Of course. I have no one else but you to love. Loads of people love *you*. For a start, all your clients with pets they'd have had to have put down if it hadn't been for your skill.'

Wickedly he added, 'And Bunty.'

Miriam smiled. 'Oh! I've known about Bunty for years. We all know how she feels about you. I should be jealous but I'm not. It's her husband Aubrey I feel sorry for. Fancy getting married knowing you're a second choice.'

'There's never any need to feel jealous; there's only you for me.'

'I know that, my darling.' Brightening up, Miriam added, 'We'll have this dinner party a month from now, so they've all got a chance to find babysitters.'

★ ★ ★

At 8 p.m. precisely Seb left for his second date with Jilly in high spirits. He was the first to arrive so he sat quietly in the bar thinking about the wonderful day he'd had. Someone came to ask if they could help. 'Name's Partridge, a table for two booked for eight-thirty.'

'Ah! Right. We're busy tonight; shall I bring you a couple of menus? Might save you time.'

'Thank you, that would be good.'

He couldn't have been there for more than five minutes when in walked Scott, carrying a beer. He spotted him immediately and came across. 'Thank God! Someone I know.' He plonked himself down with his drink. 'Got out of the habit of drinking alone, but Zoe's got school-friends coming for a meal tonight and I'm banned. So here I am. Don't mind, really. Eating

78

here is better than listening to all the girl gossip, don't you think?'

'Absolutely.'

'Can I get you a drink?'

'No, I'm fine.' Seb paused. Would he get another shooting from the hip like he'd had from Ginny earlier in the week? No, perhaps not. 'I'm waiting for Jilly Askew.'

'Ah! Right, of course. Zoe said. Second date in a week. Mmm.'

'Look, I took a real blasting in the staffroom about her. I know the opposition but there we are.'

'Seb, you go out with whom you please. If she's OK with you, she's OK with me.'

'Thanks. Are you opposed to hunting?'

'Not personally, but Zoe is. Nearly got arrested once for protesting. However, it's up to you. Your choice.' He grinned.

'Thanks. She's much nicer off the horse than on.' He smiled and Scott agreed that well she might be. 'Here she comes now.'

Seb got to his feet and so did Scott. Jilly looked perfectly splendid and Seb was proud it was him she'd come to meet. He introduced Scott.

'Ah! You're Scott the Australian,' she said. 'My uncle is full of admiration for your expertise.'

'Thank you. He has wonderful animals. I'm glad to have the opportunity to look after them. It's a privilege. Must go, I'm expected elsewhere. Have a good evening.' Scott melted tactfully away but not before, behind Jilly's back, he gave Seb a huge wink accompanied by a thumbs-up.

Seb had to hope that Jilly didn't notice him blushing.

He handed her a menu while he calmed himself down. Scott was only being friendly and where would one be without friends like him?

'Scott seems a lovely chap. Is he married?'

'He is. Well married with three children and his wife wanting a fourth. I understand they're very happy together.'

'You're not warning me off, are you? I'm not that kind of person.'

'Of course not. Sorry. It's just that he doesn't appear to be a settled kind of person, that's all. What do you fancy from the menu?'

'Haven't decided. I'll have a drink first, please. My usual.'

Seb's mind went blank. 'Your usual?'

'Vermouth and lemonade.'

'Ah! Yes, of course.' Seb went off to the bar. He felt anxious that they wouldn't be seated by eight-thirty as it was already twenty-five past. Being the sort of person he was, that worried him.

As he handed Jilly her drink she said, 'I can see you're on edge because I was late and we shan't be sitting down at eight-thirty. Don't be. They are here to serve people like you and me; that's what they're paid for.' Looking round the room, Jilly sounded surprised when she commented about how nice it was. 'Smart but very comfortable. Uncle wouldn't be seen dead here.'

'Why not?'

'Not expensive enough. He sets great store by cost. Believes it means quality and nowadays I'm

80

afraid it doesn't, not always.'

'I see.'

'What?'

Seb came out on the side of the badly paid. 'It's all right to have that opinion, but not all of us can afford to dine at The George.'

Jilly looked offended. 'You're not one of those damned socialists, are you, envious of people with money?'

'I beg your pardon. I'm so sorry if I've given offence, that wasn't my intention.'

'I should hope not. It's his money, from his land, and he works hard for it, contrary to public opinion. People always have the wrong idea about Uncle Fergal. He is the kindest and most understanding of men, but he is painfully shy.'

'Shy?'

'Yes. I think it's because he was kept in the nursery all the time when he was a child and then sent off to board at a prep school at eight years old. He's never quite recovered. Imagine being sent away to school at eight years old? Unbelievable.'

'How have his own children been brought up?'

'They all went to school locally and then on to public school at thirteen, then university, naturally Oxford, and then made their own choice of careers. They're expected to fend for themselves financially which can be nothing but good for them.'

Seb was tempted to say, 'Not the same for you, then.' But he didn't, he'd offended her once already.

Instead he asked her if she'd done anything

about applying for her postgraduate diploma.

'I thought I'd talk to you again. What do you really think?'

'From my own experience I would say do it or you will regret it for the rest of your life. Do it before it's too late.'

'But what about the family? They'll laugh.'

'Let them. You'll have the last laugh because you'll be doing exactly what you want with your life, just as they're doing.'

Jilly raised her eyebrows at the vehemence in his voice. 'You mean it, don't you?'

'Yes. Whose life is it? Yours or theirs? Ask yourself that.'

Jilly looked hard at him before she replied. 'You look very meek and mild, but underneath you're damn tough.'

'You don't struggle through five years at veterinary college without getting tough. Academically it's hard, and proving yourself in front of clients can be shattering. And I also had to make tough decisions, knowing as I did from an early age that I was expected to take over the farm.'

'Who helps your father then?'

'My brother. Lovely chap but not absolutely A1 up top. Couldn't manage the farm himself without help.'

'I see. Then you were brave.'

'I'm certain you've got the same kind of bravery.' Seb smiled at her and she smiled back. They held the glance for a moment and then both lowered their eyes.

'Better order the food. I'm starving,' Jilly said.

They enjoyed their meal and didn't leave the restaurant until after ten. Afterwards Seb saw Jilly to her car and was taken aback by the huge top-of-the-shop Jaguar, although he didn't say a word.

Jilly leaned forward and kissed Seb's cheek. 'Thank you for a lovely evening. It does me good to talk to you and I think I've decided to take your advice. It'll be hard for someone like me but I believe I could make it.' She unlocked the car, then said ruefully, 'This thing will have to go. Can't turn up at school driving this, can I? Give the wrong impression altogether. See, I am learning. Give me a ring, please.'

Seb waved her off and wondered if she really would take that first step. With a life as comfortable as hers appeared to be, it would be a tremendous hurdle to leap, to say nothing of understanding the lifestyle and ambitions of the children she would teach.

6

The new client with the alpaca farm lived a good fifteen miles from the centre of Barleybridge, and Seb had to turn back and retrace his steps twice before he found it. By the time he drove into the entrance he was already twenty minutes late for his appointment. A shining new sign announced that this was the 'Goddard Alpaca Farm'. As he went up the drive he paused to admire the alpacas in the field beside the drive. He immediately took them to his heart. They were utterly beautiful. Their colours ranged from snow-white to a light biscuit colour, with one brown and two black ones. Curiosity got the better of them and some came to the fencing to get a better view of him.

They were sweetly appealing and Seb couldn't wait to examine them. He pressed on and eventually arrived at some buildings; one obviously a private house and the rest apparently indoor stabling for the alpacas.

As he got out of his estate car he patted it. He hadn't expected a new car, only a hand-me-down from someone else in the practice, but Mungo had stretched to a new one for him and he loved it so. He'd never before felt the slightest bit sentimental about a car — so long as it started up without any trouble it was OK by him — but this one . . . well, he was drawn to the Prussian blue colour, its style and the fact it was so easy to drive. 'You're just the ticket, you are,' he said to it.

A voice called out, 'Hi! You must be Mr Partridge?'

Seb blushed bright red, feeling a complete idiot, even more so when he turned and saw who was speaking to him. She was a tall, slim, dark-haired girl, pretty in an odd kind of way.

'That's me. I'm from the Barleybridge Veter —'

'Of course you are. We've been expecting you.'

'I got lost. Twice. Sorry.'

'That's fine. Everyone gets lost, no matter how well we explain where we are. Still, next time you won't.'

As she approached him he saw she was a woman not a girl, but her clothes and the way she wore her hair — fluffed out in a great cloud almost as wide as her shoulders — made her look younger than she actually was.

She reached out her hand to shake Seb's and he found his gripped in a strong clasp. 'Maggie Goddard. My parents own this place. I'm resting at the moment.'

'I'm sorry. Have you been ill?'

Maggie laughed brightly. 'No, I've not been ill. I'm an actress. Resting is what we call it when we've no work in hand.'

'Ah! Right. Shall I be meeting your parents today?'

'Of course! Here they are, look.'

Seb turned and saw Mr and Mrs Goddard crossing the yard. They couldn't have looked more unlike their daughter if they'd set themselves out to be so. They were haphazardly dressed with nothing matching: sleeves too long or dramatically too short; jackets too bulky; boots that looked too big for their legs and faces. Even Seb, who didn't really care what people looked like, noticed their faces were heavily lined, as though they'd weathered badly or had an appallingly traumatic life.

'Good morning! Mr Partridge, I assume.' Mr Goddard marched towards him with an outstretched welcoming hand, as though he too were an actor resting from the stage.

Mrs Goddard gave her greeting as if she were about to swoon from the burdens of this life. She clutched his hand and held on to it for support, saying breathily, 'So glad you were able to come. We do need a person we can rely on . . . completely.'

Poor Seb couldn't extricate his hand and had to follow her to the field at the back of the house at a good rate of knots, with her chattering hysterically as though deprived of human contact for years. Finally they reached a small field and there were the young alpacas, en masse.

Mrs Goddard let go of his hand and propped herself against the fence, seemingly lost in thought.

Maggie came to his rescue. 'These are the babies. Weaned now and ready for sale. Well, almost.'

Seb loved the look of these fluffy junior alpacas. They were comical and full of fun. One suddenly began a crazy gallop around the field, as if trying to entice the others to follow him.

Mrs Goddard muttered, 'It's the males. We're needing them . . . we need them to be . . . '

'Castrated is the word, Mother.' Maggie raised her eyebrows at Seb and tutted.

'Maggie, you're indelicate. They're very sensitive.'

'Why do you want them castrating?' Foolishly, Seb whispered the last word but received a grateful glance of approval from Mrs Goddard.

It was Maggie who explained. 'Some of these are not good enough to be bred from. Nothing massively wrong with them, but they're not quite up to snuff.'

'I see. I'm afraid I haven't brought the necessary with me. I'll make an appointment and come back fully equipped. How many?'

Mr Goddard took charge. 'Four, that's all. Had a spate of boys, you see, and we don't want the bother of them getting frisky. In any case, we need to sell them . . . as pets. Not everyone wants to go in for this job like we've done.'

'You've certainly got some beauties here. How long have you been keeping alpacas?'

'Five years. We bought four from a champion herd, then three more and suddenly in five years there was a crowd.'

'Do you get much demand for them? For sale, I mean.'

Mrs Goddard groaned elegantly. 'Please, don't talk about selling them. It breaks my heart.' She dabbed her eyes, tucked her hand into the crook of Seb's arm and drew him away from the fence. 'Come and see.'

She took him into the nearest stable where

there were two mothers and their very young babies. 'Aren't they beautiful? This is why I can't bear to part with them. I spend a lot of time in here and get far too attached to them. Some of the people who come here wanting to buy! My dear, they are dreadful. Quite dreadful. We couldn't possibly let our babies go with them. Heaven alone knows . . . ' She rolled her eyes dramatically and Seb could see where Maggie got her acting ability from.

'Tea. A cup of tea. I've got it all ready. Come!'

The cups and saucers were an odd collection of old leftover tea services. The spoon for the sugar bowl was wiped clean on the corner of a tea towel which had seen better days, and the milk jug given a quick rinse under the tap to avoid disturbing the mountain of dishes piled in the sink.

Even though he was meticulous in his own kitchen somehow it didn't matter to Seb, because the whole amtosphere of the establishment was so kindly and relaxed, and he really rather enjoyed it.

'Call me Ruthie; everyone else does,' Mrs Goddard said as she poured the tea. 'I like being called Ruthie.'

'Ruthie it is, then.'

'And my husband is always known as Sandy. Don't ask me why because his hair couldn't have been more black as a young man.'

'Thanks for this tea. It tastes lovely.'

'You're welcome.' She seated herself at the kitchen table. 'What do you think to my Maggie?'

'I don't know her, obviously, but what I've seen of her is very pleasant.'

Ruthie bent her head closer. 'She's a brilliant actress but never seems to get the parts. Sad, really. She's on the verge of giving up. One can rest for so long and then . . . money rears its ugly head.'

Maggie came in to have her tea and seated herself at the table, hugging the mug in her elegant hands. 'Are you interested in the theatre, Mr Partridge?'

'I'm afraid I've never had the time. School, university, work to do, you know how it is.'

'No, I don't. I'm producing a show, though, and I'll see you get tickets. Two?'

'I would be delighted.'

'First week in November. Any particular night?'

'It's difficult to know if I shall be on call. I'll let you know nearer the time. But thank you very much.'

They chatted a while longer till Seb remembered he would be needed at the practice. Standing up, he replaced his chair under the table. 'Thank you for your hospitality. I've enjoyed meeting you and your alpacas. Shall we say next Monday? About three?'

Ruthie came over very solemn. 'Excellent, Mr Partridge.'

'Everyone usually calls me Seb, short for Sebastian.'

Immediately Ruthie gushed her delight, thrilled by the familiarity. 'Oh! I've never met anyone called Sebastian before. What a lovely name!' She leapt from her chair and embraced him. 'I can see we're going to get on famously.'

Maggie also got up to embrace him but hers was not the motherly one that Mrs Goddard's had been, more the embrace of someone who fancied him. Seb gently released himself and fled the kitchen. He drove away from the yard in a welter of embarrassment, red-faced and appalled. How could she? They didn't even know each other. Not the slightest little bit. But then he calmed his nerves by remembering she was an actress and of course they were in the habit of over-egging the pudding when emotions were involved.

Before he left, Seb pulled up alongside the fence to take another look at the alpacas. He got out and buried his fingers in the coat of one standing close to him. It was rich, warm and very soft and he tugged at it, thinking how warm an alpaca jumper or scarf would be in a cold winter. They clustered round him and he found himself hugging them each in turn. They were delightful. No wonder the Goddards had decided to breed them.

Yes, he'd definitely enjoy looking after them.

The whirr of bicycle wheels interrupted him and he glanced up to find Maggie racing hell for leather towards him. She braked abruptly and leapt off her bike.

'Glad to have caught you,' she said. 'I don't suppose you fancy a drink? Tonight?'

'Sorry,' Seb stuttered, 'I'm on call tonight so I have to stay in Barleybridge.'

'Well, I'm in Barleybridge tonight for rehearsals. I could see you after.'

Seb's brain was working overtime but he

couldn't come up with a credible excuse. 'If we arrange to meet and I don't arrive it's because I've been called out. It's my night, you see.'

Maggie rooted about in her pockets and gave him a business card. 'No probs. There's my mobile number. We try to finish at half past nine. St Andrew's church hall. It's the church next to the precinct. See you!'

She swept away up the drive towards the house, her hair flying out in a great cloud.

What had he done? He wasn't into acting and such, and that kind of exuberance alarmed him. He didn't really want to go.

His night on call began at seven when the practice was closed for the day, so he made sure he ate in good time so that he wouldn't have to go without his meal. He then spent the next part of the evening on tenterhooks waiting for the phone to ring, but it didn't so at 9.15 p.m. he set off to meet Maggie, feeling as though he had no other option.

There was a large car park outside St Andrew's church hall and after he'd squeezed into the very last space, Seb went inside to search out Maggie. The rehearsal was just finishing and that wild cloud of black hair helped him to pick her out.

'Seb! How lovely you've come! Look, every-one, this is Seb.'

He was greeted with loud 'hellos' and a few wolf-whistles and a couple of 'I says!', which embarrassed him to death.

'See you next time. Remember — word perfect by then. No mumbling, or sneaking a look at your script,' Maggie called out cheerfully. 'Goodnight, everyone!' Then she tucked her hand into Seb's elbow and marched him out.

They adjourned to a nearby pub and sat at the smallest table, it being the only one available. It brought them into close proximity.

'What would you like to drink, Maggie?' Seb asked politely. 'I'm having orange juice in case I'm called out.'

'I'll have a whisky and soda, please.'

'Right. Whisky and soda it is, then.'

As he put her glass down for her he said, 'Most unusual to find an English person having soda with their whisky. I mean, it's all right. I'm just a bit surprised, that's all.'

'I got used to it in the States.'

'You've been acting in the States? Wow!'

Maggie laughed loudly. 'It isn't what it seems. I say that sometimes to impress everyone. They all imagine it's Broadway at the very least; in fact, it was a high schools tour. Taking Shakespeare to the masses.'

'Wonderful opportunity, though!'

'I do love your enthusiasm. We were all second-rate, although the venues were marvellous. But the miles we travelled! God! Some days I woke up and couldn't remember which city we were in, still less which play we were doing that afternoon. I came back and needed a month to recover. I lost weight, mind you, that was a good thing. I'm always just that bit too plump. You, on the other hand, look superbly fit.'

Seb humbly agreed he rarely gained any weight at all.

'That's wonderful. Wish I was the same.' She downed the last drop of whisky and said, 'I need to apologise for Mum for being so ridiculous about what she says in front of the alpacas. As if they know what she's talking about.' Maggie smiled at him and Seb's heart thudded. She was perhaps the most extrovert person he'd ever had anything to do with and she was apparently captivated by him. Touchy-feely, too, always patting his hand or nudging him or downright flirting with him. There was no pretence, so he might as well allow himself to enjoy it. After all, it did no harm.

By the end of the evening he had willingly agreed to see her again. Seb did have a touch of conscience about Jilly Askew, but then there was nothing going on between them. They were, as they say in the celebrity columns, 'just good friends'.

For a brief moment they kissed each other. She was responsive, warm and cuddly, and it was a case of mutual attraction. It seemed to be his year for older women. He didn't think she was as old as Jilly, although not far off. But he didn't care.

What with a job so well suited to his capabilities and with Maggie so exciting and welcoming, Seb went to bed that night full of happiness. And best of all, he managed the whole night without a call-out. Bliss!

7

Seb set off for work the next morning eager to begin the day and looking forward to immersing himself in his job. Yesterday evening had been very successful. He'd thoroughly enjoyed Maggie's company and looked forward to seeing her again. She was the kind of woman he needed — jolly, fun, talkative. You'd never be short of things to talk about when you were in her company, and he loved that.

The postman left him two letters in the entrance to the flats and he'd laid them and the rest of his post on the passenger seat, so at the first set of traffic lights he flicked through them. There were three rubbish ones which would go straight in the bin when he got to work, one from his dad and — what was this? — a letter from his mother, too. That was odd.

At the practice Seb took his post inside with him and opened the letters from home immediately. From his father's letter a cheque fluttered to the floor, and another cheque was neatly stapled to his mother's. The cheque from his dad was wages paid to Seb for helping out on a nearby farm while he was waiting to start at Barleybridge, and the cheque in his mother's letter was from the local newspaper for an article he'd written: *They're asking if you'd be willing to write once a month about your experiences in veterinary practice as a series just for six months as an experiment*, she wrote.

Seb punched the air with delight. Rather more for the money than the idea of writing an article every month. His mother didn't include the editor's letter because she'd put it down somewhere and it had disappeared under his dad's pile of accountancy papers. Seb had to smile. That was typical of their house. It had been the same for as long as he could remember. Briefly he felt a longing for home and went to stand at the window. He looked out across to Beulah Bank Top and thought of the Yorkshire Dales.

Taking his eyes away from the hills he studied the car park for a moment. Surely that worn-out car that had just rolled into the car park didn't belong to the practice? It was far too early for it to be a client. Was it being dumped? No, it wasn't — there was someone still sitting in the driving seat, a woman, and she turned so her eyes scanned the building and came to look directly at him. Immediately she jumped out of the car. Carefully closing the car door behind her, she rushed to the back door, opened it and dashed in. Seb went to greet her.

'Good morning. You're too early for the clinic — it doesn't start until eight-thirty. I just happen to be early this morning. How can I help?'

She was a tiny person, lightly built and exceedingly nervous, and for some reason it took her a while to answer. 'I left home at five. It's my dog, Tatty. He's badly hurt. He fell from our cottage window. He jumps up onto the thatched roof of the outside wood store, you see, and then leaps onto the window sill of the bedroom and sits there in the sun. Someone mentioned Mungo Price to me. That he was a miracle-worker. Are you . . . Mr Price?'

'No, I'm not, but he does work here and he'll be down shortly.'

'A neighbour said . . . he'd be able to help . . . if anyone can.'

The frailty of the woman struck at Seb's heart. There was something very strange about her and he felt an overwhelming urge to solve her problems for her. 'I'm Seb Partridge.' He held out his hand.

Hers was the thinnest, boniest hand he'd ever shaken, and it trembled as he grasped it, with no strength in it at all.

'Look, let's bring Tatty inside in the warm. It'll be better for him in here.'

'I can't pick him up. He's in such pain we'll have to bring him in laid in his bed.'

'That's fine. I'll carry him in for you. What breed is he?'

The smallest hint of a smile flickered at the corner of her mouth. 'He's called Tatty because he's an all-sorts breed, but lovely . . . yes, lovely nature, you know.'

Tatty whimpered as Seb manoeuvred his bed out of the back of the woman's estate car, and whimpered again when he placed him carefully on the table in the intensive-care room. As the woman's gentle, bony hand stroked Tatty's head to soothe him Seb saw she was wearing a wedding ring.

'And you are Mrs . . . ?'

'Mrs Evie Nicholls.'

While Seb carried out a gentle examination of Tatty, Mrs Nicholls nervously chattered on. 'I knew straight away when I heard him yelp that it was very serious. He's done foolish things before, he's so adventurous. Tom wasn't up. I don't sleep, you see. I'm up at five most mornings. Yesterday that was. I took him to the vet in Culworth and he said a couple of days' rest, but if he had a bad night to bring him in today and they'd X-ray him and see what needed to be done. It's his right front leg, I'm certain. They did their best. But I knew. I knew it was very serious. This Mungo Price, he's good?'

'Well, if anyone can help him he can. I've not been here long but I've assisted at a couple of his operations and he's . . . well . . . he's brilliant. But he will tell you the truth, you must be prepared for that.' The moment the words were out of his mouth he knew he shouldn't have said it. She went three shades whiter and almost fell to the floor. He caught her and sat her down on the nearest chair.

'Have you eaten this morning?' he asked with concern.

Evie Nicholls shook her head.

As Seb was about to offer her some coffee Joy arrived, bursting in through the back door as she usually did as though she was already an hour late.

'Oh! I wondered whose car it was. My name's Joy. I'm the practice manager.'

But Mrs Nicholls was past speaking so Seb explained everything.

97

'Well, I think the best thing is for me to ring up to Miriam and get her to give you breakfast. You can freshen up in her bathroom and Mungo will come down and take a look at . . . Tatty, is it?'

Mrs Nicholls nodded vaguely, her strength almost gone.

Joy disappeared to ring Miriam from her office telephone and came back within minutes to say that Miriam would gladly give her breakfast. Then she escorted Mrs Nicholls upstairs.

Miriam and Mungo were both in the kitchen where Mungo was finishing his breakfast.

'This is Mrs Nicholls,' she said. 'Her dog Tatty is downstairs in intensive care with Seb. He fell from a bedroom window and Mrs Nicholls knows something is not quite right.' Joy gave Mungo her special look indicating a serious problem which she didn't want to discuss in front of the client.

Mungo and Joy departed, leaving Miriam with Evie Nicholls.

'Let me show you the bathroom,' Miriam said kindly, 'and I'll put the kettle on and tidy up. There's no hurry. Tea or coffee?'

'Tea and some toast, if that's possible.'

'As much toast as you like.'

Miriam swept away the detritus left by her and Mungo's breakfast and set the table again for Mrs Nicholls. Toast in the toaster, kettle filled, teabags in teapot, fresh butter, jam as well as marmalade, and a quick think about this Mrs Nicholls.

Mrs Nicholls returned from the bathroom and

surveyed the welcoming table. 'That's so kind, Mrs Price.'

Very gently Miriam said, 'Everyone calls me Miriam — will you?'

Mrs Nicholls nodded and then added, 'I'm Evie.'

A silence fell. Miriam sat down opposite Evie. She thought she'd wait until Evie had eaten something before she encouraged her to talk.

It wasn't until the toast shot out of the toaster and landed in the African violets on the window sill that the atmosphere lightened. Miriam apologised, saying it happened almost every time but that the best place in the whole flat for the violets was the kitchen window sill as it was where they thrived the best. She brushed the slices of toast down with a clean tea towel and placed them on Evie's plate. Evie giggled a little, but then the giggles turned to tears.

Instantly Miriam was sympathetic. 'My dear.'

With Miriam's arm around her shoulders Evie sobbed. Moved by the sympathy of a total stranger, she broke down for the first time since Tatty's accident.

'There's no one better than Mungo for putting things right, you can be sure of that,' Miriam comforted her. 'He'll probably be up in a while to tell you the situation. He always puts the animal first and will tell you straight from the shoulder — '

'He won't say he can't h-help, will he?'

'He will tell you the truth, and he won't allow your dog to go through hell unless he is sure he will be successful. He can't bear for animals to be in pain, you see. How old is Tatty?'

'He's about four. We got him from a dogs' home, you see, so they didn't really know. He's my life-saver, is Tatty. I was going to kill myself and just in time Tom took me to buy a dog, thinking it might do me good, and it did.'

'He's got youth on his side, then.'

Evie decided to wade into the toast so silence fell again, leaving Miriam sipping her tea and desperately wondering what on earth to say next. Kill herself? Dear God. She couldn't decide whether Evie was trembling because of her anxiety about Tatty's fate or whether she always trembled because of the delicate state of her mental health. Suddenly she wondered whether 'Tom' actually knew where his wife was.

'You told Tom where you were going, did you?'

'I didn't think. I just knew I had to get here.'

'When you've finished your breakfast you should ring him to tell him where you are.' Privately Miriam decided that Tom must be out of his mind, what with no dog and no Evie, and Evie in the state she all too obviously was.

'I came in a rush. It was Sheila Bissett told me about your husband. She brought her dog here some years ago. I never met it because it died before we moved there and she never bought another, but she said how good your husband was, so about half past four this morning I got the map book out and decided I had to come. I never drive a long way but I had no alternative. Tom is the manager at the village store, so he can't not turn up for work.'

At that moment Miriam heard Mungo coming up the stairs. With both hands under the table she crossed her fingers.

Fearing the worst, Evie got out her handkerchief.

Absorbed though he was with the animal more than the client, even Mungo recognised the desperate state of Evie's emotions, and went about his task very delicately. 'Now, Mrs . . . er . . . '

Miriam stepped in to save embarrassment. 'Mungo, it's Evie.'

'Ah! Right. Now, Evie, you have a very jolly little dog there, he's a sharp little character and I like him very much, but . . . '

Evie swallowed hard when he paused. 'He is a poorly dog. You were quite right to come here. Two days taking life easy is most definitely not the answer. Falling from a bedroom window is not a good idea, and the shock of his landing has broken his right elbow really rather badly. Other than that he appears to be sound. I shall have to scan him and see exactly what I'm talking about. He needs some fluids pumping into him as he's dehydrated and then, when the swelling has gone down, an operation. I can do it, but I have to warn you it will be expensive.'

'You mean you can make him walk? Like before?'

When Mungo nodded his head Evie almost collapsed again with relief.

'I don't promise he will be *perfectly* all right, but he will be much much better and certainly not in pain, which he is at the moment. I've given him something to relieve the pain and make him comfortable, and now I'm waiting for your decision.'

'I wouldn't want him to suffer, Mr Price. Not that. But you haven't said anything about putting him . . . well . . . to sleep so . . . ' Evie almost tore her handkerchief to shreds as she struggled to keep control of her feelings.

'If I thought I couldn't help him to have a good quality of life then I would seriously recommend putting him to sleep for his sake, not yours. But I'm confident we shall have a successful outcome.'

Evie left her chair on winged feet and flung her arms around Mungo. 'Thank you! Thank you!'

Miriam interrupted. 'Might it be a good idea to ring Tom and tell him where you are and say how expensive the operation is going to be?'

Evie, with dread in her eyes, stared hard at Mungo, who was slow replying.

'Just over a thousand pounds but that includes aftercare, like drugs, drips, supervision, my time, scans and the anaesthetic that Tatty will need. Why don't you go down to intensive care and spend some time with him? He'll be sleepy because we've given him something to ease his pain, but he'll know you're there. I have clients coming this morning and time is pressing. I certainly shan't operate today as it's too swollen, and he'd have to be here a few days after the operation for me to check him. You could ring each day for a progress report.'

After Evie had gone down to sit with Tatty,

Miriam said softly, 'A thousand pounds! That's nowhere near enough, is it?'

Mungo looked embarrassed at being caught out. 'It should be nearer two thousand but I can't tell her that because I'm sure that would be beyond their means. Don't say a word, please. The poor woman. Think what it cost her in fear driving from wherever she's come from when she's obviously on the verge of a nervous breakdown. I can't break her heart, too.' He got up, planted a kiss on Miriam's mouth, lingered there for a moment to gather strength from her love, and went back downstairs to begin his day's work.

★　★　★

While she sat beside Tatty, with one finger poked through the bars close to his nose, Evie rang Tom on the mobile he'd bought to help her feel safe. 'Tom?'

'Evie! Thank God! Where are you?'

She told him what was happening while he served customers in the village store

'But Evie, why didn't you wake me? I'd have driven you. Have you had breakfast?'

She explained that Miriam had given her something to eat.

'They sound very nice people.'

She agreed.

'Evie, how much is all this going to cost?'

'About a thousand pounds — well, over a thousand pounds — but he promises Tatty will be free of pain and have a good quality of life.

You are going to say yes, aren't you?'

'Of course. We'll find the money. Now, please keep in touch and tell me when you're coming home.'

They chatted for a few more minutes then she said, 'I promise I'll call as soon as there's any news,' and rang off. She had to do this all by herself, to prove something, although quite what she was proving she didn't know.

Bunty came in. 'How is he?'

'Sleeping. Thank goodness.'

'Good. We've a rabbit and a cat coming in here shortly; they'll be no trouble so stay where you are if you wish. The shops are quite close if you fancy a walk. I'll keep an eye on Tatty for you.'

'I'll do that. You're all so kind. I won't be long.'

'Be as long as you like. He's well doped up with his painkiller.'

It took Evie three attempts to leave the premises. She remembered she needed to comb her hair, returned to ask to use the facilities, and came back again for her handbag she'd left in the bathroom. She smiled apologetically at Bunty then gently padded out through the reception room, which was already half-filled with clients and their pets.

When Seb went to see Tatty during his morning coffee break, Evie still hadn't returned from the shops. He said, 'Hello! Tatty,' and was greeted with a slow, sleepy wag of the tail before Tatty fell asleep again.

'What's going to happen to him?' he asked Bunty.

104

'Waiting for the swelling to go down, then Mungo's hoping to operate on his elbow. Difficult and complicated. But you know Mungo, nothing defeats him. What I dreaded was him having to say that putting him down was the kindest thing. She'd have been devastated, then having to drive home . . . '

'Where is home?'

'Some obscure place. I can't remember. Don't ask me where it is.'

'Not round here, then.'

'No, definitely not.'

Evie still hadn't returned by three o'clock and Miriam had reached panic stations. She'd promised Evie lunch in the flat and had now placed it in the fridge to keep fresh. Seb and Mungo scanned Tatty and what they found made them very hopeful of success, but still no Evie. Her car remained in the practice car park looking empty and forlorn, and they were on the brink of ringing the police. Miriam wondered if she'd rung Tom and he'd said no. That had happened before, and they'd had ringside seats to witness rows between a wife who adored her dog and her husband who thought the dog meant more to his wife than he did. Which, considering what a brute he appeared to be, was probably true.

Just as they were closing at 7 p.m. Bunty's husband, Constable Dicky Bird, arrived with Evie. They could see without being told that she was exhausted and fearful.

Miriam instinctively put her arms round her and gave her a powerful hug. 'Evie, my dear!

How lovely you're back. We've got a meal all ready for you and you're just in time. Have you had a lovely time?'

Evie nodded helplessly and clung to Miriam with relief, whispering in a tiny voice, 'Thank you.'

Dicky Bird winked at Miriam and said cheerfully, 'I met her heading for here so I gave her a lift in the car. Is Bunty ready for off?'

'Yes. She is just putting her coat on.' To Evie she said, 'You go upstairs and freshen up for supper, Evie. I won't be a moment. You know the way.'

Dicky tactfully waited for Evie to get out of earshot and then, speaking softly, he told Miriam how he'd found her fast asleep on a bench in the precinct and finally sorted out that she couldn't find her way back to the practice and had become totally disorientated, hungry and desperately in need of help. 'Nice little woman, but she's too frail to be out on her own. Bunty!' His face glowed with love which he quickly masked.

Bunty had arrived in reception in her coat. 'Aubrey! What a lovely surprise! I was just going to catch the bus. My car'll be ready tomorrow lunchtime, so I'll be OK tomorrow night. Goodnight, everybody.'

She and Dicky went off arm in arm. They made an odd couple, Miriam thought, but at least they appeared to be happy.

* * *

Against all the golden rules, Evie Nicholls was invited to stay the night with Miriam and

106

Mungo. Mungo disappeared back to his office as soon as they had eaten, leaving them choosing chocolates from a huge box that lay between them on the sofa. Perkins curled comfortably on Evie's feet.

'Evie, just help yourself. If you don't I shall, and then where will my hips be?'

Miriam laughed but Evie was finding very little to laugh about because her heart and mind were with Tatty downstairs.

'How do you keep so slim, Evie?' Miriam asked.

'Worry keeps me slim. I worry about everything. Without Tom I don't know where I'd be. Well, I do — in a psychiatric hospital for sure.'

'He sounds a lovely man.' Miriam smiled.

Evie pondered hard.

'He is. As a younger man he was in the police, you know. Drug squad and all that. Sometimes I never saw him for days, although the station rang me, from time to time, to say he was all right. I've never got over it.'

'But you said he was a manager of a village store.'

'He is now. He's safe and so happy. The owner is lovely and they get on well. May I?' Evie helped herself to another chocolate.

Miriam paused while she got a hard caramel chocolate under control; she really would have to stop eating chocolate. 'So if he's safe now, why do you worry still?'

The silence was so prolonged that Miriam was convinced she'd asked the one question which was going to tip Evie ever deeper into depression. But eventually Evie answered, 'I really don't know.'

'Let's think about all the things you should be grateful for. Come on, I'll start you off: a loving, helpful husband with a job that he enjoys. That's a plus. Not all women have that.'

'A lovely house in a beautiful village where everyone likes me . . . '

And the list went on for a while until Evie admitted to being an embroiderer.

'No! Really? What a gift!' Before Miriam knew where she was, any idea she might have had that Evie embroidered tray cloths for pleasure was squashed flat as her guest talked about the banner in the church, the hanging commissioned for a cathedral, the piece her embroidery group was working on at the moment for the new council office, the tapestry she'd made . . . Miriam listened open-mouthed.

The box of chocolates was put on a side table and Miriam moved along the sofa and gave Evie a tremendous hug. 'What a wonderful talent. Just think how much pleasure you give people, how valuable you are to us all. What a fantastic contribution you make to beauty in this world when so much is so very ugly. My dear, I wish I had a talent like that. I really do.'

Evie's heart gave a leap as she acknowledged Miriam's genuine admiration. She swallowed hard.

'I don't expect you have photographs of your work that I could see?'

'Tom's taken photos although I haven't got

108

them with me. But I could send you copies if you really mean it.'

'Of course I mean it. If you lived nearer I'd come round to see them. You must believe in yourself, Evie. Most people with a heaven-sent talent like yours would be shouting it from the rooftops. I know you're not that kind of person, but you should have a quiet confidence right inside yourself, you know. Your village must be so proud of you. Anyway, look at the time! Horlicks and bed?'

As Evie was wandering off to bed in Miriam's small cosy guest room, which was all restful and inviting in soft greens and cream with one of Miriam's nightgowns awaiting her, she took Miriam's hand. 'Tom has told me the same things, but somehow you saying them ... ' Timidly she reached up and kissed Miriam's cheek. 'Thank you.'

Evie went to sleep filled with happiness. She couldn't put her finger on what it was about Miriam that had so appealed to her but as her eyes closed Evie felt contentment flooding through her mind. It was just like stepping into a warm bath.

★   ★   ★

That night Evie slept right through until the sun broke through and she could hear Miriam in the kitchen. There was a tiny shower room for her to use and this she did thankfully because she never had the confidence to share with other people, worrying overmuch about when was the best time to try the bathroom door and scurrying back to her room if she found it already occupied. When she smelt the coffee she emerged to find Mungo at the breakfast table and Miriam making a pot of tea. Mungo rose to his feet as she approached, which embarrassed her to death.

'Good morning, Evie. Do sit down. I've been to see Tatty and he's ready for the operation. He's made great strides. Why not ring Tom and see if he can come to collect you tonight and take you home? He could come on the train and then drive your car back. You'll know by then that Tatty is OK and you can go with your mind at rest. Ring every day about nine if you wish and we'll give you an update. Eh? How about it?'

Full of excitement, Evie clasped her hands together below her chin. 'Oh! That's excellent. You're more than kind.' Miriam was hovering with the teapot in hand. 'Both of you. Yes, tea, please.'

Miriam asked if she'd slept well.

'Yes, I did. Really well. I was so tired after not sleeping the previous night because of Tatty. That's a lovely bedroom.'

The morning appeared to drag but Mungo sacrificed his lunchtime and began operating as soon as his last client had left. He co-opted Seb to give him a hand and together they tackled the problem of Tatty's right elbow. They began at one, and by half past three the operation was finished. Evie had sat all morning in Miriam's sitting room silently staring out of the window at Beulah Bank Top, hoping and hoping. Miriam had gone out with Perkins and then to the shops in Barleybridge, and finally rang her to invite her out to lunch. Evie was so delighted at the idea of lunch with Miriam that she said yes straight away.

Surprised, Miriam suggested that she ask Dodie to take her to the restaurant. 'It's quite tricky to find, you see, and then I'll take you back in the car. OK?'

For Evie it was a glorious lunch. She couldn't quite put her finger on why Miriam was so good for her but she was. With Miriam there she had no doubts about the success of Tatty's operation and could talk to her like a lifelong friend.

Miriam, aware that things were difficult for Evie, still didn't sense quite how deeply demanding Evie found every aspect of her life to be, and chattered on about this and that, hoping it all might do some good. As for Evie, it was the loveliest lunch she'd ever had. Gone were her anxieties about dealing with the waitress and eating in public, which closed up her throat and made swallowing so hard, and she could talk about going into hospital and how she 'lost' the real Evie once she got in there.

'Evie! How terrible for you. It won't do, you know. With the wonderful gift you have for embroidery, what do you have to worry about? Tom is safe now, no longer do you have to fear for his life, and Tatty is going to be well, I'm sure. So?'

Evie finished buttering another cracker and piled some Brie on to it, but before she took a bite she put it down saying, 'There isn't anything, is there?'

'No.'

'I would have loved to have given Tom children but there's no way that can be now, as I'm too old.'

'Does Tom go on about that?'

'No.'

'Then . . . '

'I'm going to have to try to be cheerful and confident for Tom's sake, aren't I?'

'Yes, make that your target. Think how wonderful it would be for him to have you well and happy. And for your own sake, too.'

Evie popped the cracker into her mouth, chewed it, and swallowed it down with a gulp of coffee. 'I've been selfish, haven't I?' she said.

Miriam protested. 'No, no.'

'You're not selfish, are you? Not for one minute.'

Miriam studied this question and then had to smile. 'I try not to be.'

'Then I shall try, too. Can we go now? I want to see Tatty. Will they have finished, do you think? I can't believe that life might go right for me, because it never appears to.'

Miriam looked hard at her. 'Maybe from now on it's going to go right for you and for Tom. OK?'

When they eventually got back to the practice the operation was over and Mungo was well satisfied. Tatty would be properly awake in an hour.

Colour flooded Evie's face and she kissed Mungo on the cheek. Then she spotted Seb settling Tatty in a cage in the recovery room, and

112

he received a big kiss too, as well as a hug. He flushed with embarrassment, and so did Evie, astonished at herself for spontaneously kissing total strangers. But then they were no longer strangers but dear friends. Above all, Tatty was to be restored to her. She'd have the pleasure of taking him over the fields behind Hipkin Gardens every day with the wind blowing his rough, gingery fur in every direction and his dear bright eyes checking her whereabouts every two minutes as he ran about. In gratitude, she'd put Tom first from now on and remember each day to count her blessings, just as Miriam had taught her.

8

When Seb arrived at the practice the following morning he went first to see Tatty, and found him comparatively perky. His eyes were bright and he was munching his breakfast.

'Good morning, Tatty. You look better than you did last night.'

Sarah came in. 'Morning, Seb. He looks good, doesn't he? Very bright this morning, is our Tatty. Evie Nicholls is such a lovely lady, isn't she? I did like her.'

'Yes, she is a real lady, but so afraid of life. Has he tried standing up?'

Sarah shook her head. 'Not that I've seen, but it's early days. He's had his prescription, after some persuasion, and he's eaten most of his breakfast.'

'Excellent. Mungo never fails to impress, does he?'

'I remember only once when he didn't impress. The dog never recovered, and the owners were devastated and threatened to sue him. However, they changed their minds, thank goodness. It wasn't Mungo's fault. Oh, listen! That sounds like Kate! Must go. Come and meet her!'

So this was the famous Kate. No one had ever said a bad word about her so he wondered just what she would be like. A paragon of all the virtues, perhaps? Arrogant with it?

She was standing in the midst of what

appeared to be the whole of the staff. He stood on the fringe, listening to the excited chatter.

Mungo was saying, 'Champagne tonight when we've closed, Miriam says, in the flat. Everyone must stay. Welcome on behalf of us all. We've waited a long time for this day, haven't we, Kate?' He kissed her on both cheeks and then stood back. 'Yes, a long time. Welcome to the Barleybridge Veterinary Hospital.' He was beaming from ear to ear. Seb had never seen him looking so genuinely gleeful.

Then he looked at Kate. She appeared to him to be a clean-cut, no-nonsense sort of person, and the word that sprang to mind as he looked at her was wholesome; clear-skinned, bright blue eyes, long fair hair. Lost in admiration, he didn't notice that Dodie was saying, 'And this is Seb, our newest addition and already beginning to make a name for himself.'

'How do you do,' Seb managed. 'I hope you'll be very happy here. I've heard a lot about you.'

Privately he didn't think he could have found a more trite thing to say. He sounded like something out of a teach-yourself-social-skills manual. He felt a complete fool and wanted to creep away as fast as possible. So he did, muttering, 'First client here any minute.'

In fact, no one was due, but he hid in his consulting room trying to look busy. How could this Kate make him feel such an idiot when she'd not said a word? She was, according to what he'd heard, very bright and Seb felt intimidated by that prospect. He guessed she'd be the first with a diagnosis and a cure, one of those super-vets

115

with that special something which made every dog and cat putty in their hands.

After a long, gruelling day attending to every sort of illness, every single awkward client and a cat whose illness he simply couldn't diagnose, he crawled up the stairs to Miriam and Mungo's flat for the champagne 'do' to celebrate Kate's arrival.

What impressed him most was the enthusiasm they all had for Kate, lay staff and vets alike, and he willingly admitted to himself that Kate was something special, not to mention attractive and outgoing. He imagined she'd have been very popular at college.

He sipped two glasses of champagne, persuaded to the second one by Dodie who was determined he should enjoy himself, but he kept well to the edge of all the chatter, somehow needing time to assess Kate. She might be bright but he'd heard that, like himself, she hadn't passed her finals first time round, and had to do a re-take in November.

A great deal of the time at the get-together was spent remembering incidents which had taken place when Kate spent a year working on accounts before she went to college.

'Remember that time when she had to throw water from the old fire bucket over Perkins and Adolf fighting and most of it landed on Mungo's trousers,' said Joy. 'And that time when Scott fell in Phil Parson's slurry pit right up to his chest and came back to the practice covered in cow dung and she had to hose him down outside the back door?'

'And,' said Rhodri, 'don't forget that time when Phil Parsons came looking for Scott waving that billhook at the clients and frightening us all to death, and Kate calmly took the billhook off him and got him to sit down and wait for Scott? That was her big moment and not half!'

Kate laughed. 'I'd forgotten all about that. Joy wondered if Scott must have been making overtures to Blossom.'

Scott was indignant. 'I most certainly had not.'

Seb had no memories, of course, but he enjoyed the stories and laughed as loud as everyone else. When the party began thinning out Seb went home to cook his evening meal. Afterwards he cleared up and made his kitchen tidy, then he sat down feeling rather lonely after all the fun. So he was glad when his phone rang just as he'd decided to relax and drown his sorrows in mindless TV.

'Hello-o-o! Maggie here, Seb. We've just finished rehearsal. Fancy a drink?'

'That would be lovely. Same pub?'

He listened to the breathy excitement that was Maggie. 'Exactly. Ten minutes?'

'See you then.'

* * *

Maggie had chosen to sit at a table all by herself in the bar, leaving the raucous crowd of amateur actors to take care of themselves. Seb marched in and greeted her with a kiss.

'My treat!' he declared, seeing she had waited for him to arrive before ordering a drink. He

117

sensed a lot of nudging and winking going on in that crowd of friends but he didn't care.

'G and T, please.'

As he made his way towards the bar, the theatre crowd whistled at him. He acknowledged them with a nonchalant wave and ordered the drinks.

Returning to Maggie he caught an admiring look on her face which she quickly disguised when she realised he'd noticed. 'Had a good week so far?' she asked him when he'd sat down.

'Yes, thanks. And you?'

'Well, believe it or not, I have exciting news.' She drew in a great big breath and paused just long enough to make him tip-toed with curiosity. 'I've an audition for a new TV soap next week!'

'No! That's wonderful news. You must be so excited.' He grasped her hand and squeezed it.

'I am! But one never knows. You can get taken on and then they change their minds or the pilot doesn't work out or the script-writer can't follow it up with more good episodes. It's all so unpredictable.'

'But still, getting asked puts you in the picture, so to speak. A real plaudit for your ability as an actress.'

'Oh, yes. I've been on cloud nine since I heard. This could be my big break-through. I've always imagined I was destined for the RSC — you know, Stratford and the rest — but since I've got older I've decided to lower my sights. Got more common sense now.' Maggie tapped her glass against his. 'So wish me luck.'

'Of course. All the luck in the world. I'm very

pleased for you.' Seb was so delighted with her chance to succeed that he leaned across the table and lightly kissed her cheek, enjoying the fresh floral smell of her. 'I'll be thinking of you. Are you auditioning for a specific part?'

'Well, certainly not the young romantic lead; those days are long gone. I shall be a divorcee determined not to get ensnared again, hiding her dissatisfaction with a quick-fire sense of humour and, on occasion, an acid tongue. I'm a sad librarian. In the soap, I mean.'

Maggie asked him about his day, then, so Seb told her about Tatty and how it looked as though the operation would work out, how sad it was about Evie being so scared of life, and about their new member of staff. Maggie listened so intently to his tale, demonstrating an awareness of how Evie must feel, that Seb warmed to her more than ever before.

'And Tatty? What are his chances of a normal life?'

'With Mungo having done the operation his chances are high. He is so gifted. It's a privilege to watch him at work. I'm very lucky that he lets me assist.'

'You must be good if he lets you assist him. You've only been there a short time.'

Seb smiled. 'I've an awful lot to learn yet. Believe me.'

'Don't under-estimate yourself. I don't mean be overly confident because you're not that kind of person, I know that.'

Seb attempted to change the direction of their conversation. 'How are your alpacas?'

119

'Fine.' Maggie reached across the table to pat his hand. 'Mum was most impressed with the efficient and kindly way you dealt with them. You're her kind of vet. She thinks you're lovely because you must have a soul.' She giggled helplessly.

Seb threw back his head and laughed. 'That'll do for now. I'm not used to lots of praise. In Yorkshire you're thrilled to bits if someone says, 'Tha's done well there, lad,' and that's all you get, but when it's well meant . . . '

'Exactly.' Maggie downed the last of her gin and tonic. 'Have you seen that new film just out? The one about the mountaineer up Kilimanjaro?'

'No.'

'I know one of the minor actors in it — worked with him in a children's theatre group — and I'd like to see it.'

Seb, without being asked, checked his diary. 'I'm not on call till next Tuesday.'

There was a hint of relief in her voice when she answered him. 'You'd like to go? What about Sunday night?'

'Absolutely.'

'Good.'

'Shall I pick you up?'

'No, thanks. Too far for you to come. I'll meet you outside the cinema. You know Cineworld, the one in the precinct?'

'I don't know the screening times.'

'I thought we'd go to the late one so we'll meet at a quarter to eight outside the cinema and go for a drink first, all depending on times. OK?'

'Great.'

Outside the pub Maggie reached up and gave him a kiss on his cheek, hugging him briefly. 'Goodnight. Thanks for the G and T.'

As Seb drove home he decided that Maggie was a thoroughly pleasant person. A very lovable person, in fact, and he looked forward to seeing her on Sunday.

★ ★ ★

The next day Seb had a request from the Goddards for an afternoon visit, and a full morning clinic for the very first time. He felt enormously bucked by that because he found the slow building of a regular clientele was becoming irksome. One of his clients was the canary man, with a sickly-looking canary in a box.

'Good morning, Mr Smithson. What can I do for you this morning?'

'It's this little girl of mine. She's drooping all day long and it can't be right because all the others are springing about the aviary, singing and enjoying life, and she sits huddled up doing nothing.'

'Let's have a look. You get her out.'

Mr Smithson gently lifted the canary out. 'She's called Joan, after Joan Sutherland. You know, the singer?'

Seb nodded, wondering when Mr Smithson was going to run out of opera singers. He examined Joan very gently, not wanting to alarm the poor thing. 'Have you got the nest boxes fitted up?'

121

'Indeed I have. Ever the optimist, I've got six boxes. I'm just waiting, hopefully, for some eggs . . . ' He smiled.

'Is she eating?'

'No, that's part of my worry. I don't catch her eating.'

'I wonder if . . . Joan . . . is broody. They can have very funny moods when they are. What she's really wanting is some eggs to sit on. After all, she'd be huddled up if she had eggs.'

'My word, young man, I never thought about that. Am I glad I met up with you! Of course, that could be it.'

'I'm not saying it is, but I can find nothing wrong with her at all. So it is a possibility. They do go off their food sometimes.'

'If I got a couple of pot eggs to give her the idea, like . . . '

'It might satisfy her.'

'I'll put the pot eggs in a nesting box and see how she does. OK? That carpenter friend of mine who helped make the aviary has got so interested he's been round nearly every day since I got these, and he's decided to get some for himself. So I've recommended he uses you as his vet. How about that?'

'I'm very flattered.'

The morning wore on with clients involving him in all sorts of problems, but the last one before lunch caused him to ask for a second opinion from Valentine.

Valentine came in between clients.

'Let me see. How old is he?'

Seb explained the situation. 'This is a

122

seventeen-year-old male cat called Hector. Been fit as a flea all his life then developed kidney problems. They're new to this area and recently the tablets he's been having regularly don't appear to be working any more. He's become seriously incontinent.'

'Right.'

Seb realised he hadn't introduced the client to Valentine, so anxious was he to relay the symptoms to him. 'I'm sorry, this is Valentine Dedic. Val, this is Mrs Benton.'

'Mrs Benton.' Valentine inclined his head and clicked his heels, and the client blushed.

'Does he have free access to the outside as he's always had? Cat flap, you know?'

'Yes.'

'Has he changed at all? He is old, you see. Do you think he appears confused?'

'Funny you should say that, but, yes, he does. He gets mixed up with which doorway is which and can't always find his water bowl. He's always slept in his own bed at night, but now he goes to sleep in the silliest of places.'

Valentine examined Hector's eyes. 'Nothing wrong there, no clouding of the eyes at all. So it's not poor sight that's causing confusion. Look, if Seb here agrees, I suggest we change his prescription. His old tablets are obviously not working any more. That should do the trick. If not, he might be getting mixed up because of moving house, and his age is making it difficult for him to adapt. Seventeen is very old. Will you do as I suggest? Come back if there is no improvement. Let's face facts, Mrs Benton, an incontinent male cat is not the best thing in a nice house, is it?' He smiled at her, then clicked his heels and retired to his own consulting room leaving Seb to arrange a new prescription.

Mrs Benton heaved old Hector back into his carrying basket. Breathing heavily, she said, 'He's really saying that . . . in view of Hector's age . . . if there's no improvement, it would be kinder . . . you know . . . '

'Yes, I do believe he is.'

'Do you agree?'

'Let's wait and see. Perhaps another few weeks with the new prescription will sort him out. Find his way about your new house, you know. Give it a try.'

Mrs Benton rose to the occasion. 'Look! He's been our best friend all his life. I'm not going to have him put to sleep for my convenience. Nice house indeed! What's that to do with anything? I ask you! My old dad lives with us and I wouldn't put him to sleep just when he needs extra care. I'm not going to put Hector to sleep, either. So there.'

Mrs Benton stormed out of the consulting room in high dudgeon. Seb did consider rushing out after her but decided against it. Val's idea of putting him to sleep might be the best in the end. He rather hoped that time and the new prescription might solve everything.

In the staffroom during lunch Valentine asked Seb what Mrs Benton had decided to do.

'She was furious you implied that Hector should be put to sleep.'

'I said no such thing.'

124

'No, but you hinted at it and she's determined she's not doing it.' Seb had to laugh at Valentine's angry face.

Dodie Pilgrim, listening in to their conversation, asked Val if he always recommended the final solution when an animal proved difficult.

Now he really did get angry. 'Of course not! But can you imagine what it must be like in their house with a tom cat urinating everywhere? Disgusting. I'm afraid animal-lovers can be soft in the head at times.'

Dodie patted his arm. 'I was only teasing. Where I worked a few years ago we had a vet who put anything on four legs to sleep almost before the owner had understood his intentions. We got very good at treating clients for shock.'

'What happened to him?'

'Well, Val, his client list dwindled to a point where he had to go. Clients refused to have their pets treated by him. They'd ask for an appointment and say, 'I don't want to see Killer Kershaw, thank you very much.' It all got very embarrassing.'

'Well, rest assured that won't happen to me.' Val wandered off.

Thinking of Maggie, Seb asked, 'Dodie, this dinner we're having at The George, can we bring a friend?'

'So long as it's someone appropriate. I know you've not been here very long to have lots of friends.'

'It's Maggie Goddard, daughter of a new client of ours.'

'Oh! Right. I see. Well, yes, all right, if she's free.'

125

At the Goddards' that afternoon, Seb was asked to look at two of the alpacas.

'You see, Seb, it's nothing in particular, like walking lame or coughing or something, it's just a feeling I have.' Ruthie put her head to one side beguilingly. 'I have this instinct where animals are concerned, you see, and it's my instinct which made me ring you. This one here by the fence must know you've come to see him! Bless. And the brown female just the other side of him. Off colour is the best thing I can describe it as. Yes, off colour. Mimi! Carlos! Come to Mummy!'

Seb clambered over the fence and began an examination of the pair of them. The other ones in the field came to see what the fuss was about, pushing in with their noses and trying to take part in the examination. The two of them were definitely too thin for comfort, and not so lively as the other young ones. He climbed back over. 'Need my stethoscope. Won't be a moment.'

He came back with it slung around his neck looking every inch the professional man and, what was more, in Ruthie's eyes, very interesting. Despite the age gap between him and Maggie, because Seb couldn't be much more than twenty-six and Maggie was in her late thirties, she felt he would be a suitable match. Yes! This could be the one, she thought.

When she noticed that Seb was looking grave her heart almost stopped. 'What is it?'

'I don't know for sure. I'll have to get a second opinion. Have you ever had TB?'

'Me?'

'No, I mean have the alpacas ever shown up as having TB?'

'Oh! God. No!'

'I could be very wrong in my diagnosis. But they haven't lost weight for no reason at all.'

At that tragic moment Maggie returned home. 'Seb! I thought you'd have gone by now. How lovely I've caught you.'

Ruthie, on the point of swooning, said stoically, 'Seb thinks they've got TB.'

Seb protested. 'I said I didn't know for sure. It might be something quite different.'

Knowing how her mother would be affected by this news, Maggie put an arm round Ruthie's shoulders. 'Which ones, Mum?'

'Mimi and Carlos. My dearest ones.'

'Mum! *All* of them are your dearest ones, let's be honest.'

Ruthie reached out over the fence to catch hold of Seb's arm. 'Will it mean . . . ?'

'Let's stay positive, shall we?' He climbed back over the fence and stood leaning on it, staring at Carlos and Mimi.

'What now?' asked Maggie.

'I'll be in touch tomorrow. Just to be safe, separate them from the others.'

'Sandy saw a puma a few weeks ago, along the bottom of the hedge in the top field. Could that be to blame?'

'Really? That's interesting. No, that can't be blamed.'

'He fired his gun and it ran off. People have been sighting it for months now, although the police pooh-pooh the whole idea. But Sandy's no fool.' Ruthie said this proudly, as though Sandy were six years old and had been a clever boy at school. 'No, if he saw a puma then he saw a puma and no mistake.'

Seb remembered about the dinner and turned to tell Maggie about it. 'Would you care to go?' he asked, hoping she'd say yes.

Her face lit up. 'If you're sure that's OK. I wouldn't want to intrude where I'm not wanted. Yes, I'd love to. Dinner at The George, you say. I'll need a smart frock, then. When is it?'

'Two weeks today. Seven for seven-thirty.'

Seb said goodbye to Ruthie and he and Maggie walked back to his car.

'Thank you so much for inviting me. I feel privileged,' Maggie said.

'I'll ring in the morning about Carlos and Mimi. Don't let Ruthie worry too much. I could be completely wrong.'

'Or completely right.' She stood in the sun in the yard looking perfectly splendid, waving energetically to him until he disappeared from view. Glancing through his rear-view mirror, Seb saw her skip with delight just before he lost sight of her. He couldn't help but like her. She really was a lovely person, so fresh and attractive.

A phone call interrupted his thoughts. It was Joy asking him to call on the Parsons at Applegate Farm. 'His chickens have all died. They can't understand it. Poor Blossom is having hysterics as usual. Stay calm, Seb. Bye!'

He arrived at the farm and, as he'd been advised the first time he came, put on his

128

wellington boots before he entered the farm yard. Blossom was hovering in the doorway of the house, waving desperately.

'Seb! It's you. Joy said it might be. Oh, Seb, whatever shall we do?'

'Let me look first.'

So he studied the five chickens laid out almost reverently, side by side, in the chicken run. Blossom had covered them with a plastic sheet as though they were human corpses. Seb kept a straight face.

'Well, they've definitely not been attacked.'

'Oh, no. Hamish locks them up every night for certain. Foxes, you know.'

'Phil about?'

'No, he's very upset. This is Lavender. He bought her when he decided to go in for chickens in a big way.'

'How many did you have?'

'Twelve to start with, as an experiment, but it never got any further. These are all old. Most of them are past laying.'

'You didn't wring their necks, then?'

Blossom's reaction to this question was to draw a lace handkerchief from her skirt pocket — did he say skirt? It was more like a pelmet — and blew her nose. 'Of course not. How could we? They're our friends. The first one is Lavender, like I said, then there's Clarissa, Clementine, Goldie, on account of her lovely colour — well, it was lovely, looks a bit worse for wear now — and that's Lolita.'

'Well, I think the best thing is for me to get them to the Veterinary Investigation Centre and they'll do a post-mortem. It must be something in particular for all five to go at once. You need to know what caused it.'

Blossom gripped Seb's arm to steady herself. 'I'll have to ask Phil. Oh, God! Post-mortem. Oh, no.'

'We need to know, as I'm sure you'll want to re-stock, and knowledge is the best weapon against it happening again, you see. Bring in new stock and the same thing could happen all over again. But we will know once the centre has done the post . . . investigated them.'

Eventually Seb was allowed to depart with the chickens carefully secured inside a large plastic bag.

He reported what had happened to Joy when he got back to the practice. 'They were devastated. Phil had been hiding in the house but Blossom insisted we ask his permission for the post-mortem and he had to have a brandy to brace himself. Are they always like that?'

'Always. They are sentimentally attached to every animal they own. Not in it for the money, you see.'

'They don't *look* well off.'

Joy leaned forward over the counter. 'Between you and me, no one's supposed to know, they own Applegate Caravan Site further down the lane. Started more as a fluke than anything. Someone stopped one day and asked if they could camp in that field for a few days and it quite simply took off from there. They make a fortune between May and September, I understand, and surprisingly, considering the state of the farm, the caravan

130

site is immaculate and the facilities second to none. Anyway, we'll wait for the result on these chickens, Seb. Thanks for that. Off you go home.'

★ ★ ★

Seb got the results two days later and made space in his day to call in at Applegate Farm. Blossom was out shopping with Hamish, so it was Phil who received the news. He was standing leaning against a wall keeping his prize bull, Star, company. 'Come in, come in, Seb. Well, tell me the worst.'

'Good thing we had a post-mortem done, because if you'd re-stocked immediately exactly the same thing would have happened again.'

'No! Whatever is it?'

'An attack of red mite.'

'What's them?'

'Tiny little beggars who run along the perches, up the chickens' legs and into their feathers to suck their blood.'

Phil paled. 'But I've never seen little red things. Never. How can it be?'

'They're very crafty. They wait till it's dark and then emerge.' Seb felt he had to be very blunt otherwise he'd never get the message home. 'Eventually the chickens drop off their perches due to lack of blood in their veins.'

'I don't believe it. It can't be true. Tell the chap to do it again.'

'I'm afraid they'll have been incinerated already. So — '

'Stop right there. I'm telling you I've never

seen any red things in that chicken house.'

'When they're full of blood they go back to any nook and cranny they call home before it gets light, Phil. That's why you don't see them.'

'We've no red mites in that chicken house. Why, before we bought the farm it was a chicken house and has been all the time we've been here, we've never had a problem, ever.'

'If you re-stock immediately the same thing will happen.'

'Well, I don't believe it. They come out in the dark, you say?'

Seb nodded.

'Well, whatever it was, the end result's still the same — I've lost all my two-legged friends. Thanks, anyway, Seb. Be seeing you. I don't expect you'll forget to send the bill.' Phil took out his handkerchief and wiped his eyes. 'Blow me, they can't be that clever, the little beggars.'

★　★　★

When Blossom and Hamish came home Phil told them the bad news. They couldn't believe it, either. Blossom was incredulous. 'Something that size with a brain? I don't believe it. I honestly don't.'

Hamish, however, remembered a long-forgotten lecture at college. 'I do know there is such a thing, and they can cause havoc, but I've never seen anything red in there.'

Phil agreed. 'Neither have I.'

'What shall we do?' Blossom asked.

'Tonight I'm going in there with a torch to

look for the blighters,' Phil said.

'We could all go,' Blossom suggested.

'If we all go there'll be no room to see what's going on. No. I'm going on my tod to prove I'm right.'

Hamish doused the conversation with cold water. 'You might find he's right, this chap from the Investigation Centre. Very right.'

'And then again I might not. About six I'll go, it's well and truly dark then. Get that torch out, Hamish.'

Hamish shuffled off to the goat shed where he sat with the goats of a night before shutting them up for their own safety. He liked sitting there, especially if there were babies, which he adored. That had been the place where he'd first felt able to begin speaking again. Nursing a baby goat was what had healed the harrowing experience of watching his baby half-sister being killed in front of him by that brute his mother had taken up with. That and Blossom and Phil taking him in and not telling the Social about him being there. He stroked all the goats who were trying to get into his pockets for treats and promised them their supper titbits before bedtime. He picked up the torch from a hook specially hammered into the wood at shoulder height so the goats couldn't get it, and wandered back to the farmhouse. The welcoming kitchen lights were on and he could see Blossom doing something at the sink. The realisation came to him that this was his home for ever, that he really and truly belonged here. It was the only place in all his life where he'd found comfort and, best of all, love.

'Here we are, Dad.'

Phil was taken aback. Hamish had never called him Dad before.

'You called me Dad.' Phil shook his hand and then clasped him to his chest. 'I'm proud to be your dad, very proud. And Blossom would be delighted if you called her Mum.'

'Mum it is, then.'

'Good. Call her Mum in front of me, then I can see the pleasure on her face. Right, another hour or so and then I'm off to the chicken house.' He banged his chest with his fist. 'There'll be no damn red mites in my chicken house, you wait and see. Thanks for calling me Dad. I'm right proud. Now I can call you son.'

Phil had his supper before he went out to the chicken house and was there to see Blossom's face when Hamish said, 'Thank you, Mum,' as she passed him his plate.

'Why! Hamish.' She jumped up and flung her arms around him. 'That's lovely. I've been waiting a long time for this day.'

As Phil put on his coat in preparation for his investigation into the red mite situation, Blossom said, 'Hamish, I want you to think about this. I don't want an answer this minute, because it's an important decision. Would you like for Phil . . . your dad and me to make your name Hamish Parsons, all legal like. It's up to you but it would give us a lot of pleasure, believe me. Wouldn't it, Phil?'

'Brilliant idea. It would be great, would that, but think about it, son, it's a big step.'

'I've thought about it already and there's

nothing I'd like better. Hamish Parsons. Excellent. Thanks.'

Phil set off for the chicken house full of delight at the sudden turn of events. There'd be no more need to explain Hamish to anyone. They could call him their son and no one would question it.

He pushed open the chicken-house door, then closed it behind him and shone the torch round. Red mites, my eye. There wasn't a sign, not one sign. He shone the beam all along the perches, round the edges of the window, along the roof supports, along the walls, back to the perches. Nothing. For all their science and their la-di-da qualifications the people at the Investigation Centre were completely wrong. Phil decided to switch off the torch, wait and then try again. He leaned against a perch for comfort.

There was complete silence, but then there always was once it got dark. There was only ever the occasional car going slowly down the narrow lane that went past the farm. He heard the barn owl that used his old barn hooting as it flew across the valley. His attention went back to Hamish deciding to call him Dad and his chest swelled with pride. What a day, what an important day. He got an urge to scratch his leg, then his back, then . . . yes, it was a very important day, a milestone and . . . he'd have to scratch his back again but he couldn't reach where it itched the most. God, he itched all over. What the hell was it? His arm now, then his neck. He felt as though he was not just itching but *hurting* all over. What the hell . . . Now his hand. He switched on the torch to inspect his

135

hand and he knew at once. It was the blasted red mites! He fled back to the farmhouse faster than he'd run in years.

'Blossom! Blossom, they've got me! They're sucking my blood!'

In the panic Blossom refused to allow him in the house, insisting that he strip outside and leave his clothes out there. It was a perishing winter night and he begged to be allowed in but she wouldn't have it. Hamish sat in the kitchen helpless with laughter.

Blossom shot every bolt on the door and shouted through the keyhole, 'Get your clothes off and leave them outside.' When he continued hammering on the door she shouted, 'I said get them off!'

So he did and flung them as far from the house door as he could. When he was finally stripped bare, she let him in, but made him go straight to the shower. 'Downstairs in the utility room. Don't want any of 'em upstairs. There's hardly any hot water left but you'll have to put up with that. Hamish! Go get your dad a big towel, go on. It's all right you laughing.'

Warmed through with a brandy and sitting by the roaring fire dressed in fresh clothes, Phil made a vow. 'Once I've got my courage back, before I go to sleep, I'm going out with that can of spare petrol from the van and some matches and I'm setting light to the blasted thing.'

Hamish, still laughing, couldn't believe it. 'You mean you're burning the chicken house down?'

'Exactly!'

'I shall watch from the landing window when

you do. Can't miss a bonfire — I love 'em.' Then he burst into laughter again and Blossom joined in.

And true to his word Phil went out, pulled the hay from the nesting boxes and threw petrol on it. It took only one match to set it ablaze then he fled in case the mites came looking for his blood again.

9

The night of the dinner at The George Seb took particular care getting ready. Best shower gel, another shave just in case, best suit, newest shirt, and a stunning tie he'd bought specially for the occasion. Then he did what he always did — remembered his shoes needed cleaning after he was completely ready. He slid his shirt-sleeves up his arms to make sure they didn't get polish on them, thought that possibly furniture polish might do just as well and safeguard his shirt into the bargain. So spray polish it was and it worked just as well, thank goodness.

He checked his car keys and money, though he wouldn't need any if it was true what the others had said: that if Mungo organised anything he always went the whole hog and paid for it all. Then he was ready for a whole evening with Maggie Goddard. Dear Maggie. She was so comfortable and cuddly, though he'd never cuddled her. Perhaps tonight he might.

The car park at The George was almost full, but Seb found a space next to Mungo's Range Rover, locked his car and went to wait in the foyer for Maggie. She was already there, looking quietly sensational in a short black dress, understated but obviously classy. Her hair had been slightly tamed but not enough to make her look ordinary. As he greeted her with a kiss on her cheek he smelt that lovely floral perfume of hers and was inordinately pleased at his choice of dinner guest. Maggie was well aware of how to conduct herself at such an event and he had no qualms about her fitting in.

He began introducing Maggie to everyone, and what pleased him most was the fact that they all took to her immediately and she to them. Valentine arrived alone, looking edgy and ill at ease. At the bar Seb asked him if his guest hadn't been able to come.

'That's right,' Valentine said shortly. 'Must say, I like Maggie. She's lovely. Who is she exactly?'

'The daughter of a client. The one with the alpacas. She's an actress.'

Valentine's eyebrows shot up his forehead. 'Is she indeed? I'll get these.'

They all stood around in the bar chatting while they waited for Rose and Dan to arrive. Which they did in a last-minute flurry, explaining that the babysitter's car wouldn't start and Dan had had to go and get her, and the children, small though they were, had become fractious knowing Rose was going out.

Rose caught up with Seb while she waited for Dan to get her drink. 'Hi, Seb. My, I hear you've made a good start, what with canaries and alpacas and the dog called Dai. And this is a friend? Hi! I'm Rose, Dan's wife.'

Maggie took to Rose's open American approach and before long they were chatting about the theatre like two old friends, finally having to be called to attention by Dan, who was hungry and didn't want to miss his dinner.

'They've all gone in, Rose. Come along, darling.'

Joy's seating plan put Seb and Maggie between Valentine on one side and Scott and Zoe on the other. Scott found Maggie enchanting, and while he had very little knowledge of the theatre he did enjoy talking to her about the kind of people she met and the audition she was about to go to. Seb was delighted to listen to the pair of them.

When Seb had turned to talk to Valentine Scott said, 'We're all very pleased with the way Seb is fitting in. New clients already and doing very well indeed for someone so new to the practice.'

Maggie raised her eyebrows. 'What else can you expect? Seb is a gem. He's already won my mother over and she's very hard to please. I daren't add up the number of vets she's gone through. I haven't enough fingers anyway!' She laughed then said seriously, 'Seb looks quiet and doesn't push himself forward, but he's very deep and very passionate about being a vet. Nothing will stop him doing an excellent job, believe me.'

'Yes, I'm sure you're right. How long have you known him?'

Scott looked her straight in the face, testing her out, but Maggie was equal to his questioning. 'A few weeks, but I feel I've known him for years, and that's a good start to a relationship, isn't it?'

'Oh! Yes.' This unsophisticated, open-hearted Australian was unaccustomed to Maggie's type of conversation and felt at a loss. A relationship? After all, it was obvious to anyone that Maggie was considerably older than Seb.

'Scott, who are the partners?'

'Mungo is the senior partner. Colin is the one with the very thin wife who looks anxious all the time, but not nearly as anxious now they have a little boy. Dan Brown has the dashing American wife with a houseful of babies, though you wouldn't think it, would you? I'm the newest partner. My wife Zoe here used to be one — didn't you, darling? — but when we married she decided to give up practice and have babies instead, and I am the partner in her place.'

'How many children do you have?'

'A son at school and two babies — so far.'

'I see. I didn't say what I said about Seb because I knew I was talking to a partner, you know. I'm not that kind of person. I've very little guile.'

Scott laughed. 'I would have thought in your profession guile would have been very useful.'

Maggie gave one of her uproarious laughs which drew everyone's attention to her. 'Maybe I'd have gone further up the ladder if I had more guile.'

Mungo cut across everyone's conversation. 'The time has come for every second lady to move round to their left, please, starting with Miriam.'

During the ensuing chaos Miriam ended up next to Maggie, Valentine on his own making the even numbers awkward. 'Maggie? I'm so pleased to have a chance to talk. When will I get a chance to see you acting?'

'Well, I'm going for an audition shortly. If I get the part I shall be on TV in a series. I've seen the script and I have free choice which scene I choose to do for the audition.'

'Have you chosen your scene yet?'

The puddings came round and the two of them tasted theirs immediately because it looked so tempting. Miriam, a lover of puddings, said, 'Mmmm! Wonderful. I never know which I like best, strawberries or raspberries, but these raspberries are so sweet and tangy. Do you like puddings?'

'Much prefer them to the main course.' Maggie giggled that charming giggle which so endeared her to people.

'So do I!' Having found common ground Miriam asked, 'Well, have you chosen yet?'

'I've chosen the last scene where she confesses in a round-about way to a murder. Years ago, but she never got found out.'

'You're not a nice character, then? I mean, the part you will play!'

'The murder was almost justified.'

'I see. I can never see that murder can be justified in any way at all. Still, that's me all over. Have you known Seb long?'

'A few weeks.' Maggie smiled. 'You're the second person to ask me that tonight.'

'Sorry. We're a close-knit group, that's why we ask. The first year as a vet in a new job isn't easy. You have to prove yourself every time you see a client and they can be so touchy, so we keep an eye.'

'Seb's very adult for his years, very sympathetic. But . . . ' Maggie paused. 'But I think something happened to him . . . I don't know

142

what, but I sense it's something that almost broke him.'

'Really?' Miriam put down her spoon and fork and gave her whole attention to Maggie.

'He hasn't told me, it's just my over-sensitive emotions — actress and all that. Sometimes you see more than there is.' To divert Miriam from asking more Maggie offered, 'I understand your Mungo is much admired for his orthopaedic work. Seb is full of admiration for him.'

'He specialised in orthopaedic surgery after he'd qualified and, though I say it myself, he excels at it. But he's lovely as a person, too, and that's important.'

'Of course it is.' Maggie's eyes strayed over to Seb and they smiled at each other.

Miriam noticed the exchange of smiles and, putting two and two together, made up her mind to have a word with Joy. She'd know, would Joy. Maggie must be at least twelve years older than Seb and it simply wouldn't do. Then Miriam almost kicked herself for not remembering that nowadays people often had relationships based on friendship, and that romance never entered the equation. She wondered what had happened to Seb, this thing that Maggie sensed had gone wrong with him. But it was none of her business. After all, everyone was pleased with Seb's work and no one more so than Mungo. And that was all that was of interest to her and the practice. She glanced across at Mungo and he caught her eye. He toasted her with his wine glass and for a single second they were the only two in the dining room.

It was when Mungo stood up to make a speech of welcome to everyone, and Seb and Kate in particular, that the fun began. He was a brilliant raconteur and he had a very willing audience, well primed with drink all evening. It was a good thing that they had a private room because each of them seemed to have a speech to make.

Ginny's Gab volunteered first. 'I have an announcement to make.' He made sure he had everyone's attention before he said the next sentence. 'As the eldest of the six Bridges brothers — even if it is by only twenty minutes — it is only fitting I am the first to enter the state of matrimony and I wish to say that it is the very best thing I have ever done in my life. I asked Ginny to marry me and, believe it or not, the immediate answer, almost before I got the words out, was 'Yes!' I'm well aware that many people are of the opinion that Ginny and I make an odd sort of couple, but my mother wholeheartedly approves of Ginny. They get on like a house on fire. Both of them are opinionated, bossy and wilfully determined to have their own way, so I haven't a chance. But marriage is the best and I can honestly say that I recommend it.' He grinned all over his face and pointed at Seb. 'Come on then, Seb, get cracking!'

It came to Valentine's turn and he stood up. There was a sparkle about him they hadn't seen for a while, not since his Nina had gone back 'home'.

'I had to leave the table a few minutes ago to take a phone call. It was my wife Nina to say

144

. . . to say what I've been waiting for these long long months since she left. She is coming back next week — for good!' A great sigh of pleasure went round the room. Miriam got to her feet and put her arms around him, giving him a kiss. 'That's wonderful!'

No one else quite knew what to say. Was it 'congratulations'? Or 'more fool her'? Or 'perhaps when she's back you'll manage not to look for women outside your marriage'? They were all pleased for him, though, very pleased, but they all had long memories and remembered Nina's almost continuous distress at his extra-marital adventures.

Everyone else's speeches were good fun and lots of clapping ensued but none had quite the impact of Gab's and Valentine's.

★   ★   ★

That night in bed Maggie, who felt she'd made a good job of being Seb's dinner guest, recollected the conversation she had with Miriam and contemplated how she felt about Seb. He was a gorgeous, sympathetic man, certainly a man not a boy, even though she was years older than him. How many? Twelve years? There was a strength about him which wasn't immediately apparent to people. She loved his choice of career, his gentleness . . . Well, she had to face it . . . *she loved him*. She rolled over in bed to gaze out of her open window to the fields beyond. She was besotted. It was ridiculous of her because she scarcely knew him. He'd kissed her on her

145

cheek, held her hand, admired her with his eyes and that was all. But he was unlike any man she'd ever been out with. Though his origins were humble there was a distinction about him — his bearing, his smile, his thoughtfulness. An owl flew across from the wood. Actors, sensitive beings though they were, could be manipulative, scheming and, very often, after one thing and one thing only, and she'd never been a bed-hopper. But Seb wasn't like that. She mustn't rush things with him. She'd play it cool.

Seb, on the other hand, went to bed thinking not only about Maggie but also about Kate. They'd chanced to sit together for a while in the mad moving-about game Mungo apparently always played at these kind of events.

He'd been overcome by Kate. Tongue-tied, inadequate and wishing he was anywhere but where he was. It was stupid really because she treated him with nothing but respect and showed a lot of interest in his work, but it was how she affected him. He tried, really tried, to be interested in her, but it didn't work. It was that superior look she had — not snooty nor arrogant, just superior. It unnerved him. To add to his problems he sensed Miriam was watching their reaction to each other and it embarrassed him. As for Kate, she was completely at ease and for some ridiculous reason this fact annoyed him.

But he fell asleep thinking about her good looks and comparing her to Maggie. Maggie was crystal clear. You knew where you were with her. But they were, to quote a well-used phrase, just good friends.

146

* * *

The next morning everyone made a point of thanking either Miriam or Mungo for the splendid dinner they'd enjoyed the previous evening. When Seb thanked Mungo he replied, 'Pleasure, my boy, a pleasure. Glad you enjoyed yourself. I must say, that Maggie of yours seems a nice person. Someone said she's an actress?'

'Yes, she is.'

'And what did you think to our Kate? Lovely girl, isn't she?'

'She is indeed. She seems to have settled in well.'

'She's known us for a long time, Seb. You could do worse!' He grinned, waved a finger in the air as a goodbye, and went swiftly off to his consulting room.

* * *

Miriam couldn't help being concerned that Seb was getting involved with someone so much older than himself. She popped down to Joy's office the afternoon after the celebration party and suggested they had a cup of tea together.

'Something on your mind?'

Miriam laughed. 'You know me better than I do myself. Yes, there is.'

Joy said, 'There's no one in the staffroom; we'll make the tea there while we talk.'

'Good party, wasn't it?' Miriam said once they were ensconced.

'Excellent.' With the spoon poised over the box

147

of sugar Joy asked if Miriam was still dieting.

'Drat it, yes. But today I'll have sugar. Mungo's so good; he never has sugar in his coffee, and I know he loves it.'

Joy gave Miriam a rather sceptical look and instantly Miriam knew. 'He has sugar? He doesn't. Does he?'

Joy nodded. 'I'm afraid so. We're not supposed to tell you but — '

'I shall tell him I know. I asked him not long ago and he swore he didn't.'

'Well, there you are. Black with two sugars.'

'Two! I don't believe it.'

They settled down to drink their tea and Joy's first words were: 'I liked Maggie very much, but she's far too old for Seb.'

Miriam nodded. 'Exactly. I intercepted a look between the two of them. He likes her, that's obvious, but it's more than that on her part and I don't think Seb realises.' She sipped her tea. 'Seb is a lovely young chap. I'd hate him to be wasted on a fool. I don't mean Maggie is a fool, she's a lovely warm person, but rather that it would be *foolish* for them to get together.'

'Too true.'

'Maggie says something has happened to him in the past which he hasn't quite got over. Her instinct tells her, she says.'

'That's interesting. I wonder what.'

Miriam stirred her tea to make sure there wasn't any sugar still lurking in the bottom, then drained the mug. 'Be nice if he found someone worthy of him.'

They looked at each other with the same

thought in their minds, and said together, 'Kate!' Then they burst out laughing.

After Joy had dried her eyes and calmed down she said, 'We really mustn't, you know. This gossiping has to stop. Oh, dear! But I think Seb feels intimidated by her. He scarcely said a word to her.'

'Just give them time!' Miriam put down her mug. 'Got to go. Perkins has not been out this afternoon. At least he doesn't want to go as far as he used to do. At one time he'd have walked to Weymouth and back.' She paused at the door. 'Don't mention a word to Mungo but I do believe Perkins is on his way to doggy heaven.'

'He is old, Miriam.'

Miriam's eyes filled with tears. 'I know. I know. Be seeing you. Nice news about Valentine's Nina, by the way.'

'It is. Unfortunately we haven't a job available here at the moment, except for stepping in when we're short-handed.'

'I can't see it working, can you?'

Joy came out in his defence. 'He's been a very, very good boy since that blasted Eleanor whatever-her-name departed for the bright lights. Now she *was* a pain. I think maybe he's realised how much he loves Nina. He's been a different man since she told him she'd had enough of his affairs. One can be too tolerant and a good boot up the backside is sometimes what's needed, not just forgiveness and understanding.'

Joy's phone rang and Miriam waved a silent goodbye, opened the door and left, bumping into

Seb as she turned to go upstairs. 'Good afternoon, Seb. Did you enjoy last night? It was good, wasn't it?'

'Yes, it was and I would like to say thank you on behalf of Maggie and myself. We both thoroughly enjoyed ourselves.'

'Good. I liked Maggie very much.' She looked quizzically at him with raised eyebrows and sparkling eyes. Now was as good a time as any, she thought.

Seb sensed what she was asking and felt uneasy. 'We're only friends, you know, nothing more. She's good fun and good company.'

That's what you think, thought Miriam. But she said nothing.

10

Seb had intended to ring Ruthie and Sandy Goddard to tell them the results of the tests on the two alpacas, but Tim, who'd carried out the tests, suggested otherwise.

'It seems to me it's possible that before these two were taken ill the Goddards had another incident and never told anyone. I guess they didn't know it was TB but the animal died and they've quietly buried it, innocently, no doubt. But if they did, that's perhaps where it all started. So go to see them and find out if I'm right. There's probably more than two with it now.'

Seb planned to go that afternoon as he knew that Tatty would be coming in during the morning with Evie and Tom for his check-up. Eleven o'clock was the appointment and on the dot they arrived. Evie was breathless and Tom carried Tatty. In view of their long journey Seb suggested they might like a coffee or a drink of tea. Dodie offered to make it for them and settled them in the reception area, hoping no other clients imagined they qualified for refreshments. She really would have to tell Seb it just wasn't on. Then she saw how apprehensive Evie was and decided he'd done the right thing.

Mungo came to the door of his consulting room to say goodbye to his previous appointment. 'Glad to have been of help. We'll contact you when we've studied the scans and made a decision. In the meantime, don't worry. I think perhaps it's not as bad as you think.'

'Thank you, Mr Price,' said the client. 'I'm so grateful for your help. Tiger is, too, I'm sure. We'll wait for your call.'

Dodie carried the tray of tea into Mungo's consulting room and Bunty ushered the Nicholls in.

Mungo shook hands. 'Evie, Mr Nicholls. Good morning. How are you?'

Tom answered. 'In a much better frame of mind than when we saw you last. He gets better as each day goes by, except he's stopped climbing onto the wood store and then jumping up on to the bedroom window sill.'

Mungo laughed. 'Let's see him walk.'

Tom put Tatty down on the floor and Mungo persuaded him to walk by tempting him with a corner of a biscuit. There was a slight hesitation in his right leg, but it was nothing to worry about at all. And best of all he obviously wasn't in pain.

Evie spoke for the first time. 'We're so delighted. He can walk ever so far now, and he and I have a lovely time in the woods because he loves rabbiting. If I hadn't come to you that day . . . I can't begin to imagine . . . Thank you so much, so very much.'

Mungo gave them a warning. 'When he begins to get ancient, really ancient, he may have a limp. Arthritis always seems to go for the weakest point. Just a pet theory of mine. It's been a long way for you to come, but I'm delighted to see he's so well. He's such a jolly little chap, isn't he?'

Evie smiled. 'He is.' She bent down to pick up a carrier bag she'd laid down beside her. 'Is Miriam about?'

'She said she'd come down when you arrived. I'll give her a ring.'

'Oh! I don't want to bother her if she's busy.'

Mungo winked at her and picked up the phone. 'I'd get shot at dawn if I didn't tell her. Miriam! Evie's here with Tom. Right, see you in a minute. Here, Tatty!' He opened his arms wide and Tatty took a flying leap, landed on his knee and sat there, his tongue lolling out, enjoying being stroked by Mungo. 'Not an unpleasant bone in him. I wonder what his history was?'

'As a puppy he was bought by a family and the children were allowed to tease him, so then he began snapping and the parents took him to the dogs' home. We saw him and loved him.'

'Then you've done a good job because he's lost all that. Children do have to be taught how to care for a pet, don't they?'

Miriam walked in with Perkins, and Tatty jumped down, as if sensing that Perkins was not at all amused by another dog looking down at him from Mungo's knee. They sniffed each other and began a silly game of chase.

Mungo intervened. 'Perkins! That will do! Sit. Tatty, sit!'

They both did as he said.

Miriam kissed Evie then Tom, and said how pleased she was to see that Tatty had recovered. Secretly she rejoiced at how much happier Evie looked.

'All thanks to your dear husband.' Evie held

153

up the carrier bag she'd brought. 'Now, I've brought you a present. I do hope you like it. You were so interested in my embroidery . . . I hope you don't think me too forward.'

'Never!' Miriam opened the bag and took out a framed embroidered picture. It could have been Beulah Bank Top in the spring with all the hill flowers in bloom on the lower slopes. It brought tears to Miriam's eyes. 'This is beautiful. I love it. I shall treasure it always. Look, Mungo! Oh! There's someone here, look, walking up the path with a dog! Just like I do. Look at the flowers, such vibrant colours! How clever! Thank you so much, Evie!' Miriam hugged her.

Evie said, 'Tom framed it for you. We're so grateful.'

All this time Seb had stood quietly in the background enjoying their gratitude and delight. But Evie hadn't forgotten him. She turned to say, 'And thank you to you, too, Seb, for all you did. You were so kind to me, so very kind.' She stood up and boldly hugged him. 'Time you found yourself a wife. You know, a nice girl who loves the work you do. You'd make a lovely husband.'

Seb blushed.

Miriam said, 'We're doing our best. They're lining up to be Seb's girlfriend. He's spoiled for choice, the lucky man!'

By this time Seb was red-faced, appalled that his private life was a topic of conversation in the practice.

'In time, in time,' he said, trying hard to laugh

it all off. But it was difficult.

Tom and Evie, with an excited Tatty in tow, said goodbye to every member of staff they met. Evie told them all the same thing: 'I don't want to have to see you again, because that means we have trouble, but you will all be in our thoughts. Thank you for everything.' Shy, timid Evie that was had suddenly flowered and when she kissed Miriam goodbye for the final time she whispered, 'Thank you, Miriam, for our little talk, it's done me so much good.'

Tom, when he shook hands with Miriam, looked her directly in the face. 'Thank you for your understanding and kindness, it's meant so much to Evie.'

Seb went out into the car park to see them off and Evie was still waving as their car disappeared out onto the main road. He went inside for an early lunch, still hot under the collar about the discussion of his private life. Well, he'd have to get over it; he supposed it was better than no one caring at all.

★ ★ ★

That afternoon Seb went to see the Goddards. His heart was heavy as he knew they would all be devastated. It would probably mean a culling of their alpacas. They'd be compensated, but in their eyes that would mean nothing; they'd be losing their dear friends.

They were delighted to see him. Both Ruthie and Maggie gave him a kiss and a great big hug. Sandy shook his hand warmly. It made him feel

155

an absolute traitor and he wished more than anything that the story he had to relate was not the truth.

He headed towards the indoor housing where he'd asked them to put the two infected alpacas, but Ruthie called out, 'They're over here.' She was pointing to the nearest field.

'You didn't isolate them?'

'Well,' said Ruthie, 'they were miserable alone in the shed so I gave in and let them have the freedom to roam. I'm very keen on freedom, you see. I feel they don't thrive if they're not free.' She smiled up at him and for one terrible moment he felt like grabbing her and shaking her till her teeth rattled.

But he swallowed hard and kept control of his temper. 'It looks as though Mimi and Carlos have a serious infection.' He didn't say the dreaded words TB, as he wanted to allow them to come to it gradually, even if he felt like strangling them for their soft-hearted approach.

Ruthie clutched the front of her sweater in horror. 'What kind of infection?'

'I'm afraid the very worst kind.' He looked gravely at the three of them and saw it was Maggie who was the first to realise the fatal situation.

'Not . . . TB?'

Ruthie fell on Sandy's chest and burst into a storm of hysterical weeping. 'Oh no! Please say Maggie's wrong.'

'Tim, who did the tests, is very experienced in these matters and is one hundred and ten per cent sure he is right.'

'Another test?'

'Of no avail. I'm sorry.'

Sandy, choking with emotion but trying to keep a level head, asked, 'That means . . . ' and drew a finger across his throat, unable to say the word 'cull?'

'Yes. We have to inform the police, too, and Mimi and Carlos have to be . . . well, taken away, not buried on your land.' When he said this he eyed the three of them carefully and saw, just for a moment, a flicker of shock in Sandy's eyes.

'You see, Tim wonders if you had an instance of an animal dying before these two showed signs of TB. You know, losing weight, then looking poorly, ears down, loss of appetite.' Seb waited for a response, noting the shifty look Ruthie gave Maggie. He decided not to say anything, just wait.

The silence grew longer until eventually Sandy said, 'Yes, you're right. It was Jose. Found him dead one morning. Truthfully we didn't know what he'd died of, but we just buried him. Strapped for cash at the time so . . . ' He shrugged. 'We just did it. If we'd realised . . . '

Ruthie, on the verge of collapse, muttered, 'We didn't know, otherwise we wouldn't have done that. Believe me. Oh, God!'

'Let's have Mimi and Carlos out then and we'll inform the State Veterinary Service and they'll deal with it. This one here by the gate looks like Mimi. Is it?'

Ruthie's eyes grew wide with horror. 'No, that's Loretta, you don't mean . . . '

Seb dug his fingers into Loretta's coat and felt

for her ribs; they were already too bony for her to be healthy. He looked at Maggie and she saw his thoughts in his bleak, shocked eyes. Great tears began rolling down her cheeks and Seb's heart trembled. In the heat of the moment he opened his arms wide and she went into them and clung on. In the midst of all the sadness he still found pleasure in having Maggie in his arms, then felt ashamed of himself.

'We've got to be practical,' he said eventually, clearing his throat. 'I'll have to examine every one of your alpacas to see if there are any more that might be infected. Then we're in the hands of the State Veterinary Service.'

Ruthie, between her tears, managed to ask, 'What about this Tim? Can he do something for us? Can we cure them if they're not too bad? We do it with people nowadays, so why can't we do it with our alpacas?'

The last desperate plea from Ruthie almost finished Seb. He released himself from Maggie's grasp and tried hard to be impartial. 'Any we find testing positive for TB will have to be put to sleep and taken away for . . . disposal. There is no way round it.'

'Well,' Ruthie took a defiant stance against the gate, 'I for one shall resist. I'm not having it. What harm have they done to anyone at all? Totally innocent, they are. Totally. It's not on! I shall stay here all night and all day if necessary. I will not allow any slaughter.' She tossed her head in defiance at Seb and glared at Sandy and Maggie in turn, daring them to disagree.

Maggie, being more of a realist than her

mother and wanting quite desperately to be on the same side as Seb, said, 'Mum, you can't.'

Sandy, torn between loyalty to Ruthie and desperate not to have, in all probability, their whole herd slaughtered, hovered between joining Ruthie at the gate and accepting the law. Finally, he said, 'So they could all be infected, and it's our fault for not isolating Mimi and Carlos?'

'Most probably the damage was done before I asked you to isolate them, but worrying about their freedom and letting them mix with the others won't have helped certainly.' Seb took a huge breath and said, 'I cannot let the matter drop. Professionally. I have to report what I find, whether or not you like it. It is entirely out of my hands. Sorry.' He stood, head bowed, desperate to get away, but so very conscious of their predicament.

Maggie took the matter in hand. 'Come in the house, Seb. Bring your phone numbers and such, and we'll deal with it together. We can't bury our heads in the sand. Come along, Mum, you're only delaying the inevitable and well you know it. Dad, bring her in. Go on. *Please*. Seb's right. He doesn't want to do it but he has to. I'll make us all a drink while we try to take it in. Come on.' The last sentence she shouted impatiently, trying to hurry her parents up, anything rather than this stalemate. She walked towards the house with one arm around Seb's waist, for reassurance more than anything, and Seb found it comforting. Slowly Sandy and Ruthie followed, Sandy white-faced and tense, Ruthie still sobbing.

In the kitchen Maggie said, 'Tea, I think. All right, Seb? We have Indian *chai*, green tea, red bush, or ordinary.'

'Ordinary. I'll use my mobile but not here in the kitchen; the reception won't be any too brilliant, will it?' He glanced behind him, aware of Ruthie approaching and having to listen to his conversation.

'Go into the hall and turn first right. You'll be all right in there.'

Being new to the area, Seb didn't have the local Veterinary Service number on his phone and rang Joy. But it was Dodie Pilgrim who answered. 'Joy's day off. How can I help?'

She listened intently to his news. 'I'll attend to this for you. No problem. Very sad. They must be devastated. Don't forget to tell them they mustn't sell any of their stock; no movement off the premises at all. Emphasise that. I've known people sneakily sell some and not let on. Thoroughly irresponsible, but there you are.'

'Right. Yes. I'll be back as soon as I can. Thank you.'

'Good. Mungo's got an op you might like to watch.'

'OK. Thanks, Dodie.'

'Remember, Seb, lots of sympathy but absolutely no soft-hearted nonsense.'

Seb had to smile at her reminder.

As they all sat at the kitchen table drinking tea Seb felt humbled by their stoicism. Ruthie appeared to have accepted the inevitability of their situation, Sandy was trying to put on a brave front and Maggie, well, she was admiring

160

his forthrightness. 'You've been very kind, Seb. We do appreciate that,' she said.

'I don't feel very kind. What I must stress is that you should, under no circumstances, *sell* or move any of your alpacas off the premises for any reason. I feel rather like the Grim Reaper.'

Ruthie couldn't bear his sadness. 'My dear Seb, it's not your fault.' She squeezed his forearm. Then the sadness of their intolerable news overcame her and she wept and couldn't be consoled.

It took Seb well over an hour to look at all the alpacas. He pulled out three who already were showing signs of lost weight, plus Mimi and Carlos and Loretta, and had them all isolated. 'The Veterinary Service will contact you to say when they're coming, but it'll be within the next day or two. Let me know, OK, Maggie?'

'What I really need is to go out for a drink tonight with you.'

It was a plea he couldn't refuse. 'Fine. Same place. Half past nine? OK?'

'Yes. That's lovely.' She reached up to kiss his cheek and smiled in such a lovely way that her whole face was engaged by it. He'd never noticed before what beautiful eyes she had.

'I'll be on my way. Tonight, then.'

'Great. Thanks, Seb, for being lovely. Mum's heartbroken, but I'm glad it was you who came to tell us. It made it a bit easier.'

★ ★ ★

Seb spent what was left of the afternoon watching Mungo amputate a dog's leg. There

161

was no other answer and the dog was only two years old, so it had every possibility of adapting. Still, it didn't boost Seb's spirits after the episode at the Goddards', and he was glad when his day was finished and he could go home with the thought of meeting Maggie later that night.

Maggie was already sitting in the bar when he arrived. She got to her feet and greeted him with such pleasure he was taken aback. She reached up and kissed him on the lips, gripping his forearms, standing close. Unprepared, Seb didn't respond in the same way.

Maggie shrank with embarrassment. 'I'm so sorry. I just wanted to let you know how I felt . . . Obviously I've jumped the starting pistol. Sorry.'

'No, no, it's not you. Not at all. I'll get our drinks and then I'd be glad to tell you.'

So over two gin and tonics they mulled over the situation of the alpacas' pending demise.

'But there's nothing more to be said,' Maggie said. 'It has to be done. Hopefully we've caught it early and shan't lose the lot. Let's be glad you recognised the problem. Please cheer up.' She smiled at him and squeezed his hand. 'Please?'

Maggie knew there was more to this story than Seb was revealing and she had the idea that whatever it was, it was to do with the terrible hurt she felt always surrounded him, so any setback seemed to cause him to feel things more deeply than appeared justified.

Seb suddenly said, 'You're right, but I can't bear distress . . . At least tonight we haven't got that mob of extroverts watching our every move.'

162

He slid across to the chair next to her and took hold of her hand. 'I'm off this weekend. Shall we go somewhere interesting? I haven't had the time to visit anywhere since I arrived. Everywhere's new to me round here.'

'I enjoy walking on the coast path. It's all so varied, with no two views the same. Do you walk?'

Seb grinned at her. 'Not often, but it would be lovely with you.'

'When you smile you look like a little boy.' This gave her the opportunity to ask the question she didn't want to ask. 'How old are you, Seb?'

'I'm twenty-seven.' He nearly added, 'And you?' but held back.

'Ah.' Maggie fiddled with her glass, took a sip and then obviously made up her mind. 'I believe in being truthful, especially with someone who matters to me. I'm thirty-nine.'

Slightly fazed by this candour, Seb quickly covered his embarrassment and replied, 'I hadn't realised. You appear much younger.'

'You are a charmer, Seb Partridge. A real charmer.' An awkward silence fell, which lasted too long.

Eventually Seb said, 'What's twelve years between friends?' And he laughed and so did Maggie, who was delighted it didn't appear to be a stumbling block.

When they both finished their gin and tonics at the same moment Seb said, 'It's not far to my flat. Do you have the time to come back with me? The chairs are more comfortable.'

Maggie answered in a very level voice, terrified of appearing too forward with him and spoiling it all, 'That would be nice.'

Her mouth curved into a conspiratorial grin and they both laughed again.

Back in the flat Seb served their drinks and sat beside her on the sofa. For a reason Seb couldn't identify, after his first sip of his drink, he put the glass down on the coffee table and leaned towards Maggie to kiss her. As a tentative experiment really, because he didn't know what her response would be, but it turned out to be no experiment at all. Maggie launched herself into the kiss as though kisses had been forbidden since her adolescence and she was greedy for them. Before they knew it they were kissing frantically, short of breath and longing for more.

There seemed to be nothing to hold them back, and the sheepskin rug, so carefully selected by Miriam, saw the pair of them making love with an urgency and an empathy surpassing anything either of them had experienced before. Finally they lay exhausted in each other's arms and fell into a wonderfully deep, deep sleep.

Seb was the first to wake, a slow waking in which he felt filled to the brim with happiness. He turned to look at Maggie and gently stroked her arm. She was cold so he went to get a duvet from the bedroom to cover her.

The duvet touching her woke her, and she reached out to hold him close. They said nothing, because there was nothing to say.

Eventually she murmured, 'Must go, Seb. What time is it?'

'Oops! It's almost twelve.'

She got to her feet and began dressing as fast as she could. 'Really must go. I've that audition in London tomorrow at four. Oh! I feel fantastic.'

He nodded. 'I do, too.'

'We'll do it again some time.' She smiled joyously at him, gave him a peck on his cheek, and grabbed her bag. 'You'll ring?' she asked as she raced down the stairs.

'I will. Good luck for tomorrow.'

★ ★ ★

Maggie rang Seb from a friend's address in London the following night, obviously over-excited. He loved that about her, that almost childlike zest for life she had. It bubbled over onto anyone who was with her and one felt swept along by an irresistible tide of fun.

'It's me.'

'How did it go?'

'Millions of hopefuls there, just millions, but I know I did really well, the best audition I've ever done. I even silenced the technicians and that's going some.'

'I'm so pleased.'

'It's you.'

'What is?'

'It was you, last night, who helped me. It was wonderful and it stayed with me all day today. I'm coming back tomorrow. Shall I see you?'

'I'm working tomorrow and on call tomorrow night, so I can't stray far.'

Maggie's famous giggle came over the phone. 'I shan't lead you astray, Seb, I'm not that kind of a girl.' She giggled again.

'So long as I am in the environs of Barleybridge in case there's a call . . . '

'I'll come to your flat about eight. OK?'

'Fine. I'm so glad you've done well.'

'It doesn't mean I've got the part, but . . . I know I impressed.'

'That's excellent. I'll do a meal, shall I?'

'That would be fun. Thank you, Seb. Goodnight.'

'Goodnight, Maggie.' He added, 'Come earlier if you can.' But the phone had gone dead and he didn't think she would have heard him.

★ ★ ★

They'd just finished their meal the next evening and Seb was contemplating repeating the events of their previous date, when his phone rang.

'Good evening. Barleybridge Veterinary Hospital. Seb Partridge speaking. How may I help?'

He'd scarcely finished his opening patter when he was interrupted by an almost hysterical voice. 'Barleybridge Police here. Constable Bird speaking. There's been an accident. A horsebox has overturned; two ponies were inside. One has been badly injured when it tried to escape and the other has completely disappeared. You're on duty? Will you come?'

'Certainly.'

'Thanks. Bye!'

'Hold on! Hold on! Where are you?'

'Sorry! On the by-pass east of the turning for Tesco, near the roundabout. Know where I mean?'

'Yes. I'll be there as quick as I can.' He slapped down the receiver and called out to Maggie. 'Got to go. And I need to call at the practice for a pistol. Sorry.'

'A pistol? Can I come? What is it?'

'A badly injured pony. I need a pistol just in case. I'll ring the practice on the way.'

By the time they arrived at the practice Mungo had taken the pistol and bullets out of security and was waiting at the back door.

'Here we are, Seb. If you need help don't hesitate to ring, and I'll be there. It sounds as though the pony's in a bad way.'

'Yes, I think it is.'

'Do you want me to come anyway?'

'I'll let you know. I'm going to take a lethal dose, too, just in case there's too many people about to use the pistol. OK?'

By the time they arrived, the police, the fire engine and the ambulance were there. A large 4x4 was slewed across the road, a pony laid on the grass verge and a horsebox was standing badly damaged in the nearside lane, with another car into which it had all too obviously crashed.

Seb got out his head-torch and the big torch and went straight to the pony on the verge. It had already lost a lot of blood and was desperately struggling to rise to its feet, but Seb's examination proved that both front legs were badly broken. The worst part was the blood seeping constantly from a huge tear in its chest.

Maggie looked distressed. Seb talked to the pony, desperately trying to reassure it, but to no avail. 'It's no good, Maggie,' he said, 'it'll have to be put to sleep. Can you find out who is the owner?'

Within minutes Maggie was back, accompanied by a tall man in smart country dress.

'You the owner?'

'Yes.'

'Seb Partridge, Barleybridge Veterinary Hospital.'

'Good evening. Things are bad, aren't they? I've been trying to keep my little girl from seeing him. It's her pony, you see, and hit by our own car, damn it. What's the verdict?'

'My honest opinion is that it would be a kindness to put him to sleep. Both his front legs are badly broken, and you don't need me to tell you how much blood he's lost.' Seb held up his bloodied hands to show the owner and displayed his shirt and trousers. 'Can I get on with it?'

A little girl rushed up. 'Daddy! Daddy! Silver! Oh, no. Please, no!'

Seb deliberately shielded her from seeing all the gore issuing from Silver's chest.

'Got a gun with you?'

'I have.'

'Get on with it, then.' The owner carried the little girl away, trying to find words of comfort for her but failing miserably.

Maggie brought the gun from Seb's car and handed it to him. She was crying.

'Maggie, hush. He'll be out of his pain in a moment. Just soothe him, will you? Stroke his

168

head, you know.' But Silver had other ideas and still pursued his intention of escaping, lifting his head and then his neck in his desperate efforts. Immediately before he loaded the pistol Seb came to the conclusion that there was too much happening around the scene of the accident, and that the risk of live bullets flying about was too much to contemplate. So he put the pistol in his bag and instead prepared the syringe with a lethal dose.

As he was doing this the owner's wife emerged from the darkness and introduced herself. 'It's my daughter's pony. I'll try to quieten him from this end. Too busy to use a gun, eh? Injection's the best, then. Anne-Marie won't hear the gun shot. Loveliest pony we've every owned. Anne-Marie's heart-broken. There, there, Silver.' At the sound of a voice he recognised Silver lay more quietly, enabling Seb to inject him with safety. In a moment Silver lay still, out of his pain.

Maggie was still crying, not quite able to reconcile having to kill the pony and Seb doing it without, apparently, any emotion.

He asked the little girl's mother if she saw which way the other pony ran.

'This one, ours, ran straight at us. We were following our friend's horsebox with both the ponies in it but we got left behind at the traffic lights and were catching up. Silver ran straight at us and we couldn't avoid him. So we never did see which way the other one went. Thanks for dealing with him so quickly. Much appreciated. I'll get back to my daughter. We'll make arrangements to move ... the ... body. The Hunt will have it.'

'Thank you.'

Maggie said, 'Oh, Seb, you're so brave.'

'Hush, Maggie. I'm not brave at all. It's only the second time I've needed to do that. I had to remain absolutely unaffected by it all for the pony's sake. Now for the other pony.' He stood up and Maggie saw he was covered in the pony's blood.

'Oh! Seb, you're — '

'I've been covered in a lot worse than this, believe me. Come on. Bring the torch and we'll have a look around. Let's hope the second one isn't badly injured, too.'

She watched him store his bag with the pistol inside it in his car, carefully lock the doors and then shine the torch around, hoping to catch a glimpse of the other pony. They couldn't see it but they could hear it crashing about in the field next to the road.

They soon found the place where it had burst through the wooden fence and stepped over the broken rails. By the light of the big torch they realised he was rushing about, scared out of his wits, in a field of well-kept allotments. Suddenly he changed tack and began running up and down from the top of the field to the bottom on a wide grass verge.

'He's puffing a lot. Almost out of breath. If we keep still at the bottom here, he'll start slowing down soon. Watch.'

Indeed, Seb was right. There was a noticeable slowing-down. The pony was breathing noisily and seemed to have very little strength left.

Maggie whispered, 'I daren't catch him. Can you?'

'I'll give it a damn good try.'

'Here he comes.'

Seb stepped out to snatch his halter, but the pony was too quick for him.

'Damn.'

'Next time, perhaps. You're right — he's really slowed down.'

Seb began talking to him as he approached and this time he was able to catch hold of his halter and, putting all his weight behind him, hung on, eventually bringing to pony to a halt.

'Find Silver's owner. He needs a horsebox to get this one home. I'll wait here on the verge. Mind the traffic.'

While Maggie spoke to the man Seb checked the pony. There were a few bad cuts where he'd obviously been hurt in the crash, and some lighter cuts inflicted by bamboo sticks and panes of glass, which he'd broken in his mad rampage among the allotments, but nothing of a serious nature. 'There we are, boy. Who's a clever chap? Mmm? You've had a real fright. You're OK now, though.'

Eventually Seb and Maggie were free to leave, but first Seb had to call at the practice to return the pistol.

Mungo called from the top of the stairs to the flat. 'Come up, Seb . . . Oh! And you too, Maggie. Have a drink with us. You deserve it.'

While Seb and Mungo locked the pistol up Miriam whisked Maggie into the kitchen to

171

decide on a drink. 'Well, for me hot chocolate would be more than welcome, not alcohol as I'm driving home. I don't know about Seb.'

'He likes hot chocolate, too.'

While Miriam bustled about the kitchen she very gently probed into the relationship between Seb and Maggie. Maggie smiled to herself because she realised it was only Miriam caring about Seb.

'He's a lovely chap, isn't he? I've become very fond of him.'

Maggie agreed. 'Yes, he is lovely.'

'He's got a great future, you know, according to Mungo. He needs to stay focused.'

'Right. Shall I take the tray in?'

'Yes, please.'

Seb apologised to Miriam. 'I won't sit down, I'm such a mess. Sorry.'

He told the story of the evening's events and Mungo said, 'Anne-Marie? Tall chap, a bit commanding? Well-spoken?'

'Yes, that's right.'

'Know who that is, don't you, Miriam? One of Lord Askew's sons. Thoroughly nice guy, he is.'

Miriam agreed. 'Oh, yes, of course. I've seen his daughter competing in shows. She's a dear little thing and doesn't look like a rider at all. Frail and very pretty. I'm sorry about her pony. It'll have cost a packet, believe me. Anything to do with horses and the Askews don't worry about the price. They're horse-mad. Have you met any of them, Seb?'

'I've met Lord Askew and his niece, Jilly, but none of the others until tonight. Must go

172

— Maggie still has to drive home. Thanks for the drink.'

'Let's hope you don't get called out again tonight.' Miriam smiled one of her famous smiles and Seb felt warmed by it.

11

The following morning Dodie took a call for Mungo and put it through to the flat. 'Good morning. Mungo Price speaking.'

'Morning, Mungo. This is Jolyon Askew speaking. Just a quick call to say thank you to that young vet of yours. He came out to attend a traffic accident which involved Anne-Marie's pony having to be put down. He dealt with the whole episode very competently indeed, and very sensitively, too. Hang on to him — he's going to do you a lot of good in the future. Once you get a good man keep him sweet, I say.'

'That's very good of you to ring. Yes, he's shaping up nicely. How's Anne-Marie this morning?'

'Very distressed, of course, but we're taking her out tomorrow to buy another pony. The only way to get over it. Thanks again.'

The line went dead, leaving Mungo staring at his receiver surprised at the abruptness of the call. However, it was a good start to the day to have a fulsome compliment about a member of his staff.

Dodie told Seb when he arrived to begin work. 'The Hon. Jolyon Askew rang to thank you for the way you dealt with the road accident last night. Full of praise, he was. Keep it up, Seb, you're doing well. In fact, I've never known a new vet collect a patient list at such a speed.

You've had a call from Mr Smithson, by the way, the canary man. Two of his birds are looking distinctly seedy and he wants you to call in. Doesn't want to bring them to the clinic in case it's infectious. Such a nice man but so anxious.'

'Can you ring him back and say I'll call about twelve noon? Poor chap.'

'Of course. Your clients are already waiting, Seb, so get cracking.' Dodie smiled at him and gave him a push in the direction of his consulting room.

The waiting room was already filling up and Seb felt a powerful surge of enthusiasm as he walked through the waiting room to a concerted cheer from everyone, all of whom had obviously heard about his adventure last night. He waved his hand to acknowledge their greetings, went into his room and switched on his computer to see who his first client was. It was Miranda Costello.

He called her name from the doorway of his room and watched her dash forward wearing another of her exotic, mismatched outfits, carrying a cat basket.

'Good morning, Seb. It's little me again.' She burst in through the door and placed the basket on the examination table. 'You'll never guess what I've got in here. I found it in the garden last night, looking dazed and ravenously hungry.' She cautiously opened the door of her cat basket and, reaching inside, gently drew out a ferret, not fully grown and looking scared to death. 'Now, isn't he a beauty! Do you have any experience of ferrets?'

'None whatsoever.'

'Oh dear.'

'But I know a man who has. Rhodri Morgan used to keep a ferret called Harry. I'll go and see if he's free to take a look.'

Rhodri's face lit up when Seb explained the situation. 'Brilliant! Bring him in here. I'll be delighted to take a look.'

Miranda and Seb went together into Rhodri's room carrying the ferret.

Rhodri greeted him with such delight that Miranda was thrilled. 'I'd no idea you knew about ferrets, Rhodri. Isn't he lovely?'

Rhodri took the ferret from her. 'Actually, he's a she.'

'Oh! I imagined all ferrets were male. But then they couldn't be, could they? I am silly.'

'Where's she from. A breeder?'

'No, my ramshackle garden. Found her this morning. I wondered about keeping him . . . her . . . but I don't think so. She's not really my kind of thing. Is she fit and well?'

The ferret bit Rhodri well and truly in the soft part between his thumb and forefinger.

'Oh! I'm so sorry. Oh! Look at the blood. Oh, dear.'

Seb swiftly removed the ferret from Rhodri so he could stem the flow. It was a vicious bite and must have hurt, but Rhodri took the whole incident in his stride.

'She's a sparky little thing, isn't she? Not quite fully grown, I would have said, but lovely colouring. Give her back to me.'

Rhodri held her by her scruff but even so she

tried her best to bite him again, wriggling and scrabbling to get a hold on him. 'She's not a domestic ferret, she's certainly wild. Never been handled, you can see that. If you don't want her I'll take her on.'

'Are you sure? I'm not really into being bitten. I'll be glad for you to take her. If I hear someone's lost a ferret maybe she'd have to go back?'

'That's OK. I'll keep her as and when, and I'll be delighted to give her a home.'

'But you can't keep her in the house with babies there, can you?'

'No, but she'll be in a stable. I know the very place and I might buy another one to keep her company. I've missed having a ferret since Harry died. Thank you very much, Miranda. In fact, I'll call her Miranda, shall I?'

Miranda blushed to the roots of her hair. 'Oh, Rhodri! That would be wonderful. I'd be so pleased if you did. What do I owe?'

Rhodri shook his head. 'Nothing, Miranda. All you've done is bring me a ferret. No fee required.'

'Well, I call that decent of you, yes, very kind.'

She meandered out into the waiting room carrying her empty cat basket, recognised a neighbour and related the whole story to her and, incidentally, to all the other clients. 'So, would you believe it, Rhodri's adopted her. Isn't that lovely?'

'Good thing, too, Miranda, what with that menagerie you've got at home already. A smelly ferret would be just too much.'

'She isn't smelly.'

'She is. I can smell it on you now.'

'That's disgusting. You can't.'

'Oh yes I can. Sniff your cardy and see if I'm right.'

Not for the world would Miranda have admitted to smelling of ferret, but she did smell her cardigan and knew the neighbour was right. 'Nonsense. Not a thing does my cardigan smell of,' she said.

'That'll make a change, then, cos it always smells funny. Time you had a sort-out with them animals of yours. I'm sick of 'em coming into my garden to relieve themselves. Sick of it. As for that mess you call a garden! Well, the mind boggles. A dump, that's what it is. *A great big dump*. In fact, worse than the council tip. They do clear up sometimes, but you never do. I shall be reporting it. Definitely.'

'What? Report my garden? What about me reporting that blasted dog of yours for barking?'

'Barking? He doesn't. Do you, our Benjy? Quiet as a mouse, he is.'

Whereupon, Benjy treated Miranda to a savage barking session, and she was thankful he was on a lead.

This so enraged Miranda that she swung the cat basket at her neighbour, forgetting she hadn't fastened the door, which swung open. Her neighbour's head went right inside the basket. Miranda snatched it off but not before the smell from the basket almost choked the client sitting beside her neighbour, as the blanket inside flew out on to her lap.

Dodie dashed out from behind the reception counter in high dudgeon. 'Now, ladies, all our animals are going to be severely distressed by this behaviour. Mrs Costello, go into my office, please and . . . Now!'

The day was saved by the neighbour being called into Seb's consulting room. She marched majestically towards Seb shouting, 'Round one to me!' She punched the air with her fist and closed the door behind her.

Miranda had been a client at the High Street practice where Dodie used to work so Dodie knew her well, and the memory of the smell came back to her when she followed Miranda, who was deeply upset, into the office.

'Here! A tissue.' She thrust a tissue into Miranda's hand and sat down to wait, occupying herself with paperwork until the tears stopped.

'Miranda, you should never have let her rile you. I've no doubt your cardy does smell of ferret. It's quite a distinctive odour. They need brushing very regularly to keep the smell at bay. Rhodri's decided to adopt her, has he?'

Miranda briefly stopped weeping and nodded. 'Such a kind man, and that Seb, he's kind, too. Well, I'll be on my way. Sorry to have caused a fuss but I'm fed up of that woman, she's got no sensitivity.'

Dodie answered in her no-nonsense way. 'Frankly, I feel sorry for her.'

'Sorry for *her?* The old cow.'

'I've passed your garden and been glad I don't live next door to you.'

Miranda was horrified. In a very small voice

she said, 'Is that true?'

Dodie nodded. 'It had to be said. If she complains to the council then they'll be sending you a massive bill for clearing it up.'

'They couldn't, could they?'

'They could and they will.'

'Hell's bells. But I've got treasures in there! My mother's old mangle, a fridge I took a dislike to, a dog kennel I've never used, you name it.'

'In that case you could clean them up and sell them, and perhaps that'll go some way to paying for a man with a lorry to take all the rubbish away. Think about it, Miranda. At the very least it'll give your dogs space to run about.' A thought occurred to Dodie. 'You don't let them roam, do you?'

A silence ensued while Miranda thought about how often her dogs went missing for days at a time. As a diversionary tactic she replied, 'I'm not without money, you know.'

'Good, I'm glad to hear it.'

'Dad's money. I invested it, hardly spent any of it. So I could, couldn't I?' She cheered up enormously after this thought and got to her feet.

Dodie suggested she left by the back door so as not to encounter her neighbour, and this Miranda did, with a spring in her step and purpose in her voice. 'Thanks for talking to me. You get in the doldrums living by yourself; same thing day in day out, no comfort, just the animals. I love 'em but there's a limit, isn't there? I just needed a push.' Very softly she whispered, 'Do you really think my cardy smells?'

Dodie nodded. 'There's been a definite deterioration in your attention to your personal hygiene since I first knew you.'

'Oh, God! I am sorry.'

Miranda tiptoed down the corridor to the back door. Climbing in her van, she noticed for the first time in years that the van smelt, too, mostly of cat wee and ungroomed dog. There'd have to be a big change. She wasn't having that blasted neighbour telling everyone she smelt. No, sir! Her mother would spin in her grave if she knew. Then she remembered how lovely the garden was when her mother was alive, with lupins and delphiniums and marigolds, and that dear little pond that had now disappeared under all the mess — she spared a thought for the newts that used to be in there. That chap Fred! Fred with his ramshackle lorry, that's who she'd get. Definitely. And just as important, out would go the broken-down washing machine and she'd get a spanking new one. The very latest. Thank you, Dad. Smelly cardy, indeed. Huh!

★ ★ ★

At noon Seb left for Joe Smithson's to see his sick canaries. Various possibilities raced through his mind on the way but he decided not to pre-judge the matter and arrived at the house with an open mind.

Mr Smithson and his carpenter friend were peering at two very dead canaries laid on a piece of sheeting on the old table outside the conservatory, but Seb was more interested in

181

the living birds. There were two canaries on the floor of the aviary breathing noisily. Their feathers were fluffed out and they looked thoroughly miserable.

'The birds who've died, did they behave like these two?'

'Yes, but not for very long. They seemed to take ill and die in no time at all. Missis thinks they have pneumonia, but I said that was daft.'

'In one way she was right. I think they've got air sac mites . . . or a bad cold. But the speed makes me think it might be air sac mites. They invade the nostrils, the throat and the lungs, and eventually choke the bird to death. I can do a tracheal swab. You're more likely to get these kind of diseases with an outside aviary, because there is contact with wild birds. I know they're not in the aviary but they will pause on the aviary from time to time and it could happen then.'

'Oh, God! How can I stop it?'

'I can give you drops to use on the birds themselves and you need special stuff for cleaning the aviary. When I say clean I mean detailed cleaning in every single corner, every joint of wood, every feeding dish, every water container. And I don't just mean a swish under a running tap, because these little beggars are so small we can't see them with the naked eye and they hide *everywhere.*'

'I'd better start straight away.'

'I can't see any water for the birds to bathe.'

'I didn't know they needed any.'

'Well, they do. Every day if possible. Good

husbandry is essential. Can you hand me those two that are squatting on the floor, please? I think . . . I know . . . they're going the same way as the other two.'

Mr Smithson blanched. 'Shall I lose the lot?'

'Not if I can help it. Follow me back to the surgery and I'll get you the stuff you need. Thorough cleansing. Nothing less will do. They'll have invaded every nook and cranny if I'm right. But do a massive clean-up, even if I'm not right and all they've got is a cold.'

Seb took swabs from the throats of the two canaries and recommended that they be isolated. 'Take heart, Mr Smithson. Between us we'll sort it out.'

His carpenter friend spoke for the first time. 'Can I have some of this stuff for mine? You never know.'

'Certainly. I'll give it to Joe here. Right, Joe, we'll be off.'

Back at the practice Joe took charge of the items Seb had suggested. With an almost overwhelming gratitude he said, 'Am I glad I found you! I'd no idea there was an avian vet at this practice. It's just remarkable what life throws up at the right moment, isn't it? They say vets like you are a rare breed. There's a chap down the road from me who has a hawk, a kestrel, I think. Flies it, you know. I shall tell him he's got the very vet he needs right here.'

Seb decided not to destroy Joe's faith in him. 'Thank you. Will you pay at the desk, please, Joe? Take care.'

'I *will* take care, to the very letter.' With his

spare hand he clasped Seb's and shook it vigorously.

Seb went in to the staffroom to snatch a bite of lunch, sad that Joe Smithson was having such bad luck with his birds. Dodie was in there reading the paper. She looked up as he walked in.

'What was the problem with the canaries?'

'I've brought some samples back. I think they've got air sac mites. Two have died and another two are on their way. Poor chap, he's so upset.'

'All in a day's work, Seb, all in a day's work.' She smiled encouragingly at him and leapt to her feet to put the kettle on. 'I'll have another mug with you. Coffee or tea?'

'Coffee, please, with two sugars.'

They sat companionably drinking coffee, and Seb ate his sandwich.

'Has Maggie heard about her audition?' Dodie asked.

'Not yet but she feels she did really well. I do hope she gets what she wants. She's been sidelined for so long she's beginning to despair.'

'I hope she does, too. She'll be moving to London, then? You'll miss her.'

'Yes, I expect so but if it's her big break-through she has to go.'

'Of course. She'll want to go, especially if she's spent a long time in the wings, so to speak.'

'She lights up at the mention of it. I just hope it works out for her.'

'So do I. Must go, I've been here too long already. Mungo says you might like to help this

184

afternoon if you've no clients. Take advantage while you can. At the rate you're going you'll soon be too busy to watch anything at all.'

Seb smiled at her, crumpled up his sandwich-wrapper, threw it in the bin and went to find Joy, as he needed to get the canary swabs off to the lab.

'They'll go in the afternoon post, Seb. Wait till we get our own laboratory set up. Won't it be exciting? I overheard Mr Smithson saying about you being an avian vet and how lucky he was.'

'He gives me far more importance than I deserve. It's embarrassing.'

'So long as you keep a step ahead and don't profess to be specially trained or anything . . . '

'Right!'

They laughed together and Seb went off to enjoy his afternoon in the operating theatre. That afternoon Tim from the Investigation Centre rang to say he would visit the Goddards the following afternoon and would Seb be free? So they arranged to meet there at 2.30 p.m.

* * *

'Tim Hopkinson. Pleased to meet you.'

'Seb Partridge. Glad you could come. They've taken it very badly, because, although they sell them, each of the alpacas is a close friend. It's been hard for them. I'll introduce you.'

Sandy and Ruthie were very restrained and extremely solemn when they met Tim, and it was hard work making conversation. They stood at the gate looking at the healthy part of the herd and then showed him the ones they'd isolated in the barn.

Ruthie burst out, 'We don't like keeping them inside. They're not used to it. It doesn't seem fair. We love them all, you see, and we feel heart-broken about it. It's nothing we've done, is it?'

'Believe me, it can happen to anyone. TB is no respecter of persons. I know top-class pedigree herds of both alpacas and llamas decimated by TB, and not through bad husbandry, so don't blame yourselves. Seb has told you about not selling any of your herd, or moving any of them off your land, I expect.' Ruthie and Sandy nodded. 'That is extremely important. TB in cattle, and in alpacas and llamas, has to be controlled very rigidly. I'll examine these you've isolated.' Ruthie offered Tim a cup of tea. 'Love one.'

'I'll bring it out here, then.' She wandered off, anxious to do whatever she could to help. Sandy, shotgun in hand, watched and waited.

'Tell me, what wild animals do you have on your land?' Tim asked.

'Rabbits, rats, badgers in the farmer's top field, hares occasionally, mink that escaped from a mink farm. I keep the rats down with this.' Sandy patted his gun.

'Dairy farm next door, is it?'

'That's right.'

'Do his cows ever come into a field adjoining yours?'

'Well, yes, occasionally, in rotation.'

'So they have contact over the fence, nose to nose?'

Sandy nodded. 'Could it be from them?'

'All sorts of possibilities, but I'll go and see him just in case. I can't emphasise enough that the matter is out of my hands. I have to abide by the rules, and being kind has nothing to do with it. The State Veterinary Service must be made aware and they will deal with procedures. You are not able to sell any alpacas or move any off your land until you are given the all-clear.' Tim, in response to a dig from Ruthie's elbow, turned to see what she wanted. 'Tea! Lovely. Just what I need.'

Ruthie gave it to him in one of her best cups and saucers and smiled sweetly. Seb saw she was about to launch into a campaign of charming him to get her own way.

'No one would know if none of us said anything about this?'

'*I* would.'

'Yes, but you could say . . . I mean, they're so lovely, so appealing, it's not right. Couldn't you cure them?'

Tim downed his tea in one long drink, put the cup in the saucer and handed it back to Ruthie. 'No.'

She tried again but to no avail.

'Mrs Goddard, lovely, appealing, yes, they are, but my hands are tied. I should be failing in my duty if I ignored this situation. Putting them to sleep and keeping a watchful eye on the others for several months, perhaps for as long as a year, is what is going to happen and no matter how hard you plead, I'm afraid . . . ' Sadly Tim shook his head at her.

Ruthie slowly nodded her agreement. 'It's so hard, you see. So hard.'

'I know. I know. I'll take my leave when I've done a thorough inspection. We'll be in touch almost immediately.'

Seb and Sandy tried to console her but it was no good; she was going to grieve and that was that. Sandy, with an apologetic smile at Seb, guided her into the house and Seb left. He passed Maggie coming up the drive on her bike, pedalling like mad as always. She slewed to a stop and he wound down his window.

'Maggie!'

'Seb!' She reached her hand inside the car and grabbed his. 'Well?'

'He's here and it's like I said.'

'Ah. Well. I expect Mum tried her best to persuade him?'

'She did, but there was no way he could change his mind.'

'I knew she would. I can never understand why she thinks she can persuade people when they've a job to do. Do we know why they've got it?'

Seb shook his head. 'Maggie?'

'Mmm?'

'Maggie? Are you free right now?'

'Yes.'

'Do you fancy . . . ?' Seb looked at her, so obviously asking her . . .

'Yes!'

She flung her bike into the grass at the side of the road, got into his car and they fled at speed to Seb's flat, raced up the stairs, stripped off and fell into bed.

An hour later Seb opened a bottle of wine and they spent another two hours enjoying themselves in his bed. They woke and Seb saw it was already seven o'clock. 'Shall we go for a meal? I should have shopped tonight but I haven't. We'll treat ourselves, shall we?'

'Why not? I'll shower before I dress. That Italian restaurant?'

Seb nodded. 'We'll shower together. It's a double shower so there's lots of room.'

So they lathered each other with some aromatic shower gel he'd bought in a mad moment, and they laughed and enjoyed themselves like two children, but with adult matters in mind.

'Oh, Sebastian Partridge, I do love you,' Maggie said. 'You are such fun. It's as if some sadness has fallen away from you now and you have permission to enjoy yourself at last.'

Her unexpected insight came as a shock to Seb, and he paused as he reached into the airing cupboard to get her a towel. 'I didn't know you knew.'

'Well, I don't, it was a shot in the dark, but I've thought you had a sadness about you right from the first time we met. I'm right, aren't I?'

He didn't answer.

'I'm sorry. I've spoken when I shouldn't. I'm so sorry.'

'You're right. But making love to you has . . . helped me. You see, you give your all without any hidden agenda and that's wonderful for me.'

'Hidden agenda. Of course I haven't. Why would I?'

He wrapped the towel sarong-wise around her and put his own around his waist, and they stood in his tiny bathroom in the lingering steam while he told her what he hadn't told anyone before.

'A year before my finals, I met someone called Carly at a party at college. She was a friend of a friend of a friend, not a student. I was completely dazzled by her, and I wasn't the only one. She dressed outlandishly and expensively, and compared to the women students she looked fantastic. For some reason she took a fancy to me, and got my phone number. Was I flattered when she rang a couple of days later and suggested we met. I believe the expression is swept off my feet. She was every bit as good as I'd first thought. Every bit. We had a whirlwind time and when she suggested she came to share my bedroom in the student house I lived in, well, I most certainly didn't say no. When I look back on it I never told my parents what had happened. I mentioned I had a girlfriend but not the fact that we were living together. Stupid really, but something . . . something held me back.

'We lived together all that year and when it came round to my finals I knew I had to work to catch up, never mind just revise. So I had to spend long hours working in the college library, I couldn't settle in the house as it was always so full of people. She was so generous she never once complained. Three days before finals started I knew I couldn't study any more. I had to get some sleep because I'd ground to a halt, reached complete saturation point.'

At this moment Maggie propped herself on the edge of the washbasin and Seb, glad of a reason not to say any more, said, 'I'm sorry, I'm boring you.'

'No, Seb, you're not boring me, not at all. Go on.'

Seb shook his head.

'Please, go on. You need to tell someone and I'm honoured it's me.' She reached up and kissed his lips so sympathetically . . .

'Well, I went home on the bus and when I got there two of the other students were watching sport on the TV. I stuck my head round the door and said something about being exhausted and I was going to sleep for a couple of hours. They both leapt to their feet and tried to persuade me to sit down and watch the football, but I'd have none of it and raced upstairs. I thought it odd that they came into the hall and persisted in shouting up the stairs asking me to watch TV. I walked into the bedroom and there was Carly naked in bed with a man I didn't know. In *our* bed where we'd *loved* . . . Through the haze she kept saying, 'I'm so sorry. I'm so sorry.' *Apologising? For* . . . '

Seb couldn't go on. Maggie held him close until his voice returned to him. 'No wonder she'd been quite happy for me not to spend much time with her. I just blacked out with exhaustion and shock. I had to leave college and go home I was so ill. The college was very understanding and said something would be sorted out for me once I was better, and I'd be able to take my finals as and when. The

191

upshot of it was I never saw her again. You see, I thought she loved me as I loved her, and I was convinced we'd marry and be together for life. But Carly was conducting, as she saw it, a sexual initiation for this dope.' He tapped his chest. 'I simply had no clue that that was what she was doing. That was why the betrayal was so . . . appalling to me. The others told me they knew what she was up to but had to assume I knew because they'd kept telling me in all sorts of ways, which I'd not been willing to recognise, me being so completely in love.'

The steam had cleared now and Seb could see Maggie more clearly than before. He knew how much she meant to him, but perhaps she didn't want him after what she'd heard. He braced himself. 'Sorry, I should never have told you. If you don't want me . . . don't want that meal . . . I'll drive you home.'

But they did go to the Italian restaurant, and Maggie restored something of Seb's natural happiness for him and told him how much she cared for him. 'After a betrayal like that, no wonder . . . Anyway, now we've cleared the air, can we still be friends?'

Her mobile rang. It was Ruthie. She listened intently then said, 'I'll be home in an hour. Thanks for telling me. Yes, I'll ring them first thing. Yes, I am.'

Maggie put the phone back in her bag and looked at Seb, positively bubbling with excitement. 'Can you bear to listen to some good news? Very good news?'

Seb nodded.

'I've to go for a second audition!'

'No!'

'It's absolutely excellent news, the best I've ever had. It doesn't mean I've got the part but . . . Mum was bursting to tell me.'

'I'm so pleased, so very pleased. When it's something you really, really want you've got to go for it.'

'Oh, Seb, have I really done *you* some good? You've done *me* good. That was why I acted my socks off at the first audition because I felt so lit up by you after that first time, and I'm sure that's why they want me back.'

The Goddards were so delighted at Maggie's news that it took a bottle of champagne and a lot of laughing before Seb could leave. He kissed Maggie passionately before he left, and as she waved him off she shouted, 'I'll ring you tomorrow morning after I've spoken to them.'

Of course, the news the next day was that she had to go to London straight away. She'd see him when she got back.

Seb faced the fact that the comfort she gave him was going to be lost to him for ever if she got the part. But he would have to steel himself to let her go without allowing her to feel she was abandoning him. He wanted none of her joy to be spoiled by regret. That was the best of gifts he could give her — his full permission for her to leave him with no strings attached.

12

Seb's phone rang at 7 a.m. the following morning and he didn't need to be told who was speaking. He knew instantly that it was Maggie. She was full of excitement.

'I know it's early, but the audition yesterday went excellently well and . . . we'll wait and see. But they did ask me when I would be free, which sounds promising. I'm coming straight home. Can I see you for a meal tonight? Our favourite Italian restaurant? Yes?'

'Yes. I'm glad it all went well. Fingers crossed. Seven-thirty? I'll book a table. Shall I see you in the multi-storey? That'll be easier, won't it?'

'Yes, it will. I'll tell you all about it when I see you. Love from me to you, Seb, darling.'

'See you, then. I am looking forward to it, Maggie.'

They'd just met and were taking time to greet each other after being apart for two days when Maggie's phone rang. She rooted in her handbag and eventually found it amongst all the vital debris she carried around with her.

Maggie listened intently. 'But why didn't they ring me? I gave them my mobile number. Anyway, what did they say?' She began to hop up and down, then she ran round in circles, kissed Seb on his cheek, leapt up and down like a child on a trampoline and shrieked.

She switched off her phone and said, 'I've got

it. Oh, God! I've got it. They need me on Monday.' The people in the car park stared at her but Maggie continued springing up and down until Seb felt breathless. 'That's marvellous!' he kept saying. Maggie apparently hadn't heard him, because she took hold of his jacket lapels, looked directly into his face and breathed excitedly, 'Do you realise I've got a part in a TV series, and it's the best part of the whole lot. The *lead* part! I can't believe it. I've done it at last, what I've been waiting for all these years. Isn't it wonderful? Kiss me, Seb, kiss me like you've never kissed me before.'

So he did. He felt he had no alternative because her excitement was so catching, and they were still kissing five minutes later. 'Oh, Maggie, I'm so pleased for you. So very pleased.'

'Should we go to your flat? You know, the two of us? What do you think?'

'I don't think I can. I haven't eaten since breakfast and I'm truly starving right now.'

Maggie burst out laughing. 'Honest to God! Well, I never. Right, food it is, and then . . . Can't have you under-performing from lack of sustenance, now can we?'

They found their favourite table vacant and their favourite waiter in attendance, and they knew that it was so perfect it couldn't be bettered, especially on a night as important as this one. Seb chose one of the most expensive wines on the list, with the best steak dish, side orders of mushrooms and green salad, and they sat gazing at one another, dreaming of world-wide success for Maggie.

'You never know, Maggie, what it might lead to. The West End! All sorts of opportunities! Scripts will be landing on your doormat every other day. It's so wonderful, Maggie, just unbelievable.'

'Hey! Just a minute, why is it unbelievable, eh?'

'Well, I didn't mean it was impossible for *you* to get a good part, I meant . . . well, I don't know what I meant, it's just so fantastic. I'm sorry, I didn't mean to offend.'

Maggie sobered up and went from being drunk with success to being downcast. 'It's a terrible responsibility, isn't it? I mean, if I don't get it right I could ruin it for everyone. No more series, no more anything. From high profile to zilch.'

'You were wild with excitement not five minutes ago. Come on, now.' He took hold of her hand with both of his. 'Smile?'

But Maggie couldn't. She'd just faced up to what she would lose by becoming totally absorbed in her acting career; and she would need to be totally absorbed to make a success of it. Then she remembered her life-long ambition was about to happen, the one thing she'd worked towards for years. Could she let it slip away for Seb's sake?

Seb recognised in her eyes the dilemma she was facing and did what he knew he must. 'You have got to go for it. You *have* to step out on to the world's stage and see where it leads. If I was selfish and self-seeking I'd beg you not to go, but I'm not going to. I'm going to say, at whatever cost to myself, *go*, Maggie. Go.'

Tears slid slowly down Maggie's cheeks. She nodded very slowly. 'We've only known each other a matter of weeks, but I love you as dearly as if I'd known you ten years, not ten weeks. I could marry you tomorrow and not go to London and — '

'No, you won't, because I shan't propose.'

A broad grin spread across Maggie's face. 'Oh, you heartless man, you. Cruel, that's what you are.'

'No, not cruel to you, only to myself. I should never forgive myself if I persuaded you not to go. My parents expected me to run the farm for them, but I knew I had to disappoint them because I simply could not do it. I would have withered away. Now I'm doing what I love best in all the world. Despite the disapproval and the upset, I stepped out and so can you. That doesn't mean I shan't miss you, because I shall . . . I . . . I . . . '

Their main course arrived and put an end to their conversation and they didn't get back to it until after the waiter had cleared away their plates.

'Maggie, I . . . I think it would be best if . . . ' Seb said.

'Yes?'

He breathed deeply. 'I think it would be best if we make this our last evening together. It's so beautifully perfect — our favourite table, our favourite restaurant, our very own waiter . . . we . . . '

Maggie was devastated because she had plans

197

for the evening to go on well into the night. 'You do?'

'We know we have to make the break. I've to let you concentrate on the job in hand and be able to give your all to it without me hanging on your coat-tails.'

'But I haven't got any coat-tails!'

'You know what I mean. You need to be free.' He spelt out the word for her, writing it with his finger on the palm of her hand as he spoke. 'F.R.E.E. So I'm suggesting that's what we do, free you to . . . devote yourself to what it is you have to do.' Seb's eyes filled with tears and for one terrible moment he thought he would break down. Maggie clutched his hand.

Then the dessert arrived and it looked so tempting they couldn't sit looking at it.

They each picked up their long-handled spoons. He scooped some cream onto his spoon and fed it to Maggie, and she did the same for him until the dish was empty; the bananas, the raspberries, the cream, the meringues, the honey sauce, the toasted almonds . . . a beautiful memory. They laid their spoons together side by side and looked long and lovingly at each other. Seb tenderly ran the back of his forefinger up and down her cheek, enjoying the incredible softness of her skin.

Maggie whispered, 'You're right. We must finish tonight before we get too . . . '

Seb drove her to the multi-storey car park. He got out of his car and watched her searching in her bag for her car keys. It took a while, but he didn't mind, he loved watching her expressive hands as they found one thing after another that proved not to be her keys, realising she couldn't see properly for the tears flooding her eyes.

'Oh! Here we are.' She held up her keys triumphantly. 'It doesn't mean we shan't see each other again, does it?'

'No.'

'When I come home for a break.'

'Of course.'

'Thank you, Seb, for a wonderful summer. Carlos, Mimi and Loretta went yesterday. Mum wore black all day. Three more tomorrow. Hopefully that'll be the end. Look after Mum and Dad for me. Mum's very down about me leaving home. Anyone would think I was going to be put down, too, not leaving because of a fantastic career move.' Maggie paused for a moment, then forced herself to look up at him. 'I'm sure you're right, Seb, to say goodnight now, but it's very hard to c-cope.' With her voice barely audible she whispered, 'I've fallen for you in a big way. What a lovely man you are.'

'You're lovelier. Goodnight, Maggie, and thanks . . . for . . . you know . . . '

Maggie reached up and kissed Seb's mouth sweetly, bravely, almost tremblingly. She waved briefly and drove erratically away.

13

The devastation and loneliness Seb suffered after Maggie left for London was far worse than he'd ever imagined it would be. He'd been so sure and so brave the night he'd suggested they said goodbye, he'd had no idea how badly he would be affected by not seeing her.

She'd phoned him a few times and sent him a silly postcard; he'd phoned her and sent her a beautiful art deco card. But still, for Seb, the pain dragged on. Maggie had a whole new world to contend with and she was so thoroughly absorbed in it he could feel the bonds which had held them loosening and he didn't quite know what he could do about it. Even though they'd agreed to part, Seb contemplated a weekend in London and rang her to suggest it, but she was so full of her first week's rehearsals that he knew he mustn't. After all, it was he who'd suggested she needed to be free so it was he who had to keep his word.

So he decided to go to Sarah Cockroft's engagement party and make himself enjoy it. She was celebrating her engagement to a soldier from the local military barracks and she'd invited absolutely everyone at the practice to a night at the Fox and Grapes with a meal, dancing and free drinks.

Seb didn't feel the slightest bit interested in someone else's happiness and almost said he couldn't go, but couldn't come up with a single genuine reason why not. He'd tried offering to be on call but Mungo had said absolutely not. He, Mungo, would be on call so long as Seb brought Miriam home when she was ready.

'Seems to me you need cheering up, Seb,' said Mungo. 'I don't know why, but you do.'

'But I'd much rather — '

'You're going. She'd much prefer you to be there than an old has-been like me, so there's an end to it. Party and drinks and dancing and laughing are just the right recipe for a chap in the doldrums. That's an order!'

Seb arrived late, had to park outside in the road and then felt anxious most of the evening about his car and the possibility of damage being done to it until Kate asked him to dance.

They danced well together, chatting, laughing and perfectly in time with each other. He could have danced with her all night, but she was in demand so he had to relinquish her to Rhodri and then Scott and then all the other male members of staff.

The little band Sarah had booked to provide the music played the hottest tunes possible and Seb found it grated on his nerves after a while. He escaped into the bar to find a quiet corner, but that was denied him as the bar was packed and everyone knew him so he had a constant supply of colleagues willing to talk, or rather shout at him. His phone rang and because it was impossible to hear what was said he went outside into the garden so he could hear better, desperately hoping, he had to confess, that it

201

would be Mungo needing help. But it wasn't. It was Jilly Askew.

Seb sat down at one of the tables and greeted her with enthusiasm, glad to have someone to talk to who wasn't full to the brim with alcohol.

'Seb, long time no see. Drink tomorrow night? I'm still at Uncle Fergal's so shall we meet at the Fox? How about it?'

'I'd like that. Yes. How are you? Made any plans?'

'That's what the drink is about. Tell you then. Eight-thirty? No, I'm eating with my cousins and Aunt Cecilia and Uncle tomorrow night, so better make it nine-thirty. They always drag it out. See you then. Bye.'

As Seb switched off his phone he heard a voice say, 'Can't hack it, then?'

Seb looked up and found Kate standing at the end of the table he was sitting at.

She happened to be standing under an arc light which the pub used to illuminate the garden on summer nights with an eye to keeping everyone buying drinks long after dark. He didn't reply for one long minute. Instead he gazed up at her, collecting his thoughts. She looked at him, thought he didn't want company and began to move away.

'No! Don't go. Sit down and finish your drink. Please.'

He patted his end of the long bench he was sitting on and she sat.

Seb offered his excuses. 'I can't stand the noise. That's why I'm out here just for a while.' The light still shone on her hair and lit her face, that face he'd thought was arrogant but tonight looked . . . vulnerable. 'Not enjoying life?'

Kate nodded. 'Exhausted. Had a long night on call and I'm not used to it.'

'On call already? They gave me a fortnight's grace before I started and then I was lucky. One call and I was back in bed by midnight.'

'Mmm. I got up at two and didn't get back to bed till seven, by which time I had to be up for a day's work, and this party. Couldn't not come. I've known Sarah a long while, seven years, and she has always had time for me. But all I want is to go to bed.' Kate smiled at him.

'Have a quick kip here if you like.' He studied her face and decided that perhaps she wasn't arrogant. She looked it only because she had classic good looks. With her fine-boned straight nose, large blue eyes, discreet make-up, elegant forehead and lovely smile, she was exceptional.

'If I fell asleep here, right now, I'd still be here tomorrow morning.'

Seb laughed. 'I recognise the feeling. Why do we do it? We must be mad.'

'On the other hand we could be dedicated and devoted. I've fought every fight to get myself to veterinary college and stay there, and then at the end failed one of my finals and had to take it again last month.'

'I did wonder why you started so late.'

'Now you know. My stepmother almost died of disappointment for me. But at last here I am.' Kate finished her drink.

'Would you like another? I'll get it for you.'

'Thanks. Orange juice this time or I really will be fast asleep. I've no head for alcohol.'

Seb disentangled his legs from the bench, picked up her glass and disappeared into the bar. It took a while for him to get served and when he came back she was fast asleep, her head resting on her forearms on the table, dead to the world.

She'd put her coat beside her on the bench so he picked it up and carefully placed it over her shoulders and tucked it around her to help keep her warm. He sat down with her to enjoy his drink. Miriam came by so he put a forefinger to his lips and nodded his head towards Kate.

Miriam sat down opposite him, saying softly, 'I've come to escape the noise.'

'So have we.'

Miriam was delighted by this situation. It was just what she and Joy wanted, the two of them making contact. Well, not contact exactly, because Kate was fast asleep, but it was progress.

'Kate was on call last night and didn't get much sleep. Not used to it, you see.'

'Of course. Wonderful party. The food's coming soon. We shall lose Sarah, you know, because Steven's going out to Germany and of course Sarah will go with him. I'm glad she's found someone so worthwhile. She's a lovely girl. How's Maggie doing? I suppose you've heard from her?'

'Maggie's doing well. We've agreed not to see each other.'

'You have?' Inside Miriam almost rejoiced.

'This chance is what she's been wanting for years and years, right from being at school, and I

204

knew we had to let go. So she could be free.' Seb swallowed hard, taking a mouthful of his drink to cover his distress.

'Maggie was . . . I mean . . . is a lovely person. She thought the world of you. Did you realise?'

Seb nodded.

'It's too cold out here. I'm going in. I'm sorry Kate is so weary. All part of a vet's life, though, isn't it? She's a lovely person, just like Maggie was . . . is . . . ' Miriam wandered off to find Joy and tell her what she'd seen in the garden.

Shortly after Miriam returned inside it was announced that food was to be served, so Seb gently shook Kate's shoulder, because he didn't want her to wake up and find she'd been abandoned.

She struggled to sit up and rubbed her eyes. 'Oh, God! I didn't fall asleep, did I? I'm so sorry. Food? Well, I am hungry. I'll collect a plate of food and come back out here to eat it, then I'm going home.'

Kate disappeared, embarrassed by being so tired and wondering if ever she would get used to being on call. At college there'd been a member of staff with her on night calls. Maybe she'd chosen the wrong profession. Still, Seb appeared to survive OK. Maybe she would.

★ ★ ★

Seb dragged himself into his consulting room the next day. He grunted his good mornings, checked his appointment list with bleary eyes and wished himself anywhere but where he was.

His first appointment was Mrs Bookbinder with her Chang.

'Do you mind? I usually see Valentine, I know, but it's his day off and it's urgent. Chang here has been poorly all night. I rang first thing and they said I could see you.'

'What's the problem?'

'Well, that's why I've come. There's something wrong but I don't know what it is. He had no dinner last night and this morning, when I thought he'd be starving, he didn't even have his breakfast.'

'What would he normally have for his breakfast?'

'Something hard to chew on, like a Bonio or something to clean his teeth. That's all. I don't want him to have rotten teeth in his old age, you see. But he's behaving most oddly.'

'Let's put him up on the table and I'll have a feel.'

Mrs Bookbinder was trembling with anxiety and Seb sensed something was very wrong because she'd intimidated him when he'd had dealings with her before and here she was almost a total wreck.

Seb felt all over Chang's body and found it swollen and obviously painful. Chang jerked away from him and was close to snapping at him. He felt his undercarriage again from the end of his ribs right down to between his back legs, very, very gently. 'It seems to me that he needs an X-ray because there's something causing him great pain in his abdomen. Has he passed a motion this morning or yesterday?'

So as not to mention such intimate matters in Chang's hearing Mrs Bookbinder whispered, 'Friday first thing but not since.'

'I see. Mmm. That's four days. An X-ray it is, then.'

'Oh, dear. It's serious?'

'Does he play with stones when he's out? Pick up sticks?'

'No, not usually.'

'Will you leave him with us? I'll get him X-rayed and give you a ring when I've had a look.'

Mrs Bookbinder, was horrified. 'Leave him? Leave him here on his own?'

'Mrs Bookbinder, he couldn't be in better hands, now could he? There's definitely a blockage of some sort. You must face the fact that he may need an operation . . . '

'An operation?' She sank down on a chair, suddenly white and faint.

'Put your head between your knees, please.' Seb rang his emergency bell and Dodie came rushing in.

'Yes?'

'Mrs Bookbinder feels faint. Could she have a glass of water, please? I'm admitting Chang here for an X-ray, you see.'

Dodie got the silent message from Seb and set about quietly removing Mrs Bookbinder in a very sympathetic manner from the consulting room. 'I'll send Sarah in for Chang.' She nodded to him and left with Mrs Bookbinder.

'I'm so sorry. It's the shock, you see. He has a blockage and we all know what that means.'

Whereupon Dodie had to call for help, as she couldn't support Mrs Bookbinder in total collapse all by herself, as she weighed twice what Dodie weighed, so Joy had to lend a hand to get her seated.

The clients waiting their turns secretly enjoyed this happening to Mrs Bookbinder as they all knew her as a very domineering woman, and several of them had personal experience of her sharp tongue. Poor Chang, though. He was a sparky little dog.

The word went round the waiting room and back again, softly so Mrs B. didn't hear what they were saying. The glass of water did wonders for her, and gradually the rapid breathing and trembling slowed and she looked more like herself.

Dodie relieved her of the empty glass and said soothingly, 'Seb knows what he's doing. So sit quietly and when you feel better let me know and one of us will drive you home.'

'I thought I'd stay here and take him home with me.'

'Not today. If he needs an operation the very earliest he can go will be tomorrow.'

'I see. But my car's here.'

'Well, we'll see how you feel, shall we? Tea?' Dodie got a nod. 'Sugar, for shock?' Another nod but no words. After half an hour Mrs Bookbinder got to her feet and said she felt well enough to drive home and she'd ring in a while. 'Tell Mr Partridge I am relying on him *completely*.'

'Of course. Now take care, Mrs Bookbinder,

as you drive. I'm sure it won't be as bad as you think.'

In a gap between clients Dodie went in to see Seb. 'What is it?'

'What?'

'Chang, what's wrong with him?'

'I think he's swallowed something and it's got lodged in his stomach.'

'She says you used the word blockage.'

Seb agreed he had.

'You see, 'blockage' to a lay person implies cancer, and that's what's made her almost faint.'

'Ah! Right. Sorry.'

'Choose your words carefully.' She smiled so sweetly that Seb knew it wasn't a reprimand, simply good advice, and he accepted that.

'Thanks, I didn't think about that.'

'Don't worry, you'll learn. She's gone now, so let's have the X-ray done a.s.a.p. and then we can let her know. She's a good client of ours. We don't want her upset, OK?'

'OK.'

The X-ray showed that in fact Chang had swallowed a child's toy of some sort, which was too big to pass into his intestine, and would have to be removed surgically. So Seb rang Mrs Bookbinder and reassured her that he would be operated on that very afternoon. 'He'll never be able to pass it through. I'm amazed he managed to swallow it in the first place, but there we are.'

'I know exactly what it is. Two of my grandchildren stayed the night on Friday and brought toys with them, and when they went home on Saturday they couldn't find a nasty metal alien from outer space. That must be where it went. It made a vile whirring noise when they wound it up and Chang didn't like it. He must have decided to chew it up to get rid of it. The naughty boy! I'm so relieved.' She burst into tears.

Seb managed to make himself heard above her sobbing and told her to ring about five, but no, Chang wouldn't be able to go home tonight. Post-operative care, you see.

'Of course, of course. Thank you so much, you're so clever. Five o'clock it is.'

Having handed Chang over to Bunty, Seb called for his next client. 'Tyrone Foster, please.'

There was a message from reception on the screen warning him that they were concerned about the dog and that this was a new client. Tyrone was a cross pitbull terrier and big with it. He walked awkwardly into the consulting room, looking mortally afraid.

'Good morning, Mr Foster. This is Tyrone, then?'

'Yes. He's been in a road accident and he seems to be in pain.'

'Did you see the accident?'

'Well, no, I didn't. Why?'

'Because if you saw it you could tell me if he went under the wheels, or merely got bumped by it, or trapped underneath. You weren't with him, then?'

'Well, no, he slipped out and I didn't realise.'

'I see. So how do we know it was a road accident?'

'Well, I guessed as much, the way he is.'

'Seeing as we don't know where he got hit I'll examine him standing on the floor. Lifting him up could only make it worse for him. Is he accustomed to being examined by a vet?'

'No, he isn't.'

'How old is he?'

'Two years old.'

'Good with children?'

'Well, yes, if he ever meets 'em.'

'You haven't got any, then?'

'No. Can we get on with it? I can't waste time like this.'

Seb began by trying to reassure the dog. It was difficult because he shrank away when he tried to stroke him, shivered when he did get touched and tried to growl but didn't quite succeed, presumably because of the pain he was in.

'He's very nervous.'

'Well, so would you be if you'd been hit . . . by a car.'

'I expect I would. If you don't mind, I'm going to put a muzzle on him. He's far too unhappy to be examined without one.'

Mr Foster didn't answer, so Seb left him in the consulting room for a moment while he went to get one. 'Joy, I need a muzzle for this dog. He won't let me near him.'

'I'll be hard put to find one. It's ages since one was needed. This is the pitbull cross?'

'He's certainly unsafe to touch never mind examine.'

'Hold on.' Joy disappeared into the back and came out with an almost new muzzle. 'I'll give Rhodri a shout. Two opinions are better than one. Just as a safeguard, you know.'

Seb took the muzzle back in and told Mr Foster that if he wanted to use a muzzle, legally he needed another vet in attendance and someone was coming. Seb didn't know if it was a legal requirement but felt safer saying that.

'Well, that'll cost me.'

'Let's wait and see.' Seb offered Tyrone a couple of chocolate drops but he wasn't having any of it, which was very unusual. Many a difficult situation had been resolved by the consumption of chocolate drops, but not this time.

Rhodri came in. Between them they fixed the muzzle and fastened a leash on Tyrone so Rhodri could keep hold of him while Seb did the examination. By this time Mr Foster was becoming agitated. 'Well, all this fuss about a few bruises. What a carry on. I think I'll just go and let you get on with it. I'm doing my best for him, and here you are making a song and dance about it.'

'He could have cracked ribs if he's been in a car accident.'

'Well, I expect he could, but what's a cracked rib? They don't even do anything for humans nowadays. Not even strapped up, they aren't.'

Seb began examining Tyrone. It was taking all Rhodri's strength to hold on because Tyrone was absolutely frantic to escape. Seb managed to feel along his ribs, gently squeezed his flanks, tested his legs in view of the difficulty he had walking when he first came in, felt his jaw, but it was the ribs where Tyrone hurt the most.

'I think we shall have to X-ray him. He's in such pain a broken rib may have punctured a lung. Can you leave him with us? We'll sedate him and X-ray the vital bits.'

'Well, not Pygmalion likely. I'm not leaving 'im 'ere. 'eaven alone knows what you might do. Charge me the earth, I've no doubt. Take that blasted muzzle off and I'll be off. Then you can't charge me a penny 'cos you've done nothing.' Mr Foster grabbed at the leash but Rhodri was too quick for him.

'I agree with my colleague that this dog needs veterinary attention and we would be lacking in our duty of care if we allowed you to go. The dog is the important one in this situation. So leave him with us, give us your telephone number and we'll be in touch later today.' Rhodri's lilting Welsh voice must have reassured Mr Foster because he eventually nodded his head and gave him a number.

'Is this a landline number? It doesn't look like it.'

'Well . . . no, it's my mobile number.'

'And your address in Barleybridge?'

'I'm just passing through. Been helping on the new road they're building. We've been using Tyrone as a guard dog, but he ain't no use as he is now. I'll be off.'

Rhodri grew suspicious and with it very firm indeed. 'I think you're going to do a runner. To abandon a dog is an offence and I'm not going to allow you to do it. Tell me the truth: who was it who injured this dog?'

'*Who* was it? I said it was a car accident.' Mr

213

Foster began eyeing the door out of the corner of his eye.

'No.' Rhodri roared this word and Mr Foster jumped. 'I asked for the truth. It can't be that hard.'

Seb asked why the dog was so nervous. 'Someone's been maltreating this dog, haven't they? Who is it? You?'

Mr Foster stripped off his sweater and showed them his bare arms. Both of them had several deep teeth marks made by a big dog. The one on his right arm was already going septic with inflammation circling it, almost visibly spreading. Seb was appalled and saw that his first instinct to muzzle the dog had been all too right.

'It's me what's been maltreated, not 'im.'

'Well?'

Rhodri blanched when he saw the wounds. 'Have you had a tetanus injection?'

'Never.'

Seb, angrier than he had ever been, said, 'Sit down, Mr Foster, will you. I'm taking Tyrone and tying him up in one of our isolation rooms, out of harm's way. Then I'm coming back to you to ask you some questions. So you'd better have some answers ready. The truth this time.'

Rhodri stayed with Mr Foster. Seb took the dog and locked him up as he said he would and then went to find Joy. 'We've got a problem. I've locked the dog in the isolation room, fastened him tightly to the hook that's there for the purpose. I'm keeping the key. No one is to go in there, no matter what. He's too dangerous. Apologies to my next client.'

'Don't worry. I'll get Kate to see them.'

By the time Seb returned to his consulting room Rhodri had got the truth from Mr Foster. 'All right. All right. I use him for fighting. Betting and that, you know. He's a killer. Best dog I've ever had. Never a mark on 'im. Then he turned on me two days ago. He was asleep and I caught him unawares and startled him. I spoke to him like I always do, so he knows it's me what feeds him, but he went for me, something he'd never done before. Could always rely on 'im, I could, but I must admit to being a bit nervous of him just lately. Different, he's been. Gave me a right shock, he did, the daft beggar. Couldn't get him off and my mate had to kick him hard as he could, in his ribs, to get me free. If my mate hadn't been there . . . I just don't know what to do.'

'So you're not just passing through while you work on the road?'

'Well, no.'

'It's my opinion that this is a pitbull terrier.'

'Well, it ain't. On his papers it says he's a cross.'

'Where do you meet for the fights?' Rhodri could tell that Mr Foster was getting a lot of pain from his arms so he knew this was the moment to get the truth.

'I . . . this doesn't half hurt.'

'Tell us. Now is your moment and then we'll have a word with the police and say how much you helped us.'

'The police! My God! They'll make me have him put down.'

'Exactly. The poor thing, when it's not his fault. Life isn't fair, is it?' Seb was so angry now he had difficulty speaking without venom in his voice. 'So we're still waiting for the answer. Where do the fights take place?'

Mr Foster delayed answering while he examined yet again the great gashes Tyrone's teeth had made on his arms, some of them fifteen centimetres long and jagged, too.

'Imagine the damage he could do to a small child if he'd startled him? Mmm? He'd have been killed.' Seb left that to sink in for a moment and then said in a persuasive tone of voice, 'Come on, then, tell us. You know it's for the best.'

'Well, I love Tyrone. He's always been my best friend.'

'Best friend? I don't think so. He's lived in fear of you, hasn't he? I'm afraid that my experience tells me that Tyrone is a dangerous dog and that he must, I repeat, *must* be put down.'

Rhodri said, 'If you tell all, and you sign a paper to say you gave your permission for us to put your dog to sleep, then the police will be impressed, believe me. I know from experience. I'm not saying you'll be let off but it will certainly improve your chances. Is Tyrone your only dog?'

Mr Foster nodded. 'Well, at the moment, yes, he is.' He winced again, then his words tumbled out in a rush. 'A farm over Beulah Bank Top, in that giant barn they have there. That's all I can say. We only go at dark. Don't know its name even.'

216

Seb wrote a declaration on his computer and printed it out for Mr Foster to sign. They had to read it out to him as he said he couldn't read. The signature was written painfully slowly in an almost child-like script. Then Seb asked him for his address and wrote it below Mr Foster's signature: 'The Dark Blue Bus, Station Car Park, (back of) Barleybridge, Dorset.'

As sympathetically as he could Seb said, 'You live in a bus?'

The man nodded.

'Now, Mr Foster, we'll attend to Tyrone. He won't know a thing, he'll simply fall asleep and that will be that, he'll be beyond pain. What you must do is get yourself straight to hospital before those wounds get any worse. You don't want septicaemia to set in. I've never seen such a serious dog bite.'

'Well, you haven't lived. I've seen a lot worse. Do it gently to him, the blasted daft beggar. What did he have to turn on me for, eh? I ask yer? Me what feeds him.'

Rhodri, in a very controlled tone, said, 'Out of fear, Mr Foster, out of fear. Good afternoon. Pay at the desk on your way out.'

Seb prepared to put Tyrone to sleep. 'I wouldn't mind if Tyrone was to blame, but he isn't. It feels so cruel.'

'It isn't, Seb. He's had one hell of a life, the poor thing, and we're putting him out of his misery. I've recorded our conversation, OK? Didn't get a chance to tell you. We'll get it transcribed and then fasten the letter he signed and the tape and the printout in a big envelope and put them in the safe for security. I don't trust that chap further than I can throw him. Come on, let's get the job done.'

So they both went to the isolation room, unlocked the door and found that Tyrone had spent his time attempting to drag the strong steel hook the leash had been tied to, out of the wall. Another five minutes and he would have been loose. In his eyes was the same frantic fear he'd shown when he first arrived.

'Get that needle in quicko, Seb,' Rhodri said. 'No conscience about it, if you please.'

Tyrone collapsed immediately. Seb stroked his head, knowing it was all too late, but not liking the poor dog to go without what was perhaps the first compassionate touch he'd had since he was born.

★ ★ ★

That night Maggie rang. She was full of excitement, thrilled to bits at being with her theatrical soul mates, and wondering how her darling Seb was getting on. She'd known the moment he answered her call that things were not right with him. 'What's the matter, Seb?'

'I'm being ridiculous really. It's nothing.'

'It is, I can tell. Tell me, please. I wish I were there to hug you.'

'I had to put a dog to sleep today and it wasn't his fault.'

'He was too ill, you mean?'

'No, he was dangerous through no fault of his own. You see, he'd been used for dog-fighting, betting and that. There's big money in it apparently. When they're going to use them for fighting they don't get loved and cared for like they should. Don't want to make them soft, you see, but he turned on his owner and they had to kick his ribs in to make him let go. I know we couldn't let him live, obviously, because he was dangerous, but I rather felt it would have been a good idea to stick the syringe in the owner not the dog.'

'You sound so angry about it.'

'I am.'

'In Barleybridge, though? Sleepy old Barleybridge. Whereabouts?'

'The other side of Beulah Bank Top. We've informed the police.'

'Good. They deserve all they get. Don't worry about the dog any more. It wasn't his fault but it would have been yours if, knowing what you knew, you'd not put him down and he'd then killed someone. At least you've nothing on your conscience.'

'No, you're right.' Seb felt consoled by Maggie's sound common sense.

'Change of subject. Seb, I'm having a wonderful time here, it's all going so well, but I do miss you.' Maggie hesitated, and had to clear her throat.

'I miss you, Maggie, very much. You know we're all rooting for you, willing you to come out tops. Do you feel happy with what you're doing?'

'So happy, Seb. Got to go, there's someone at the door. Goodnight. Miss you.' She sent a kiss down the line and Seb returned it. 'Soon be

Christmas. See you.'

The receiver went down before Seb could tell her he had all of Christmas off and was going home. He'd tell her next time.

* * *

Tyrone's death never left Seb's mind. Joy's Duncan, who for years had walked on Beulah Bank Top, guessed exactly which farm it was.

'That's Beulah Heights Farm,' he said. 'They built a huge barn for some reason or another years ago and the idea for it fell through so it's never been used since. The farmer's not a bad chap; let me shelter there one day for an hour when it was tippling down. Not making much of a living, though, I shouldn't think.'

Bunty's Dicky was celebrated at the police station for being hot on animal cruelty and the news stirred him like nothing else could. 'Right! That's me sorted for a few days,' he said. 'Foster? Foster? I'm sure that name rings a bell. Little chap, like a weasel, nasty little face.'

So Seb knew that something would be done, but the whole episode had left a nasty taste in his mouth.

14

While his head was still full of the dog-fighting problem there came a knock at his consulting-room door. Kate put her head round. 'It's only me. Are you free?'

Seb smiled. 'Of course!'

She came in and closed the door behind her. 'Feeling better after the party?'

'Yes, thanks. And you?'

'I went home, fell into bed and slept the sleep of the innocent until half past seven. Mia, my stepmother, knocked on the door to wake me up. God, I was tired. She'd like to invite you to a meal one night, by the way. Thinks you won't be feeding yourself properly.'

'That sounds lovely. Yes, I'd like that. It gets boring eating all on your own. When would she like me to come?'

'Tonight?'

'Sorry, I'm seeing someone tonight.'

'Friday night, then?'

'That'd be great.'

'Best explain. I call Mia my stepmother but she looked after me from when I was two weeks old, because my mother walked out on me. Thoughtful, wasn't she? Then Mia married my dad while I was still a baby, but he died of a heart attack six years ago so we've stayed together in a new flat ever since. She's now married again to a very nice man she met

221

through the art gallery where she works. His name's Gordon Buchanan. Scottish obviously. We get on very well indeed. He's kindness itself to me. So now you know. Best for me to tell you, then you won't drop a clanger.'

'Thanks for putting me in the picture. I'll look forward to that. What time?'

'About seven?'

'Right, seven it is.'

'I've been in to see Chang. He's looking good, isn't he?'

'Yes, he is.'

* * *

Seb went to check on Chang Bookbinder for himself. He stood in front of his cage in the intensive-care room as Bunty called it. He felt in a daze. Automatically he checked the notes tucked into the front of it where Chang couldn't chew them, read them, opened the cage door to be greeted by Chang struggling to wake. He stretched and yawned and wagged his tail.

Seb rolled him over onto his back and examined the site of his operation and felt satisfied with it. He was so absorbed he didn't notice Bunty come in.

'He's doing fine. I reckon he could go home tonight, don't you?' she suggested.

But she got no answer. All that happened was Seb scratched Chang behind his ear. The dog loved it and braced himself to get the maximum enjoyment.

'Are you all right?' Bunty asked loudly.

222

Seb, his eyes glazed, said, 'Yes, of course. I think he could go home tonight, don't you?'

'That's what I thought. I'll give Mrs Bookbinder a ring, shall I?'

He still wasn't hearing what she said. 'I'll ring Mrs Bookbinder and let her know, shall I?'

'Good idea.'

Bunty reported back to the staffroom that she wondered if Seb was losing his marbles.

'Really?' replied Joy. 'Well, I never.'

Bunty saw the grin on her face. 'Is there something I don't know?'

'Nothing at all. Just a joke between Miriam and myself. Right, Bunty, get your lunch. Mungo's wanting to make an early start this afternoon. That grey cat that he's operating on isn't looking any too clever. His owners will be distraught if it doesn't work out. Mungo's told them it's risky and that he's not sure about it, but they're willing to take the risk, so I'm keeping my fingers crossed all afternoon. They're the sort who won't find it at all funny to have to pay for the operation and no cat to take home. Have you noticed the decorations? I wonder, shall we have a Christmas mince pies and drinks event to show them off? Mulled wine, that kind of thing. I'll ask Mungo, see what he thinks.'

Christmas events were not uppermost in Bunty's mind. 'Why not? Are you *sure* Seb's all right? He was very upset about that dog he had to put down yesterday. But he'll have to learn, won't he?'

'Exactly. Don't worry. Off you go.' But she still had that unfathomable smile on her face.

Seb could not concentrate on the job in hand the rest of the afternoon. From the operating theatre he couldn't hear Miriam and Kate's voices but in his mind he could see Kate's face, hear her voice, see her smile. She was so good-looking, so very good-looking. Not pretty, more distinguished. Classical almost. He couldn't understand why he hadn't noticed her at college . . . he knew Mungo had spoken to him, but he hadn't the faintest idea what he'd said.

'Seb! Did you hear me?'

'I'm sorry, no.'

'I said, ask Bunty to come and take . . . what's this cat called?'

Seb referred to its notes. 'Sweetie.'

'That's right, what a godawful name. No dignity. No wonder the poor thing hasn't any interest in staying alive.'

'But she has. Stayed alive, that is.'

'Yes, thank goodness. The owners would have gone berserk if she hadn't. But I did say she might not. However, we're not out of the woods yet.'

Seb didn't make a move at all, but stood staring at Sweetie. Neatly stitched up and off the anaesthetic and waiting . . . waiting . . .

'Seb! Bunty, please. You do realise that Bunty's nose is out of joint with you assisting me. All we need is you arriving in intensive care with dear little Sweetie then the balloon really will go up. I can't afford to have her storming out in a temper, she's too valuable. Now, shift yourself.'

Mungo confided in Miriam that evening when he got up to the flat. 'It's no good. Seb's going off the boil. He was useless this afternoon. Absolutely useless. Didn't hear a word I said. I'm having serious doubts about him. Dazed he was, absolutely dazed, and it won't do.'

Miriam kissed him and handed him a whisky. 'You deserve that.'

'Why?'

'For . . . for operating on that poor cat's hips when you weren't at all sure you should, but you did and it worked well. Just be thankful.'

'I'm not talking about the cat. Didn't you hear what I said?'

Miriam smiled. 'Perfectly.'

'What's the secrecy?'

'There isn't any.'

'Miriam! It's not that scheme of yours and Joy's, is it?'

'She gets lovelier, you know. Just . . . lovelier.' Miriam stared out of the window for a minute, lost in thought. 'Joy says how about mince pies and mulled wine for the clients one afternoon before Christmas? Then they can see the decorations. They are especially lovely this year. Kate has quite an artistic bent, you know.' Miriam paused, then said softly, 'In a way she's the daughter we lost. We get on so well.'

'She's the daughter Joy never had, too.'

'That's perceptive of you.'

'Well, she is. I wonder. Is that what's the matter with Seb? Has he gone all gooey-eyed over her? You know, I may be right.'

'Oh! Surely not.' She was still looking out of the window so she could afford to smile because Mungo couldn't see her face. 'Must check the supper. You sit down, darling. After such a strenuous, perceptive day, you must be tired.'

In the kitchen Miriam smiled. He was the dearest man. Then she chuckled as she lifted the casserole from the oven. Seb being absent-minded was a very good sign. Had she and Joy been successful with their match-making? Only time would tell.

★ ★ ★

Seb used his mouthwash before he left the flat, changed his shirt, put on his smart jacket, went back to the bathroom to use his electric razor and his aftershave, and rushed to meet Jilly. He was curious to know what decision she'd taken about her career. It was all very well him telling her to go for it, just as he had done, and as he'd advised Maggie to do, but Jilly had a far greater problem with a big family all entrenched in money, estates, horses and the Hunt. Jilly was stepping right out of the mould and that took courage.

Dressed impeccably, she was waiting for him to arrive, without a drink in front of her and deep in thought.

'Jilly! Good evening. How are you? No drink? What can I get for you?'

'A double whisky and soda.'

Seb made no comment on the word 'double'.

She tossed half of it down in one gulp before she added any soda. Then she said, 'The dinner tonight was a disaster.'

'I'm so sorry.'

'Even Aunt Cecilia joined in the fray. No one but Uncle was on my side.'

'What about your parents? How do they feel about you being a teacher?'

'I haven't got any. That's why I spend a lot of time at Uncle's. My father was his younger brother. I don't know what to do. I told them I'd got the offer of an interview and how thrilled I was about it, and they all fell about laughing except for Uncle.'

'You've got an interview? That's brilliant, I'm so pleased.'

'Pleased? That makes only two who approve.'

'Does it matter? You're not wanting to train as a pole-dancer, or a variety artist, are you? It's completely sane and very worthwhile. You'll be magnificent at it — stylish, charismatic, fabulous.'

'Seb! You are good for me.'

'When's the interview?'

'Ten days away.'

'Another drink?'

'I'll get these. My turn.'

'You'll be a sensation in a secondary school,' Seb said when she returned.

'Shall I be able to cope, though? Behaviour problems, disinterest, scorn.'

'I can remember waiting for a new teacher to enter the classroom and knowing in an instant whether or not they had a grip on discipline.

That's the secret, going in meaning business. You knew exactly which teachers could control a class and which ones couldn't. It's a technique, I suppose, and it has to be there. Don't you remember that?'

'My dear Seb, I always went to schools with very small classes that were very much under control. No one got away with anything at all.'

'I see. Whatever I say, it is *your* decision to make. And as for your family, it's still your decision. They might think it ridiculous for an Askew to teach, but if that's what you want . . . '

'I'm more lost than ever. But you are right. I'm not asking *them* to go to university again, am I? Only me. Come to think of it, I'll do it. Yes, I definitely will. I'll do it. I'm going back to tell them all that and to hell with it.' Jilly rose to her feet, with the light of battle in her eyes. Seb stood up to find himself being kissed by Jilly. 'That's my thank-you for making me brave. You're very good for me, did you know that? You put fire in my belly. I'm going. Don't think this is the last of me, I shall be ringing you up when things get too difficult and asking for advice. OK?'

She left Seb with his drink still to finish. Jilly had smelt wealthy, he thought. Even her handbag had smelt of money, gloriously soft and smooth, as he'd handed it to her. He admired her determination but sincerely wondered if she had any idea what she was in for.

* * *

Mungo burst into the staffroom at lunchtime with an announcement. 'I'm sorry to have to tell you this but I've just heard on the veterinary grapevine that Harvey Johnson-Munt has died this morning. Only thirty-nine. Can't believe it. Right out of the blue. Out riding with some friends and he came off. He was dead the minute he hit the ground. Terrible. Leaves a wife and four little girls. The eldest is eight. Tragic. I'm very upset. Very upset. Thought you ought to know . . . just in case.' He paused in the doorway as though about to say something else, then apparently changed his mind and left.

Kate, who couldn't for the life of her recollect who the man was, opened her mouth to ask, but was stopped by Ginny. 'If anyone here dares to suggest that we take on being Hunt vet instead of that man, I for one will — '

'Good for the practice, though, if we were. I mean, I'm sorry he's dead, of course,' Kate said innocently.

Colin, being anti-Hunt, stood quietly to one side, allowing the explosion to occur without his assistance. Rhodri muttered under his breath. Seb prayed Kate wouldn't put her foot in it any more than she already had done. Dan, who'd walked in just in time to catch Mungo's announcement, said, 'Now is not the time to discuss the matter. The poor fellow's scarcely cold. Let's show some respect.' Though he knew he was only postponing the argument, what he said sufficed for the moment and cooled things down.

Ginny stormed out.

Kate caught up with Seb before his first client.

'I said something terribly wrong in there, didn't I?'

'Mmm. 'Fraid so. Someone saw me having a drink with Jilly Askew after I'd examined a hound that her horse had struck when it reared. You know, Lord Askew's niece? They mentioned it in the staffroom and it all blew up from there. There's only Dan and myself and Mungo who have no strong anti-Hunt views; the rest are dead against it. So this Harvey man dying has opened up a whole can of worms.'

'I see. Thanks. Well, I can honestly say that I don't mind either way. After all, they'll have to find another vet, won't they?'

'Mungo would be very pleased if they came to us. Nowadays a veterinary practice can't afford to turn away business. Unfortunately, Ginny's threatened to resign if we take the Hunt on.'

'Whoops! I shall watch out in future, then. I like Ginny, even though she's so forthright, but she can be stroppy and sometimes very wrong.'

★ ★ ★

Mungo attended Harvey's funeral, seeing as they had met on several occasions in the course of their work, and Harvey had been a prominent member of the county veterinary profession for the last ten years. When Ginny heard he was going she sniffed derisively and turned her back on him. The other anti-Hunt staff just quietly allowed him to get on with it, because they were generous enough to recognise that his reasons for attending were right.

The whole matter blew up a week later when Lord Askew arrived without an appointment to see Mungo. Seb happened to be in reception by the 'knick-knack' shelf, talking to a client about suitable toys for her new puppy.

'I want to get it right, Seb. I'm determined this puppy is going to be intelligent, you see. Oh!' The client covered her mouth with her hand and muttered, 'I say, look who's here!'

Seb turned and saw Lord Askew waiting. 'Good afternoon, Lord Askew. Can I help?'

'You're the new vet who's been seeing my niece, Jilly, aren't you?'

Seb agreed he was.

'Thank you for the support you've given her. My brood can't believe it of her, but I think one should do what one feels is right for one to do. My life was mapped out for me the second I was born, you see, so I approve of freedom of choice. She went yesterday for her interview and it appears to have gone well. Now, my business is with Mungo Price. Is he about?'

'He's operating, I believe. If you'll take a seat, I'll find out.'

Mungo was doing exactly that, but guessing what Lord Askew's business would be he decided Seb had better get a gown on and continue with the operation for him.

'Bunty knows what we're doing. The X-rays are up. It's a fractured femur job, very simple, good experience. Where is he?' Mungo dragged off his gloves, Bunty untied his gown, and Mungo marched into reception, hand outstretched in welcome.

'Lord Askew, good afternoon. My office is this way. Pot of tea, Dodie, please.' Just in time, he remembered to ask his lordship if tea would be satisfactory.

'Absolutely right, with a drop of whisky in it if that's possible.' So Dodie unearthed the medicinal whisky from the back of Joy's cupboard and took the tray in for the two of them, best cups and saucers without question.

Reception echoed with the gossiping of the clients all trying to second-guess why on earth his lordship wanted to speak to Mungo. Various theories were aired but nobody really knew. Some were lucky enough still to be waiting when he departed but they learned nothing, because Mungo saw him out and rushed straight back to oversee the operation he'd left with Seb. In fact, he said nothing to anyone, except to Miriam, and that was up in the flat at the end of his working day.

'I had to leave Seb with the operation and he did magnificently. Most impressed I was. He went as white as a sheet when I said he'd to take over, but he excelled himself.'

'No time for preparation, either.'

'Exactly.'

'So what *did* his lordship want?'

'You know full well.'

'The Hunt?'

'Naturally. Who else is there to turn to? He wants us all right, but I've got our staff to deal with. So far, Dan and Seb appear to be on my side. Ginny will resign; she's already said so and I shan't cry in my soup over that! Rhodri won't

232

know what to do, Colin will simply keep quiet and hope it'll go away, and Scott will say no because he can't do any other owing to Zoe's strong objection. So that leaves me.'

'And Kate.'

'Ah! Yes, Kate. If Ginny leaves, Kate'll be very necessary. Anyway, she's got her head screwed on OK so I've no doubts she'll agree with me. You see, we can't afford not to go for it. What with the extra consulting room over and above the first extension, and now the lab, which still needs fitting out, we need the brass, as they would say in Yorkshire. If we're offered it I shall definitely say yes. After all, the hounds are kept in spanking good health, far better than any dogs we have coming in here, so we shan't be running backwards and forwards caring for a host of overweight, sick dogs, shall we? There'll be only a handful of horses, and the added bonus is the prestige of the appointment.'

'My word, Mungo, you will have to travel slowly and very carefully. You may even lose clients if they're anti-Hunt. It's a very delicate subject, and I can't possibly imagine any new government daring to rescind the legislation.'

'They should never have voted for it in the first place. Face it, it's an impossible task, policing all the hunts. Is my food ready? I'm starving. Can I smell beef and ale casserole? Excellent!'

★ ★ ★

That evening Kate put her head round Seb's door when she heard the last of his clients leaving and asked Seb if he had any plans.

'No, I haven't. Have you?'

'Well, Mia and Gordon are both out tonight and I don't fancy cooking just for one.'

'Neither do I.'

'Do you like the idea of a meal out with me? I'll pay my share.'

'I fancy the idea very much indeed but it's my treat.'

'I didn't mean for it to be your treat, I can pay my way.'

'Well . . . mind if I pay this once? It would give me much pleasure.' He gave her a very charming smile as he said this and she could do nothing but agree.

'With a smile like that, how can a girl refuse? What about the Italian? It's my favourite.'

Seb felt embarrassed by her choice, more so when they were shown to the same table he and Maggie had preferred and got the same waiter.

'Good evening to you, sir,' he said with a wink at Seb. 'Good evening, madam. What can I get for you?' With notebook poised he waited but received no reply. 'I'll come back later, shall I?'

'Yes, please.'

'So-o-o, how did the op go?'

Seb had to confess it went fine. 'I was almost shaking with the horror of it, but Mungo disappeared so quickly I just had to get on with it. The X-ray was excellent and of course Bunty could do it herself, I swear, she's so experienced. My hands trembled a bit but once I got involved

234

and Bunty had pointed out one or two things suddenly my confidence was there and Bunty and I coped very well. We were just closing when Mungo came back.'

'Did he say anything about what Lord Askew wanted?'

'Nothing at all. Bunty was really disappointed. Come to that, so was I.'

'So it was a triumph?'

'Come on, not a triumph. All right, though.'

'Did Mungo criticise it in any way?'

'No, he just said, 'Excellent, I knew you could do it.''

'Praise indeed from Mungo. What was the problem?'

'A fractured femur that had pierced through the skin.'

He looked at her eager face and completely lost himself in his admiration of it. Even to the shape of her eyebrows. She was wearing a softly tinted pink lipstick that flattered her skin tones so perfectly and he wished . . . then he noticed she was blushing.

'Sorry, shall we order?'

Kate nodded, embarrassed to death. She sneaked a quick glance at Seb's face and thought how handsome he looked, not conventionally but in an unusual, well-proportioned kind of way, and greatly in need of mothering. 'Have you chosen?'

Once they'd got food inside them and the greater part of a bottle of wine, the two of them relaxed and as suddenly as switching on a light they became tuned in to the same wavelength

235

and everything felt right between them.

They kissed goodnight in the multi-storey when they went to collect their cars. Just once, but it seemed to seal a bond.

'So it's Friday for the meal at the flat. I'm looking forward to meeting your stepmother and Gordon.'

'Good. Gordon's a lovely man. You'll like him, I know. Goodnight, Seb, thanks for the meal. Next time I'll pay.'

'Not till you get your second month's salary. I know what it's like.'

They stood close, admiring each other, silent, simply absorbing and liking. Then they said goodnight again and parted reluctantly.

★   ★   ★

Seb was still awake a whole hour after he'd got to bed, going over and over what they'd talked about, what she'd said, what he'd said, how she'd laughed at a joke he told her about one of the tutors at college, which had led them on to talking about college life and their prospects in the veterinary world and . . . then she'd jumped up and said, 'Must go. Look at the time. I promised I'd be home well before bedtime because Mia worries about me being so tired all the time. Which I am but it's par for the course in our job, isn't it?'

He went over again in his mind how they'd said goodbye in the car park. He'd wanted to kiss Kate more than once, but it occurred to him just in time that the pair of them had to go so slowly, so very slowly, because this relationship was suddenly precious to him and, he was almost sure, precious to her, too. He didn't want to ruin everything by rushing in. As he fell asleep Kate's face filled his mind.

15

The shock news they received from Dicky Bird the following afternoon was that Mr Foster had died in hospital during the night. Dicky laid his uniform hat on the reception desk and told Dodie the whole story. 'I need to see Seb really but he's got clients, I expect, so I'll tell you. This Fred Foster went to the hospital with his dog bites yesterday morning. Very, very ill, he was, and they diagnosed possible septicaemia. They began treatment immediately, hoping for the best, but he had a heart attack and died, a direct result of the bites, of course. They took pictures of them for their records so I've seen them. They were . . . horrific.' Dicky looked as though he might fetch up all over the desk.

Dodie moved back a bit, just in case. 'Poor chap.'

'Poor chap! My sympathies are with the dog. Foster was a brute of the first order. I could almost say he deserved to die.'

'Dicky!'

'Dicky nothing! The high-ups want to interview Seb. He said he had some evidence so they want to see it. If they come later today — say four o'clock — would that be all right?'

Dodie wrote it down. 'I'll tell him. Rhodri was there, too. Shall they want to speak to him?'

'Of course.' He turned to look at the new decorations. 'I always know Christmas is coming when I see these. Looks like Kate's been to do it?'

'Well, she's just started work here now she's qualified and so she helped Miriam as she does every year. They are beautiful, aren't they?'

'It's them silvery bits cascading down between the windows that make it special, and them baubles, stunning they are. Why, the walls are almost covered with 'em.'

'Her stepmother bought them at a Christmas market in France or Belgium somewhere.'

Dicky leaned closer. 'That Kate is a stunner, isn't she? I keep wondering who I could find to marry her. Me and my Bunty are so happy I want everyone to be married.'

Dodie tapped the side of her nose. 'The matter is in hand. I can say no more.'

He was too short to get really close but try he did and whispered, 'Who is it?'

'Ah-ha! Mum's the word. Now I'll pass the message on about the police. Oh, look, Seb's here. You can tell him yourself.'

One of the waiting clients, whose son had had far more to do with the police than she liked, shouted out, 'Dicky! What're you whispering about? Can't we all have a listen?'

'Constable Bird to you, madam.'

She positively crackled with amusement. 'Ooo! Listen to 'im. Constable Bird indeed. You're Dicky to me and to everyone else. Come on then, tell all.'

Dicky wasn't nearly the self-confident constable he purported to be, and brash women like this client almost always got the better of him, him being small and she being tall and big with it.

'I'll be off. Seb, a word outside?' He nodded his head pointedly at the main door and set off, expecting Seb to follow. But Seb had other things on his mind, in particular the client he was currently dealing with, and couldn't go. Constable Bird, disappointed he wouldn't be able to tell Seb the whole story, got into his car and texted Seb on his mobile to tell him about the dog fight that had been arranged. He just hoped Seb might manage to get there. Constable Aubrey Bird would be there — in disguise, of course. What do you wear when going to a dog fight? He couldn't ask Bunty's advice because she would forbid him to go. He'd learned in the past not to disobey Bunty when she got a protective note in her voice. Gardening clothes. Yes! Just scruffy enough without being too obvious.

★ ★ ★

Quite by coincidence Mungo took Perkins out for his evening walk that night as Miriam had a cold coming on and was feeling pretty grotty. 'Look, it'll do me good, I spend far too much time inside and you certainly can't go at this time of night in weather like this with that awful cold. Perkins!' But he was already at the door waiting for the off. 'Oh! There you are. We're going for a long walk tonight, Perkins, so brace yourself. I need the exercise even if you don't. Whisky and hot lemon, Miriam, and in bed when I get back.'

'OK. Thanks.'

'You're doing me a good turn, believe me.'

He dug out his old anorak he used for fishing, his thickest scarf, and a pair of holey gloves, and in the pocket of his anorak he discovered a woolly hat. Just right for the night. He glanced in the hall mirror and said, 'God! I look like a burglar. A real rogue.'

He began by striding out vigorously, but as the slope up Beulah Bank Top became steeper he slowed and so did Perkins, and by the time they reached the top they were plodding along, heads down against the wind. Perkins made up his mind that Mungo had taken leave of his senses, and quietly and unobtrusively turned round and set off for home. By the time Mungo lifted his head to check for Perkins he was already out of sight, steadily marching home to Miriam and his warm bed. Mungo paused to survey the side of Beulah Bank he hardly ever saw. Below him there were lights on in a big barn towards his right and men with dogs walking up the farm track towards it. The barn door opened briefly, and he saw in the light three men and a dog entering the barn. His hackles rose. What was this? Something illegal? Then he remembered how Seb, only a day or two ago, had been upset at having to put that dangerous fighting dog to sleep. His scalp tingled with trepidation. Had he stumbled on a dog fight?

He turned to go home, then saw a van coming from the opposite direction, its headlights turned off, its shape outlined by the lights in the barn windows. Two men got out from the back of the van with a dog, which looked muzzled. Curiosity drowned out any caution he might have felt. He remembered the camera he always had with him when he went fishing so he could convince Miriam without any doubt about the size of the fish he'd caught, and patted his pockets. It was still there, long-forgotten.

This was a golden opportunity. He checked to see if he had any money with him, because he would need to look genuine by betting on a fight. His wallet was in his back pocket. Good.

He walked steadily downhill towards the barn, conscious of keeping out of sight as much as possible as he didn't imagine that men involved in betting on dog fighting would be choosy about who they clobbered in order to keep the event from the police.

For a few moments he paused behind some rocks and peered over them into the gloom to estimate how much open ground he had to cover before he reached the barn, and if he should go in or find a window he could look through without anyone knowing he was there. Feeling that was the safer option, Mungo decided to creep away to his right, approaching the barn from the back rather than the front.

Just as he'd decided to move off, someone joined him behind the rocks. The hair on the back of his neck stood on end and his heart pumped hard. A hand grabbed his collar and a voice muttered in a fierce whisper, 'Got yer!'

Two men had hold of him. His woolly hat was snatched off, his arms grabbed, and a small torch shone into his face. Mungo couldn't see who'd got him, and he braced himself for a thumping.

Instead, a shocked voice whispered, 'My God! It's Mr Price!'

Constable Bird was stunned, and so was Seb.

'What are you doing here?' Dicky whispered.

'I could ask the same of you,' said Mungo.

'We're on police business.'

'You gave me a terrible fright.'

Dicky was amazed that Mungo had got through the police cordon without being spotted. 'Don't know how you got so far. The place is surrounded.'

'Really? I didn't know. I was out with Perkins and saw the lights.'

Seb asked where was Perkins now.

'Gone home, I suspect. He likes his bed at this time of night. What are we going to do?'

Dicky declared firmly, 'Wait, that's what. Just wait. We're moving in in ten minutes. Got to give them time to begin otherwise it's their word against ours. We need to catch 'em at it in full swing.'

Mungo was disappointed, having hyped himself up to pretend he was attending the dog fight as a spectator. 'I'll go in and pretend to be one of them. Got all my old gear on. They'll never know the difference.'

'What? They'd spot you a mile off, believe me. You're staying where you are. Don't want the whole plan ruined before we get 'em.'

But Mungo wanted to get in on the action and suggested to Seb that they both went in as punters, flashing their money. 'What do you say?'

'I think we should keep out of the way,' Seb said. 'The place is swarming with police, and I've no intention of getting a beating just for the fun of it. Sorry, Mr Price.'

The whole of their conversation had been conducted in stage whispers, but Dicky put his fingers to his lips and tapped his ear, indicating they should listen and not talk. It became all too obvious that the dog fighting had begun, judging by the fearsome snarling they could hear. The sounds coming across the desolate hill in the darkness were horrible and both Seb and Mungo shuddered. They waited another five minutes, in which absolutely nothing happened except for the bone-shattering snarling of the fighting dogs. Then torches were switched on all over the hill and what seemed to be a score of men running silently towards the barn and all hell was let loose.

The three of them heard the barn door being slid back as the first of the police went in. Some men escaped, dragging their dogs with them; some leapt into their vans and tried to drive away; others simply headed away on foot down the hill and out of sight. Dicky raced forward to help. From nowhere police vans were there and men and dogs were bundled in. In minutes it was all over, and the vans were driving away.

Seb said, 'Let's go down and see if any dogs need help.'

By using the headlights of the vans driving away and Dicky's torch they went down to the barn and walked in. In a fenced-off ring lay two dogs, panting heavily, way beyond struggling to escape. Dicky was searching every nook and cranny for punters who'd tried to hide.

Fortunately for him, there was no one left.

Seb cautiously approached the dogs but the smell of him was wrong and they were immediately on their guard and on their feet. Both of them were covered in blood. One in particular had a huge tear down the front of its throat and had obviously been losing the fight.

Mungo roared, 'Leave 'em, Seb.'

Dicky shouted, 'Get away, you fool!'

Seb sprang back, recollecting the wounds Fred Foster had received.

Mungo, not fancying the idea of being sympathetic to two dogs in fighting mood, said, 'Those dogs are pitbulls, without a doubt. They'll need putting down. They're illegal. You'll have to get your police vet out, Dicky. Can't leave them all night. There's a bucket of water here; I'll put it in the ring for them. Now out!'

The three of them trudged up to the top of Beulah Bank, then walked down the other side towards the practice.

'Come in for a swift whisky to warm you up, Dicky, Seb?'

Dicky refrained. 'I ought to get back to the station. Sorry, lots to do. Thanks, both of you.'

But Seb accepted. 'I'm glad I went. At least we've got them. Put a stop to it for a while.'

Sitting propped against the back door was Perkins, waiting for someone to let him in. He was shivering with the cold and looking thoroughly miserable.

'Perkins! Serves you right for running back home. Come on, in you go.' Mungo unlocked the back door and the two of them went up to the flat with Perkins trailing behind them, looking weary.

'Miriam's in bed with a bad cold, Seb. Help yourself to some whisky, or a brandy if you prefer. Give Perkins a splash in his bowl; he's getting a bit old for midnight shenanigans. I'll just check on Miriam.'

Perkins had had whisky before, it was obvious, because he lapped up what Seb had put in his bowl and then looked up, hoping for more. 'You'll be rolling drunk, you will, Perkins, but go on, then — one more splash and that's it.'

Mungo came back, gave Perkins a good pat, took off his collar and sent him off to his basket. 'In your bed! Goodnight!' he said, then sat down companionably with Seb to drink his own whisky.

'Miriam's going to have a really bad cold tomorrow. Just hope it isn't going to be 'flu.'

'Let's hope not.'

'You did that dog a good turn when you put it to sleep. I hope you're not letting it upset you too much. It's a cruel, devilish sport is dog fighting. Those dogs never know what kindness is. When I think how much love and care our Perkins gets . . . ' he shook his head, 'and how a fighting dog gets none, we'd be doing them a good turn to put them all to sleep, pitbull or not. Enjoying working here, Seb?'

'I do, very much indeed. I'm learning so much, and I should thank you for taking me on and letting me help with the operations.'

'They're a good bunch, aren't they, the staff?'

'Absolutely, and always so helpful to me.'

246

Mungo cleared his throat, wagged a forefinger at Seb and launched into his advice mode. 'What you need is a good wife. Makes such a difference when you've been out on a night call and you get back and the bed's warm and there's a pair of welcoming arms. Anyway, there's time for that, you're still young, but when you choose, choose wisely. A vet's life isn't easy. Right, I'm off to bed.'

Seb finished the last of his whisky and got to his feet. 'I gave Perkins some whisky as you said and he asked for more. He really enjoys it, doesn't he?'

'Bad habits, but there we are. I shall miss him when he goes. Goodnight, Seb.'

★ ★ ★

Dicky Bird screeched to a halt in the practice car park at eight-fifteen the next day, bubbling over with the news about last night's raid.

'Seb in? Or Mr Price?'

Joy loved Dicky's enthusiasm and always played up to it with verve. 'They both are. Which would you prefer?'

'I'll speak to Seb, then, seeing as he was my co-conspirator last night.'

'Come on, Dicky, I can't imagine Seb or Mungo conspiring to anything.'

Dicky leaned on the desk, placed his hat beside his elbow and confided in Joy. 'They were both with me up Beulah last night in a raid on an organised dog fight. I nearly arrested Mr Price by mistake. You should have seen his face.

Scared to death, he was.'

Joy found this piece of information more than a little surprising, as no one believed that Dicky could put the fear of God in anyone, still less someone as self-possessed as Mungo.

'Arrested him? I think you were going above and beyond your call of duty, Dicky.'

'Hiding behind some rocks he was, dressed in a woolly hat and an old anorak, having threaded his way between a host of armed policemen.'

'This I don't believe.'

Indignantly, Dicky drew himself up to his full height and was about to explain in full about last night when Seb appeared.

'Hello, Dicky. How many did you arrest, then?'

'We got twelve of the bas — beggars. A good haul, eh? Just telling Joy about me nearly arresting Mungo.'

'To use common parlance, Mungo got his collar felt.'

Joy burst out laughing. 'No! Wait till I see him.'

'Seb. About those two dogs. The duty vet put 'em down. They were both in a bad way, poor things.'

'Well, I must say last night proved very interesting. Thanks for letting me in on it, Dicky. My first appointment, Joy?'

'Not till nine so you can relax for a bit. New client. Don't know where she's been going before. Male dog can hardly walk, but he's only three. Sounds like bad news. A Jack Russell, it is.'

Dicky clapped his hat back on and made his

248

departure, delighted with his success in the dog fight matter. He just wished he worked in a place where everyone was so happy and helpful. A police station wasn't exactly a happy place; you were more likely to be harassed and threatened.

Mrs Prior, Seb's nine o'clock appointment, carried her dog into his consulting room. 'This is Patch, Mr Partridge. Shall I lay him on your examination table?'

'Yes, please. Hello, Patch!' The dog was white except for a black patch over his left eye. 'Will you explain to me as clearly as possible what the matter is?' Seb looked carefully at Patch, who looked back with a baleful eye, and for a moment Seb felt as though Patch was telling him something but he didn't know what.

'He can barely walk. I can't take him out for a run. I have to carry him outside when I see the signs he needs to go . . . you know. He manages to stand long enough to relieve himself. Other than that he just lies around all day long. I can't understand it. We've had him since he was a puppy and loved him and taken care of him, fed him properly — '

'He isn't overweight, so you must have done well on that score.'

'No, I know he isn't. For a Jack Russell cross he's got just the right amount of flesh on his bones, hasn't he?'

'Does he eat well now he can't walk?'

'Average. Not like he did when he was growing, of course.'

'How long has he not been walking?'

'It started about a year ago, just a bit, but then

it got worse and worse, and now it's like I said — a slow stagger in the garden to find his favourite spot, and then I carry him back in and he collapses. I tell you, it's his legs, it must be. Or his hips.'

Seb began examining Patch. He listened to his heart and his lungs and felt his legs, pumping them up and down. There was nothing wrong there, no obstruction to movement, no wincing, no resistance. His hips too were perfectly flexible. He stood Patch up but Patch wasn't having it and crumpled down again, and once more there was that baleful look which Seb found unnerving.

Mrs Prior gasped when Seb tried to stand him up, and immediately went to Patch's aid. She stroked him, kissed his head and sympathised with him, and Patch wallowed in it.

Seb had to admit that he honestly couldn't find anything wrong with him.

'Look! We'll give him a vitamin boost, shall we?' he said. 'See if that helps at all. Come back if there's no improvement.'

'I'll give it a try, but I don't hold out much hope.' Mrs Prior stroked Patch's head. 'I've left my purse in the car. Will you take care of him while I go? I'll just get it and pay, and then I'll pick up Patch and the medicine and we'll be off. My poor darling Patch. Who's a poorly boy, then? I'm just sorry you can't sort him out.'

Seb turned away to put some notes on the computer. What the heck was he missing? He turned round again to find Patch standing up on the table wagging his tail, the baleful look replaced by a pair of sparkling eyes. Seb couldn't believe what he was seeing.

Then he heard Mrs Prior calling out to someone on her way back to his consulting room and Patch immediately collapsed back onto the table.

Seb was speechless.

Mrs Prior came back, purse in hand. 'My poor pet, Mummy's back. The medicine, Mr Partridge?'

'Oh! Yes. Now, Mrs Prior, you will not believe what I am going to tell you.'

Mrs Prior's face lit up. 'Have you found out what's wrong with him?'

'Well, no. I mean, yes, in a way. You see, when you went out Patch here stood up immediately.'

Horrified, Mrs Prior clutched her chest. 'Oh, no! He might have fallen off.' She stroked his head more vigorously.

'No, not at all. His tail was wagging and he was . . . well, he was almost laughing.'

'Laughing?' Mrs Prior was shocked. 'Laughing?'

Seb nodded. 'Then he heard your voice in reception and flopped down again. Look at him now, laid out. I can't believe it. You know what it is, don't you?'

Mystified, Mrs Prior shook her head.

'I guess when he lies down you sympathise with him, kiss him, love him, stroke him, give him treats, and he likes that. So he's learned to do it to get your attention. You see, he doesn't get all the patting and sympathy when he's running about, does he? He's got you right

251

where he wants you — under his thumb, so to speak.'

Mrs Prior had to sit down on the chair rather heavily. She was aghast. 'It can't be true. How can a dog work that out?'

Seb tapped his temple. 'Your Patch is extra-clever for a dog and *he's* worked it out, no doubt about that.'

'What shall I do? I can't not love him.'

'Of course not! Look, let's try something. Give him a wave, tell him you're leaving and go out, stand outside my door, but don't make a *sound*, then he'll think you've gone away. Count silently to twenty-five slowly and come back in, quickly. Go on, let's try it.'

Mrs Prior gave Patch a kiss then waved bye and left, closing the door behind her. After twenty-five seconds she came quietly back in and caught Patch standing up wagging his tail. He quickly dropped down when he saw her but he was too late. She'd seen him.

'I can't believe it. What have I done to him? How can it have happened? Have I got it all wrong? For his sake should I give him to someone else? Should I? But I couldn't, I love him too much.'

Seb had to laugh. 'There's no need for that. He's a clever dog, but you and I will put a stop to his antics. It will take a while. Be patient and from now on, when he's lying down, ignore him. Not even eye contact. If he does move about give him lots of attention, even to the extent of rewarding him with a chocolate drop, or something you know he likes. Got the picture?

Walking about must be the one thing that brings him rewards. Come back in two weeks and tell me the result.'

Seb picked Patch up and laid him on the floor and then dipped his hand into his plastic box full of doggy chocolate drops. He placed four in a line towards the door, then opened the door and made another line across the waiting room floor towards the main exit, then went back to put one in Patch's mouth and stood by to watch. Patch ate the drop in a trice, hovered and then slowly got to his feet.

'Quick! Tell him what a good boy he is. Go on. Quick!'

Mrs Prior said the magic words with real enthusiasm. 'Good boy. Patch is a good boy. Who's a clever boy! What a good dog!'

In no time at all Patch was walking, whisking up the drops with an eager pink tongue, with Mrs Prior walking alongside him. The clients watching this procedure shouted encouragement.

'My God! Look at that, Seb's got 'im to walk!'

'Why, it's a miracle and not half! Good on yer, Seb!'

'He hasn't walked for months!'

'Well, did you ever!'

Mrs Prior, half embarrassed at having made the dog ill and half triumphant to find him cured, punched the air with both hands as she reached the door and called out, 'See you in two weeks! Thank you, Mr Partridge.' Out of habit she bent down to pick up Patch, reminded herself she mustn't, picked up the last two drops instead and placed them outside the main door and got him out.

The clients clapped and cheered Seb's expertise.

Seb, grinning from ear to ear, bowed ostentatiously and called for his next client. It was Mrs Benton about her old cat Hector.

'I've come not to say how ill Hector is but to let you know how well he is. Remember he was weeing all over our new house and he didn't know where he was?'

Seb nodded. 'Of course I remember.'

'Well, those new tablets you prescribed have done the trick. He's as good as new, and what's more, now that's sorted he's settled into the new house. Knows exactly where to sleep, where the door is, so I thought I'd come and ask for a further prescription of the magic tablets and tell you the good news. Truth is, it made me wonder about my dad and his tablets, so I took him to the doctor's instead of collecting a repeat prescription for him and he's had his tablets changed and he's like a new man, too. So you see, Mr Partridge, what you've done. You've changed the Benton household in one fell swoop. In fact, I could kiss you for what you've done for us, and I will.'

Mrs Benton leaned across the examination table and planted a great big sloppy kiss on Seb's cheek, squeezed hold of his hand, and said, 'You're the best vet anywhere at all. Good morning to you.'

'A pleasure. Don't forget Hector's prescription!'

'Oh! Yes. Thanks.'

It was Joe Smithson next, on his own without a cardboard box.

On a high after his successful morning Seb greeted him with enthusiasm. 'And you're more than welcome, Mr Smithson. What can I do for you this morning?'

'I've joined a canary society. Well, the Barleybridge Cage Bird Society. Thought I'd mingle with them who's as keen as me. Believe it or not, they didn't know they had an avian vet here in Barleybridge, no idea at all. So I've suggested that we make you our official vet for the society. They said I should come along and talk to you about it, so here I am. What do you think?'

'I'm very flattered, Joe. Very. But I don't know if I'm qualified enough to be your official avian vet. I'd hate to let anyone down.'

Joe Smithson puffed out his chest. 'Not qualified enough? That's ridiculous. Of course you are. Look what you've done for me. Taught me all I know.'

'Yes, but — '

'All right then, think about it. It'd mean all the members would use you when they had a problem, and if we had an annual show, which I intend to start up, you could be vet in residence on the day. Just think, eh!' Inspired, he came up with another idea. 'I know, you could come and give us a talk. How's that for an idea?'

Seb swallowed hard. 'I'd have to consult Mr Price. He's the senior vet and it's his practice, but I've no official avian qualification, you see.

It's just what I've . . . learned, kind of.'

'So? You've learned it, that's what counts. Anyway, talk to Mr Price and if you need a letter of recommendation or anything, let me know. You saved my canaries that day when they had them thingumabobs. I'd have lost the lot if you hadn't told me what to do.'

Seb smiled. 'Can I let you know? I can't just say yes as I'm not a partner, you see.'

'No, but one day you will be with talent like yours. They're all right impressed in the waiting room. Got that dog to walk when he couldn't. How's that for a miracle? I saw her carry him in. I shan't forget this morning in a hurry, believe me. You, Mr Partridge,' Joe pointed at Seb, 'made the paralysed walk. My word! What a story.' He turned to go. 'Right. Let me know. You've got my number, haven't you?'

'But Mr Smithson, I didn't — '

'Hush yourself and take credit where it's due. Good morning.'

By the end of the morning there didn't appear to be a single client who hadn't heard of Seb's miracle. Even Mungo came in to have a word. 'God, what have you been up to, making the lame walk? They're all full of it.'

Seb protested. 'He could walk, but he simply wouldn't because he'd worked out that if he didn't walk he got all sorts of loving care, and titbits and sympathy and cuddles, and it served his purpose to lie down.'

'Never mind, it'll have done the practice a lot of good. They'll be queuing up for an appointment with you and the ones you can't

256

solve with your magic chocolate drops, *I will* with an operation! Good work!'

Seb had to laugh. 'The other thing is, Mr Smithson, of canary fame, wants me to be the official vet for the Barleybridge Cage Bird Society. I said I'd have to ask you.'

'Is there no end to his talents?' He clapped Seb on the shoulder in his delight.

'Yes, but I'm not qualified. All I've done is learn about birds.'

'Does that matter?'

'Well, I think it does.'

'Swot up on it in your spare time. We shall have 'em coming from far and wide — owls, hawks, budgies, eagles, you name it. Have we got room for another extension, I ask myself? I'll think about that. Must dash, I need my lunch.'

'How's Miriam today?'

'Bit low, but we don't think it's 'flu. Thanks for asking. Keep up the good work! After lunch I have a very interesting operation — are you free?'

'Yes, I am.'

'Then come. Bunty's day off, so I need your help. See you.'

The next person to call in his consulting room was Kate, brimming with *joie de vivre*, and, in Seb's eyes, looking ravishing.

'Thought I'd call to say how pleased I am that the wonder vet works in the same practice as me! A miracle-worker no less!'

'OK, OK. All I did — '

'You made the lame walk! What more can a man do?'

To divert the attention away from himself Seb asked her how she felt this morning. 'Not so tired?'

'I seem to have caught up on my sleep debt, thanks. See you tonight?'

'Of course. Looking forward to it.'

At lunchtime he went to the precinct and bought flowers and a box of chocolates for Mia. He got back for his lunch to find Jilly Askew waiting for him.

They stood in reception to talk as there were no waiting clients. 'I hope you don't mind but I had to come.'

'That's fine. How are you?'

'Excited! I couldn't wait to tell you. I got the letter this morning, I'm going to college next September to do my post-grad! Isn't it wonderful?'

Delighted for Jilly's sake Seb kissed her there and then on both cheeks. 'I am so pleased. So very pleased.'

'Also, I've got a temporary student place at a secondary school near home so I can get some practice in! At least I shan't be completely wet behind the ears when I start.'

'That is excellent. Really brill.'

'So I'm saying *au revoir* for now as I'm leaving Uncle's tomorrow and going home to begin at the school on Monday.'

'I shan't see you, then.'

'No, but I can always give you a ring when I come to Barleybridge to see my Uncle, can't I? I did wonder — '

They were interrupted by Ginny marching in

to reception. 'You must be Jilly Askew!' she said. 'You've got the Askew nose.' She shook Jilly's hand very vigorously in an 'I'm taking charge here' manner.

'That's right. Just called in to see Seb.'

'Didn't know you two were an item.'

'We're not, just friends.' Jilly knew instinctively that Ginny was on the war path. 'Just called in to give Seb some good news, that's all.'

'You ride to hounds with the Barleybridge Hunt?'

'Occasionally.'

'You do know that as a practice we're opposed to hunting?'

'So am I.'

This statement completely took the wind out of Ginny's sails. 'But you ride to hounds.'

'That's right. But I'm still opposed to it.'

'So why do it?'

'Because I don't want to give offence.'

'To whom?'

'My uncle.'

'What about the offence you give to a poor helpless fox who's never done you any harm?'

'My uncle frequently gives me bed and board without question and is the best uncle anyone could hope to have. I'm not prepared to hurt his feelings. Horses and riding are his life and very important to him.' Jilly's accent had become more and more upper-class with each word she spoke, and Seb could see the superiority of her accent was becoming exceedingly aggravating to Ginny.

So he interrupted their dialogue, saying

mildly, 'You have butted in on a private conversation, actually, Ginny.'

Ginny's hackles rose. 'I don't know who the hell you think you are, Seb Partridge. It's a free country and if I wish to make a point I shall.'

Seb said between gritted teeth, 'In fact, you're being rude. Jilly is a friend of mine and should be treated with respect by you and anyone else on these premises.'

'Seb,' Jilly laid a soothing hand on his arm, 'don't worry, I am well able to take care of myself.' To Ginny she said very softly and without rancour, 'I shall hunt or not hunt exactly as I like, and neither you nor anyone else is going to dictate to me whether I do or not. So go away and leave us alone.' She turned away so Ginny couldn't see her face and winked at Seb. 'Are you free tonight to celebrate? Thought you could come to Uncle's place and have a meal. Just tête-à-tête, not all the family.'

'I'm so sorry but I'm busy tonight.'

'That's fine. I don't own you.' Jilly kissed his cheek. 'Bye, Seb. I'll be in touch and let you know how I get on.' She turned to Ginny and smiled graciously at her, and knowing she would annoy Ginny by being excessively polite she said as sweetly as possible, 'A pleasure to have met you.'

Seb escorted Jilly to the main door to say goodbye.

Ginny was waiting for him when he returned. 'How dare she treat me like that? Who does she think she is? You should choose your friends more carefully, Seb.'

260

'My friends are nothing whatsoever to do with you. Are you expecting me to ask you to vet them?'

'Of course not, but you know my views about hunting.'

'Only too well. I have mine. You have yours. So be it.' He walked away from her before he said more than he should. He couldn't remember when he'd been so steaming with temper.

Joy met him in the staffroom. 'My word, Seb, I didn't know you had it in you. I wondered if I should wade in on your behalf but you managed very nicely on your own. The consultative paper's going out on Monday, then the balloon will go up and no mistake.' Joy noted the flowers and chocolates. 'My, my. What's the celebration?'

'They're for Mia Buchanan, Kate's step-mother. She's invited me for a meal tonight as she's convinced I'm not eating properly living on my own.'

'Ah! You'll enjoy that. She's a lovely person, is Mia. Get your lunch — Mungo's starting operating soon. You know, he's very pleased with your surgery skills. Thinks you're very impressive. Perhaps that might be the way for you to go. Think about it.'

16

Kate got home early that evening and began preparing the meal. She'd had friends home for a meal more times than she could remember but tonight felt especially important to her. Mia arrived home only half an hour after Kate.

'I've skipped off early. Business has been so slow today. I can't think what to do to buck things up. Running a gallery, as 'she' calls it, is a dodgy way of earning a living at best, and I have a feeling she's concentrating on all the wrong things for the area in which we live. After all, how many hippies do you know in Barleybridge?'

'None. Shall I cut the carrots into wheels or strips?'

'Strips. No, and neither do I. But it's not my business so . . . when she retires in the New Year — because it will carry on in the same vein, seeing as the new owner thinks along the same lines as she does — I might even give in my notice. It's so maddening when you know what needs doing but you can't have any influence.'

'Just a pity you can't buy it yourself.'

'That's not likely. Selling that old house of your dad's and buying this modern flat took all the money from the house and then some, so that's out of the question. Anyway, I'm so looking forward to meeting Seb. He sounds lovely.'

Mia got no reply to this statement and when

she looked at Kate's face she saw that inscrutable look she knew so well. It occurred to her that maybe this Seb was rather more important than she'd realised.

Kate filled the carrots' pan with water. 'Can I leave the rest to you? I need a shower.'

'Of course. Do I have to be on my best behaviour tonight?'

'Certainly not. He's the most comfortable person to be with, believe me.'

'Gordon said he's looking forward to meeting him.'

'Good. Are you?'

'Am I what?'

'Looking forward to meeting him.'

'If he's important to you then yes I am.'

Kate turned away and looked out of the window. 'I think maybe he is.'

'In that case he's appeared on the scene at just the right time, hasn't he?' Mia couldn't resist smiling when she said this.

Kate looked at her and smiled, too. 'Maybe. I've just seen Gordon's car pull up. I'll go and have a shower.'

★   ★   ★

When the doorbell rang, and the three of them knew it must be Seb at the door, Kate became incredibly embarrassed and hid in the kitchen, doubting everything she'd ever felt about Seb and wishing she hadn't invited him as Mia had asked her to do.

Gordon opened the door, shaking hands and

introducing himself. 'Come in, Seb, come in, very pleased to meet you. Go through. Kate and Mia are in the kitchen. Still raining, I see.'

Seb, who'd been looking forward to the evening, suddenly found himself shy, something he hadn't experienced since leaving home to go to college. He was convinced he'd gone bright red and was so nervous the flowers in the bouquet were trembling. He handed them over to Mia as quickly as he decently could and found her so delighted with her flowers and the chocolates and her greeting so very warm that the nerves began to subside. But then he had to greet Kate for the first time in front of her parents. Well, not parents but he knew what he meant.

'Hi, Kate.'

As soon as he looked at her he knew that she was embarrassed, too, and concern about her nervousness filled his kind heart with confidence and he walked across the kitchen floor and kissed her on both cheeks. 'OK?'

'Yes, thanks. Gordon, have you got the drinks ready?'

'Indeed I have, Kate. Come along, Seb, we'll leave the kitchen to the ladies.'

'It's almost ready, Gordon, we shan't be long.' But of course the white sauce had gone too thick, the carrots hadn't cooked yet, they'd forgotten to put out the napkins, and Kate and Mia felt themselves to be in the middle of a huge disaster.

Mia sighed heavily in desperation. 'This is ridiculous. Since when did I last make such a

264

mess of a simple white sauce? I'll start it all over again. Wash the pan out for me, there's a love.'

With the second lot of white sauce a complete success and the napkins found and the carrots cooked to a T, Mia muttered, 'He is lovely, I'm so impressed. He's nervous too, don't forget. I like him already.' She gave Kate a kiss. 'Right, give them a shout. Gordon likes him, and that's a good sign. He's a good judge of character, is Gordon.'

★ ★ ★

Mia went to bed that night bursting to hear Gordon's verdict. She found Seb lovely, kind and warm-hearted. Yet at the same time he was a man who knew his own mind and was principled to boot.

Mia settled herself under the duvet and asked the inevitable. 'Well?'

'Well?'

'Don't tease, Gordon, you know what I mean.'

He too got under the duvet, turned out the light and then gave her his verdict. Hands behind his head he stared up at the ceiling. 'It is my opinion that with a bit of care and a following wind those two could be just right for one another.'

'Bit of care? What does that mean?'

'I mean, we need to leave them alone and they'll find their own way together. They're both lovely people and I'm sure — '

'So am I sure! Oh, if they're half as happy as I am they'll do fine.'

'Think so? Is that Kate coming to bed?' They stayed quiet and listened but no.

Mia grew anxious. 'They're taking a long time to say goodnight.'

'Of course they are. One does at their age. He's a very nice young man, but we must wait and see.'

'Yes, you're quite right. Do you have any regrets?'

In the dark Gordon grinned. 'About what?'

Mia nudged him. 'You know what I mean — about marrying me.'

'Absolutely none. In fact, the longer we're married the better it gets.' He kissed her. 'Goodnight, Mia. Love you.'

Oddly enough that was just what Seb was saying downstairs in the sitting room. 'Goodnight, Kate. Love you. Do you mind me saying that?'

Kate hesitated before she replied. 'No, I don't. But I can't say it back just yet. I've always been slow with decisions about people. It's not that I don't like you because I do very much, but saying 'I love you' is something very different. I'm enjoying your company and feel we are compatible, absolutely on the same wavelength, but I can't say those three words, not just yet. You see, all my life I've been aware of the fact that my mother walked out on me when I was two weeks old and somehow it's made me cautious. I can't trust people till I know them better . . . Sorry.'

'Don't be sorry. We've only known each other a matter of weeks, and I like the idea that you're taking your time.'

'And there's someone else, isn't there?'

Seb looked puzzled.

'Jilly Askew. I saw her in reception having that row with Ginny.'

'Jilly is simply a friend. We met by chance and she needed someone to keep her feet on the ground. All I've done is advise her to follow her star, that's all.'

'Which is?'

'Taking a post-grad teaching diploma.'

Kate was stunned. 'An Askew? Teaching? Really?'

'Yes, honestly. Everyone in the family disapproves and finds it amusing. Only Lord Askew backs her, but then his life was mapped out for him from the second he was born, obviously, so he sympathises with her. And I back her because I followed my star instead of doing what everyone expected.'

'I can see her show-jumping or running an art gallery or being a researcher for an MP with an eye on the bigger picture, but teaching! Well, I must say, I admire her for sticking to her guns.'

'Exactly.'

Kate found her hands of particular interest at this moment and examined them closely. Seb saw that something was obviously still worrying her. Finally she came out with, 'And Maggie?'

Seb laughed. 'What's this, an inquisition? It's supposed to be the father who asks questions like these.'

'Sorry, just needed to know. Someone mentioned her . . . and I wondered.'

So the whole story of Maggie came to light,

but Seb avoided telling her about how she'd healed him after his disastrous affair at college. That could be left to another time. One thing he did know for certain was he wouldn't be thinking in love-making terms with Kate, not for a long time. She needed more space in this relationship than he'd dreamt, and space she would have because she had become so important to him.

'Must go. Early start.'

'And me, too. Thanks for coming, and being so frank with me, it's cleared the air. Goodnight, Seb.' Kate stood up. 'I can see why you have all these women after you. You're lovely and sympathetic.'

She kissed his cheek and in return he tenderly kissed her lips. 'Goodnight. I love you, Kate, and I'm more than willing to wait. Please thank Mia for that lovely meal. I've really enjoyed myself. I'll let myself out.'

★ ★ ★

Monday morning arrived and there was a copy of the consultative document in everyone's pigeon hole along with their post. At the bottom in larger print was the notice of a meeting on Friday morning at eight-thirty in reception. In brackets it said consultations would not begin until 10 a.m. that day. Seb didn't have a chance to talk to anyone about it because his first client was there waiting so he had to begin work immediately.

This first client brought Seb back down to earth with a bump. As she strode in, his consulting room was flooded with a sensuous eastern perfume that almost clogged Seb's lungs it was so overwhelming. She was well dressed in a smart indigo top coat with matching trousers, a sensational scarf peeping out from her coat collar, her hair was shining and beautifully braided, and her face glowed. No garish lipstick emphasising the usual surprising pallor of her make-up, no strangely misplaced eye shadow, no rouge lavishly applied. Was it her?

Seb checked the screen. Yes, it was Miranda Costello. It definitely was because he recognised Goliath, the smallest adult Yorkshire terrier he'd ever seen.

'Good morning, Mrs Costello, very nice to see you. You're looking stunning this morning. How's things?'

'Miranda! Miranda, if you please. Extremely good, thank you, and how charming of you to comment on my appearance. It's Goliath's time for his booster, that's all. I got your card.'

'Right. Booster it is, then.' He managed to keep a straight face but it was very difficult, because she'd even changed her behaviour, too.

Miranda lifted Goliath onto the examination table and closed her eyes to avoid watching the needle going in.

'I'll give him a quick examination while he's here. He must be getting quite old.'

'Well, I reckon he could be at least ten. I took him over from neighbours, you see, and they couldn't remember how old he was. He's very energetic still. I've got rid of my other dogs.'

'You have?'

'Yes, it all got too much for me. So difficult to keep everywhere clean and tidy. Someone had wanted the lurcher, Jack, ever since I took him in, so he's gone, and the two Jack Russells, Bill and Ben, they've gone — couldn't be separated 'cos they're brothers. My cousin's got them and they're real happy with him. He's got hours in the day to walk 'em in the woods, and they love that. The little Heinz 57 terrier, well, he disappeared one day and I've not seen him since. Been run over p'rhaps. And the two King Charles, well, believe it or not I sold them. I was given their pedigree papers when I took them on from that old lady so they went for a good price. Embarrassing, really. As for the cats, they're coming in to be neutered next week. Can't stand no more kittens, though it's easier to get rid of 'em nowadays now everyone has their cats done. But all the same, you can't go away, you know, it's hopeless.'

'So what about the mice and the rabbits?'

'Had the vermin people in, and though it broke my heart so see, they got rid of the mice and I've cleared out the shed so there's nowhere for any to hide and the last rabbit I gave to a boy what's disabled and it's giving him a lot of pleasure. Hutch and the lot gone with it. I never felt the same after poor Lettice. Remember you put her to sleep, the one I thought was pregnant except she wasn't.'

'Ah! Yes. So there's been a real clear-out at your place?'

'Yes, even the rubbish in the garden. I've started planting things out and I've rescued the pond. And best of all, I've got a job. Gets me out of the house three days a week.'

'Where at?'

'Pet shop in the High Street. I love it.'

'Wonderful. You'll be good at that. Well, Goliath appears to be in robust health.'

'Good. Ta-ta for now. Be seeing you. You're a great vet, you know. Stick at it. Bye!'

Somehow, the aggravating pleasure that had been Miranda Costello was all gone, and it was quite disappointing because there was nothing to be amazed about any more, though he expected the neighbours must be glad. He'd tell Kate at coffee-time, because she would remember Miranda.

But when he went to get his coffee he found the staffroom heaving with argument and Miranda Costello's transformation was the last thing on anyone's mind.

Ginny had engineered her morning rounds to make sure she was in the staffroom at the appropriate time and it was she who raised the temperature.

'If any of you decide to back Mungo on this and it goes through then I for one will resign. It is an abomination. I've read every word of this . . . paper and I disagree with everything in it. Colin, how about you? It's no good behaving like an ostrich. It won't go away, believe me, so stand up and be counted. Well?'

Colin appeared to shrink. 'It is my opin-ion . . . '

'Yes?'

'It is my opinion that I shall have as little to do

271

with the Hunt as I can because my clients — and I have a longer list than most of the large animal vets — keep me fully occupied.'

Ginny exploded. 'Hell's bells, Colin! Have you been in touch with your solicitor? That sounds like a typical statement from a lawyer. A great yes and no statement all at the same time. Come out with it, man. Don't hide behind Letty.'

Colin took exception to this and drawing himself up to his full height, which was only 5ft 8in at best, he said, 'If I have listened to Letty it's no business of yours. She does have some very sound opinions.' He put his mug, still three-quarters full, down in the sink and quietly took his leave.

Ginny attacked her next victim. 'Seb, how about you? How do you stand?'

'I stand where I stood before. If the practice needs the income then we should go ahead, and I am willing to take my turn.'

'How dare you? I'm astounded.'

'You can be astounded as much as you like. That's my stance and I'm sticking to it.'

Ginny swung round to tackle Kate, who'd been hoping to melt away before she was challenged. Some of the old animosity which had flared between Ginny and Kate when Kate had been seeing practice as a student came between them and Kate, hating the way she'd been put on the front line, said, 'I shall react as I see fit.'

'That's called sitting on the fence and there's no place for that in this situation. Declare yourself.' Ginny glared at her and Kate shrivelled.

Seb, anxious on Kate's behalf, interrupted Ginny's attack. 'We don't have to answer to you, Ginny. In fact, we don't have to tell anyone at all besides Mungo how we feel, so just drop it, please. Did anyone see Miranda in reception this morning? She's a changed woman. I got a shock.'

Dodie, who'd been on the fringe of the argument, quickly picked up on Seb's change of subject.

'I saw her. Amazing improvement. Couldn't believe my eyes. Just goes to show what some outspoken words can do. I told her in no uncertain terms that she wasn't hygienic and she'd to smarten up her act, and she has done. Got a job, too.'

Ginny, furious that the heat had been taken out of her coffee-break opportunity to get everyone on her side, flung her mug in the sink with such anger that it smashed. She paused for a moment and then marched out.

The row rolled on in varying degrees all week and most of the staff were glad when it was Friday so that they could get the whole matter thrashed out. Frankly some of them wished Ginny would resign because they were sick of going over the subject again and again, and they'd taken to avoiding her if they could.

Miriam provided croissants with their tea and coffee for the meeting and by eight-thirty all the chairs in reception were occupied. Dodie and Joy stayed behind the reception desk so they could hear but were available to answer the phones if they rang.

273

Mungo, a sheaf of papers in his hands, walked masterfully in to stand behind the table provided for him and said in quiet tones, 'Hands up everyone who is willing to support me in this new venture.'

Ginny stood up before anyone could raise their hands. 'We have yet to decide whether we take the Hunt on or not. You speak as though it has already been decided, and I object to that. It has not.' She sat down and in her anger almost missed her chair. Only a quick reaction from Scott saved her from falling on the floor. Quiet sniggers could be heard but Mungo glared so angrily at them all that the sniggers quickly faded.

'I beg your pardon. Yes, I phrased that rather awkwardly. Of course we haven't agreed, so I'll begin again. Hands up everyone who would be willing to support us in this new proposition offered to us by the Barleybridge Hunt.'

Seb's hand went up first, followed by Dan's, Kate's, Valentine's, Rhodri's and, surprisingly, Scott's.

'With the addition of my name that makes seven of us willing to take it on, five of whom are partners, so their decision carries more weight. Well, that settles it.'

Scott stood up. 'Could I add something to this?' At a nod from Mungo he continued, 'I know Zoe, my wife, is totally opposed to this idea and I had to take her opposition into account. However, I have decided that with money getting tighter and costs going up, the practice cannot afford to ignore this offer. So I agree to assist whenever. Also, it will, one would imagine, bring in more business because of the prestige of being the Hunt vet. Zoe accepts my decision, albeit reluctantly.'

Ginny sprang to her feet trembling with anger. 'Money! What's money got to do with it? It's principles and morals that count, not money. I am resigning here and now, this minute. No notice. Sorry. But seeing as we've set on two qualified vets in the space of a few weeks I'm sure *my* absence won't be even noticed.' She glanced piercingly at both Seb and Kate. 'And as for you, Colin, you can add some of my clients to your list to make sure you're far too busy to help. Then you truly will be hiding your head in the sand — as usual.'

Ginny fled, and Miriam rapidly got to her feet and followed her into the staffroom.

A sigh of relief passed round reception. In some ways none of them regretted Ginny leaving. Was she actually going this minute? She must be very passionate in her opposition. In particular, Mungo, who'd found her a thorn in the flesh since the first week he'd employed her, felt bucked by her decision.

In the staffroom Miriam found Ginny in tears. 'Here, my dear, a tissue. Sit yourself down.'

Miriam waited for a few moments but still the tears flowed. 'Now see here, who made this decision? You or Gab?'

'I did.' The tears flowed even faster.

'If you're so upset about it tell me why you decided on this course of action when apparently you didn't really want to.'

'Because I'm too good at being cussed.'

Miriam had to laugh, but she smothered her mirth when Ginny looked like opening the floodgates again. 'I'm sure that's not the case. Now pull yourself together and tell me the truth.'

'Gab's told me I'm being foolish and I do believe he's right. I get a bee in my bonnet and . . . No, that's not it, I'll be frank. There's something about Mungo that gets my back up. Always has done since the first day. I've felt an element of superiority in him and I'm sure he's not aware of it, but there is and it angers me, and I don't know why. It's a question of a conflict of personalities. We just don't get on. I know I'm difficult — '

'No more than everyone else. Now stop this self-pity. You've made a decision so stand by it. You're a well-experienced vet with plenty of good qualities and you should get a job in no time at all. Is what I'm saying the truth? Are you? Have you?'

The real Ginny came to the fore. 'Of course I am. There's no reason why not, is there? Except . . . no, I'm being ridiculous. No, I won't say it.'

'Go on, there's no one here but me, and I won't tell anyone — you can rely on that.'

'Of course I can. Yes, you of all people I can rely on. When I lost my first fiancé in that car crash along with my parents, I decided that never as long as I lived would I have children, not if they couldn't be Simon's. Now, right out of the blue, I've found myself pregnant. With Gab, of course.'

Miriam's face lit up with pleasure at her news.

But she didn't get a chance to say how delighted she was because Ginny rushed on. 'Totally unexpectedly, as you might say. You see, I've kind of primed myself not to think about children. The shock, you know, of Simon's death did that. So I think being pregnant is what's made this Hunt business even more important to me, or else it's skewed my thinking and I've gone nuts. So it's not due for six months but I shall leave now, like I said, give myself time to adapt to this whole new path my life is taking.'

'I'm very pleased for you both. I'm sure, though I haven't spoken to him about it obviously, that Gab would be delighted to have children, coming from a large family as he does, and I'm also certain that they would be beautiful children with you both as parents.'

There was a long silence in the staffroom and Miriam prayed that no one would come in to interrupt them. No one did, and eventually Ginny said, 'Would I be any good as a mother?'

'It's something you grow into, believe me. After all, we're not born as mothers, are we? The miracle of loving a baby will happen in a flash, you know. It happens as we mature, and when the baby is the child of someone you love, well, that makes all the difference, believe me. That's a bit jumbled but I expect you get my drift.'

'I'm a complete fool, aren't I?'

'No, just a loving person who will keep being bossy, and it's got to *stop*.'

'You're right there. Gab would like it better if I stopped it. I don't know why I'm like it.'

'It's never too late to change, Ginny, especially now you've *acknowledged* you're bossy. Now, I have Perkins to attend to. He hasn't been out yet due to the meeting. Are you going home this very minute?'

'Yes, the sooner the better. I shan't miss the clients, honestly I shan't, although I should. But I am going to try not to be so bossy, especially to Gab.'

'Good idea. There's more ways of getting your own way than being bossy all the time.' Miriam reached across and kissed Ginny. 'Take care, my dear. There's lots of compassion in you; it just needs unwrapping. Love to you both.'

'Thanks.' For a brief moment Ginny hugged Miriam and then left.

$$\star \quad \star \quad \star$$

Back in reception Mungo continued the meeting.

'Right, so that's that,' he said firmly. 'So we can get on with organising and discussing how best to deal with the Hunt as and when. We've found someone to work afternoons in charge of the laboratory so that will be set up as soon as possible. Then we certainly will be a fully kitted-out practice with nothing, absolutely nothing — and no one — to stand in our way.' Mungo didn't mention Ginny by name but they all knew what he was thinking.

Kate felt quite sad that Ginny was leaving, because, although she was a pain in the whatsit, Kate never forgot that terrible tragedy she suffered just before her wedding when her parents and her fiancé had been killed in that road accident. There was no wonder she was bitter sometimes. Kate thought about Seb and how she would feel if anything happened to him. She felt sick at the thought.

Suddenly the first of the clients with appointments began arriving and the meeting had to close. They all went their various ways.

Mungo, hugely satisfied by the outcome of the meeting, didn't get a chance to speak to Miriam until he went upstairs for his lunch.

'Not got much time. I've two operations this afternoon. What is there for lunch?'

'Plenty — it's almost organised. The meeting went well. You must be pleased.'

Mungo sat down at the kitchen table, flicked the newspaper open and began reading. 'Yes.' He put the paper down and added, 'Ginny was a bit of a surprise, wasn't she? Thought she might at least work her notice, but oh no! Blasted awkward, right to the end.'

'Well, Mungo, she never has quite fitted in, has she?'

'Did you calm her down?'

'Here's your lunch. Mustard on the ham?'

'Yes, please.'

'Of course I did. She wept bitter tears.'

Mungo looked up in surprise. 'Bitter tears? Ginny?'

'Yes, she's not made of stone, you know.'

Disbelievingly Mungo answered, 'No?'

'No. If I tell you something it's strictly between ourselves.'

'Yes?'

'She's expecting a baby.'

Mungo choked on his sandwich, and needed a drink of water to sort him out.

'Is she, honestly? I can't believe it. Ginny with a baby? That's a laugh.'

'You've never got on with her, and I think you're being unkind.'

Mungo sobered up. 'You're right, I am unkind. But she is damned difficult. At least all the others are absolutely fine. Seb and Kate are brand-new, but they've slipped into their slots so easily. I spotted them gazing at one another during the meeting. Anything in it, do you think?'

Miriam poured more tea. 'Could be, could be.'

'I'm off. Got some X-rays to study before I begin. Complicated. Lovely lunch, thanks. Where is Perkins?'

'Asleep in his bed. He's been there ever since we got back from our walk, but not for much longer, I'm taking him out for his lunchtime walk shortly.'

'OK, see you soon. Kiss?'

Miriam cleared up then called Perkins. 'Walkies!' She'd got her warm jacket out and the woolly hat she wore on cold windy days and still he hadn't emerged. 'Come on, you silly old thing!'

His bed was by the radiator in the utility room so she went to find him. He was laid as he so often was, his head hanging over the edge of his bed with his chin resting on the floor. But his head when she touched it, was floppy and lifeless. Miriam's heart felt to burst with the horror of it. He'd passed away. Perkins had quietly died in his sleep. All alone.

If only she'd known she would have sat with him, but she hadn't and that brought her the greatest grief. Perkins, whom she'd deeply loved for all of his life, was alone when he died. Only that morning she'd sat out of the wind in a hollow behind some rocks up Beulah Bank Top and he'd come to sit beside her, leaning on her so companionably, so relaxed, and she'd stroked his head and said, 'You're a love, did you know that, Perkins? An absolute love.'

And he had been, right from the age of eight weeks old when they first brought him home. She'd chosen his name, and where it came from she didn't know, but it suited him, rather as though he were a superior butler. Now she had no companion upstairs in their flat, when Mungo was busy saving lives. How could she tell him what had happened?

She kissed the top of Perkins' head and slowly went downstairs to find someone who would understand. She knew Joy wasn't on duty but perhaps Dodie would listen.

She was in Joy's office doing paperwork and looked up at Miriam as she walked in.

'Why, Miriam! Whatever's the matter?'

'It's Perkins.'

'Oh, no!' She came round the end of the desk and put her arms around Miriam. 'Let me get someone, perhaps . . . '

'No, it's all too late. Much too late. I've got to tell Mungo, and I don't know how.' Miriam burst into tears and sat down in the spare chair, sobbing as if her heart would break.

Dodie had never seen Miriam like this before, she was usually so composed and contented, and she was at a loss to know what to do. 'Look, I'll see if anyone is free.' Kate was between clients and when Dodie explained what had apparently happened, Kate raced upstairs to the flat to see for herself.

But Miriam was only too right.

Kate fled downstairs to find Seb. 'It's Perkins. He's died, and Mungo doesn't know yet.'

'Oh! Poor old Perkins. Mungo's operating, isn't he?'

'Could you take over?'

'I don't know.'

'Go and see. Go on.'

So Seb went in to find Mungo and stood anxiously hovering.

Mungo looked up. 'Yes?'

Seb didn't reply.

'Come to watch?'

'No, just wondered if I could take over.'

'Help the old man out, is that it?' Mungo looked up and laughed.

'No-o-o. There's a crisis, you see.'

'Crisis?' Mungo straightened his back and, scalpel in hand, stared hard at Seb.

'Upstairs in the flat.'

'*Miriam*?'

'No, no. We think . . . it's . . . Perkins. Can I take over?'

'I've almost finished. Bunty will tell you . . . ' Mungo left the operating theatre at a run.

A minute later he walked out of the utility room at a snail's pace and found Miriam waiting, for she'd come upstairs when she heard him rushing past the office. Mungo opened his arms wide and hugged her. She clung to him, and neither of them could find the right words to say.

17

But whatever happened in their personal lives
the work of the practice had to go on as usual
and the open Saturday simply couldn't be
cancelled. Since Perkins had died Mungo had
been intolerable to work with, and everyone had
avoided him as much as possible, sympathetic
though they were to his sadness. It was Miriam
who'd faced the fact that Perkins had gone and
Mungo who could not.

Dodie and Joy had taken on the brunt of the
organisation and were both becoming more and
more harassed the closer Saturday came.

'It's the catering, Dodie. Do I ask Miriam or
not? Are we being fair expecting her to organise
the mince pies and all the usual stuff?'

'Let's face it, it is only a dog that's died . . . '

'Dodie! Honestly!'

'Well, it is. He's not a child that's had no
chance of a life . . . '

'Well, that's it, you see. They lost both their
children to a genetic disease when they were
quite young. So perhaps this death has affected
them more than it would have normally. Perkins
used to go out walking with the children and
Miriam, you see, so in a way it's brought it all
back.'

'Ah! I didn't know that. So they haven't tried
for any more then?'

'Too late now, anyway, but I don't think they

dared. What if it happened all over again? They couldn't, could they?'

Dodie apologised for being brusque. 'But the trouble is we still have to deal with this open day. We can't not have mince pies and mulled wine, can we? And we need napkins and tea for everyone, in case, and extra cups and saucers and wine glasses. Joy, you'll have to face up to it and *ask*.'

Joy opened her mouth to retort, 'All very well for you to say.' But she didn't. Instead, she marched upstairs to see Miriam and get everything sorted out. The whole idea was abhorrent to her but she chose to blurt it out rather than Miriam feel they were shutting her out.

'Miriam? Oh! There you are! Only me. Are you free?'

'Of course. Come in. Cup of tea?'

'Yes, please. Only if you're having one, that is. I don't want to be any trouble.'

Miriam smiled rather sadly at Joy. 'Glad of something to do and someone to talk to. Sit down. I have to say this . . . I'm sorry Mungo is being so difficult. No, no, don't pretend he isn't because I know he is. I've heard the shouting. I've tried but he won't be consoled.'

'Well, it'll pass, eventually.'

'Thank you for being so understanding. I'll pour the tea. I'm glad you came I was just about to sit down and have a cup myself. The days feel so empty. No walking to do, you know. I'd never realised how my days were punctuated by taking him out. I suppose if we lived in a house with a garden it wouldn't be so important to go out, would it?'

While Joy stirred her tea she had an idea. 'I've had a thought! We urgently need more office space, with the practice getting so big. If you don't like the idea, ignore me, but it would be wonderful if we had this flat for administration and you and Mungo went to live in a house. After all, that was what you always did until we had these premises built.'

'Joy! What a wonderful idea! Of course we could!'

'See! I do have bright ideas sometimes.'

'Then Mungo could have another dog. You see, we couldn't possibly have a young Airedale in a flat — it would go mad up here. Come to think of it, so would I!'

'I shan't say a word, I'll leave it all to you.'

'It's inspired. Truly inspired.'

Miriam sipped her tea with ideas spinning around in her head. Joy decided that now was her moment to mention the mince pies.

'I hope you don't mind me mentioning this but . . . have you thought, this Saturday is . . . well, it's the open day and I . . . '

'Oh! That's all in hand. It's what's saved my sanity this week, organising it all. I've made a list, bought everything, dug out the big pan I use for the mulled wine, collecting the fresh mince pies at nine a.m. Saturday . . . '

Joy leapt to her feet and flung her arms around Miriam. 'You absolute angel. I told Dodie I didn't know what on earth to do about it all.'

'Worry no more. I wouldn't let you down no

matter what had taken place. It'll do Mungo good to have to pull himself together, too.'

Joy put down her cup and stood up. 'Must go. Time for Dodie's tea break. She's been on duty since eight. Thank you, thank you. You're a brick. It's all been so upsetting for us. Remember how Perkins always knew when Mr Featherstonehough and Adolf, that thumping great Rottweiler he used to have, were due, and the fights they had? The old fire bucket with the water was always ready. Happy memories!' She leaned over and kissed Miriam's cheek. 'Looking forward to Saturday, eh?'

Miriam nodded but didn't answer.

★   ★   ★

Saturday dawned bright and sunny but icy cold, so Joy turned up the heating and the clients arriving for their morning appointments roasted in reception but were glad they did.

Every member of staff had their own designated duties and Kate, Seb and Dan were delighted to find themselves completely in charge of guiding people around the practice, explaining the use of the different areas and the equipment that had become more high tech as the years went by. Ginny, of course, having left in such an abrupt manner, was not involved. In some ways Kate quite missed her busy presence, then decided she didn't because she'd only have been dictating to the three of them what to say.

The door to the drugs store was the stable-door type so the visitors could see all the drugs but had no access to them apart from standing at the door and looking through the top half. Colin had decided he'd stand in the drugs store and talk about drugs, old and new, to anyone who hesitated even for a moment. He'd done a great deal of thinking about what he should say and with Letty's help had planned a short talk to highlight the most important drugs. He'd even found some old packaging buried away in his memorabilia cupboard at home and dug them out to illustrate the huge changes there had been in prescriptions, along with some appallingly antique tubing and whatnots that had been in use some fifty years ago when his own father was a vet.

Scott was organising the parking, but by three o'clock he'd almost abandoned the whole idea because the car park was packed and he had begun refusing drivers entrance to the premises and asking them to park out in the road. The number of children arriving caused him anxiety, too, as they would wander off from their parents and get lost amongst the cars.

What fascinated everyone was the window in the rear corridor which gave people a view of the main operating room where Mungo, completely unaware of the people peering through the window, was working on Declan Tattersall's huge Irish wolf hound that had wandered away from the farm while Declan's back was turned and been accidentally shot by someone shooting rabbits. It was his left hip that had been hit and the Tattersall family had gone into a state of mass grief over the incident. Consequently, all seven children and Declan were camping out in the car park in their minibus awaiting news. One or two visitors went green at the sight of Mungo's protective gloves covered in blood and had to be revived with cups of tea. The two Sarahs were in charge of serving wine, mince pies and tea.

The 'knick-knack' area, which Dan had introduced against such strong opposition, did a brisk trade, partly due to Miriam having inspired ideas by continually sourcing new toys on the internet and any large pet shops. She always kept in mind the strong opposition to the 'knick-knack' shelves and was determined to keep them popular just to prove how right the decision had been.

By the time Kate had seen three groups of visitors round the building she was gasping for a mince pie and a glass of mulled wine. To her surprise she found Seb already wolfing mince pies.

'What's this? You're supposed to be working, Seb!'

'Needed a break. Here, look, a mince pie for you and I've saved a glass of the wine in case they ran out before you got here.'

'Seb?'

'Mmm?' he answered, spraying mince pie crumbs into the air. 'Sorry!'

'Mia's right, you don't feed yourself properly!'

'I do, but I love home baking. I just never get round to it myself. Tell you what, Kate, I wish my family lived nearer, then I could take you to see them.'

'So do I. I'd like to meet your mum, dad and brother.'

'They're all supposed to be coming down for a few days in the New Year. Would you like to meet them then?'

Kate studied his face and saw how important it was to him. 'OK. But for now I'm just a friend as far as they are concerned.'

Slightly disappointed by her response he answered, 'Of course.' He paused. 'Are you free tonight?'

Kate nodded.

'Meal first?'

Kate nodded. 'Yes, although you won't want much feeding after three mince pies.'

'Actually it's four, but don't let on.'

'Seb, that is disgusting. I say, shall we skip a restaurant meal and have fish and chips out of a bag sitting in the car? I'd like that.'

Seb studied her face, preferring to treat her to a good meal but not at the Italian restaurant again in case they ever said something about Maggie. 'That's fine. We could park part-way up Beulah Bank Top and watch the stars while we eat. I don't fancy those ghastly fizzy drinks they sell in the fish and chip shop. How about if I get a bottle of wine and borrow two glasses from the staffroom?'

'Wonderful! There's Dan waving. Got to go. That's a lovely idea, Seb.'

She'd no sooner disappeared than in walked Maggie.

He knew she might be home this weekend but it had gone completely out of his mind. She looked different, smarter and more sophisticated, with her hair shorter and not sticking out in a cloud. London had obviously changed her.

She weaved her way towards him between the visitors and kissed him without further ado. The two Sarahs, heads together behind the mulled wine pan, had been listening to Seb and Kate's plans for the evening and could be heard tut-tutting.

'Seb! How lovely to see you! It seems ages. Are you free?'

'Just for a few minutes, I've got to relieve Dan in a little while as I'm supposed to be doing guided tours.'

The two Sarahs decided to join in the fun. 'Wine, Maggie? A mince pie?'

'That would be lovely. I missed lunch.'

'How's the TV series going? It must be exciting!'

'We've three more weeks of rehearsals and filming, then there's a break for Christmas and New Year. It's going really well. The producer is thrilled with it, which is a blessing, believe me.' She turned to look at the crowd. 'I must say, it's much busier than I thought it would be. The decorations are beautiful. Did the two of you do them? They're very artistic.'

'No, we don't do them. A bit of holly behind the pictures, mistletoe over the door, and a few balloons, that's more us. No, it's Miriam and Kate who do it each year. Kate does the design and buys some new baubles or whatever, and Miriam follows her directions. She's very talented, is our Kate, isn't she, Seb?'

'She is.' Seb began to feel very awkward as he sensed the way the conversation was leading, and he was going to be in a fix tonight because Maggie would expect ... 'Kate is our newest vet,' he went on. 'She worked here for a while before she went to veterinary college, before my time.'

He'd under-estimated Maggie if he thought he was going to get away with this subterfuge, inferring that Kate had no place in his life. She was too astute for that and one look at the two Sarahs was enough to make her realise that this weekend things were not to be as she'd visualised.

Sarah Cockroft said, 'Dan's signalling to you, Seb.'

'So he is. Sorry, Maggie, got to go. Do you want a tour? You can come with me now, if you like?'

'I'll finish my wine and have another mince pie, then I'll catch you up. You go on.'

Maggie turned her back on Seb so he wouldn't see the disappointment she felt. The two Sarahs were busy again which gave Maggie a chance to take another mince pie without them thinking she was greedy. Which she did and then stood with her back to them, apparently watching the crowd. At this very moment she had to face the fact that the twelve years there was between her and Seb had suddenly become an issue.

She remembered seeing Kate at the dinner at The George but they hadn't really spoken so she'd wait her chance and see for herself. The wonderful evening with Seb she'd promised herself was not to be, she could see that. Never the less, she'd see Kate first and feel the vibes between them before she finally gave up hope. Perhaps Kate only needed brushing aside and Seb would be hers all over again. Her heart thumped as she saw Kate shepherding a group of visitors straight towards her. There was something rather stunning about her, a grace and a charm not many girls her age possessed. She could see now the possibility of she and Seb being fascinated by each other.

Despite the flood of visitors needing serving, one of the Sarah's, fancying spicing up the afternoon with a bit of gossip, said, 'Maggie, this is Kate who's done the decorations.'

The other Sarah said between ladling mulled wine, 'Maggie's been admiring the decorations. We told her they were your brain child.'

Kate blushed slightly. 'Thank you. I'm afraid I don't know your name, sorry. I know we were both at Mungo's dinner.'

Maggie was about to say 'I'm a friend of Seb's', but she rapidly changed that to, 'Seb's been dealing with some alpacas belonging to my parents so I thought I'd come and see the hub of his empire.'

Sarah Cockroft reported that Maggie was an actress.

Kate, being the well-mannered person she was, genuinely showed interest, turning to Maggie to ask what she was working on right now.

They chatted together for a few minutes and

while they were doing so Maggie knew at the very bottom of her heart she'd never be anything other than a client's daughter to Seb, not now he'd met Kate; they were made for each other.

Maggie put down her half-empty glass of mulled wine, and her paper plate with its half-eaten mince pie in the bin provided, and said hastily, 'Must go. Busy, busy. You know how it is.'

Kate was disappointed. 'Oh! But I haven't shown you round. There's an operation in progress to watch — '

'Very kind, Kate, but I must go. Things to do. Tell Seb I'll be in touch when I get back to London.'

'Of course I will. Nice to have met you.' Kate reached out to shake hands and, as Maggie took hold of Kate's hand, she knew she was right about her. The girl was just the one for Seb. Something in her forthrightness, in the good-heartedness that shone from her communicated itself to Maggie, and she felt her own heart throb with a sharp pain.

She left Kate and dashed out into the car park, head down, wishing she'd never come and then she wouldn't have known for certain.

*　*　*

Seb remembered a bottle of wine he had in the fridge back at the flat so when the crowds began thinning out, he drove home and picked up the wine, a kitchen roll to do duty as napkins, and two glasses. He paused for a moment to look at himself in the mirror to gauge if he needed to rinse his face before going back to pick up Kate, but the image he saw in the mirror was Maggie's. The new Maggie, with the smart clothes and the restrained hair. The new Maggie whom he knew had sensed things were not as they had been. And they weren't. There was still a corner of his heart holding Maggie very dear, but for him it was Kate now. Had Maggie realised this? After all, the two Sarahs told him they'd met, so she may well have done. She was very astute where emotions were concerned.

Seb washed his face, brushed his hair, checked his wallet for money for the fish and chip shop, and headed back to pick up Kate.

She was waiting for him in reception, well wrapped up and looking fabulous. Her cheery red beret, matching scarf and tweed coat with a small red fleck in it enhanced her good looks, and he could have taken her in his arms and kissed her then and there. But he didn't because Dan, Mungo and Scott were there with Colin hovering on the fringe of the group.

'It's been a good afternoon, hasn't it?' he said. 'Everyone seems to have enjoyed themselves.'

Mungo agreed. 'Never been better, I couldn't believe the crowds. All good for business.' He rubbed his hands together and they all laughed. 'We're going from strength to strength. I'm delighted and thank you all for the hard work you've put in. Bit of a log jam outside the drugs store with Colin and his ghastly old instruments, but they loved it, didn't they?'

Dan asked him how his operation had gone.

'Very well indeed. He's sleeping it off as we speak, though we couldn't put him in a cage to recover. He's just too blinking big. We should have drawn the curtains over that window but when I saw how pleased people were to be witnessing an operation I decided to leave them open. Bunty was delighted we were so popular.'

'You'll have to plan to do an operation next time, seeing it was such a success!'

'Good thinking, Scott! Yes. Thanks, anyway, all of you.'

Seb and Kate bought their fish and chips in the shop Seb had patronised that first week he came to Barleybridge, and drove quickly up to Beulah Bank Top to park.

'I asked for salt and vinegar — is that OK for you?'

'Shows how little we know about each other.'

'We've got all the time in the world to learn.'

Kate turned to look at him. 'Yes, we have. Plenty of time.'

They ate in silence. The only words they exchanged were when Seb asked her if she wanted more wine.

'Yes, please, although I shan't be able to drive home for at least an hour. I'm hopeless with alcohol. One glass and I'm away; two glasses and I don't know what I'm doing.'

'Well, we can sit here as long as you like, or I could drive you home.'

'Do you mind sitting here?'

'With you? No, I don't mind.'

'I can't see any stars, can you?'

They both peered through the windscreen.

Seb faked the sight of a star. 'There's just one I can see. Look, over my side.'

Kate bent across Seb to see and found the back of her neck being kissed.

'There wasn't one actually, but I did fancy a kiss,' he said.

She gave him a polite peck. 'That's all you're going to get, for now.'

'That's fine by me.'

'Seb?'

'Yes.'

'Seb, in the future . . . if you and I have one . . . you remember little Mrs Nicholls with Tatty? Well, when she was sitting with Tatty while he waited for his operation, she showed me some photos of where she lives, place called Turnham something or other, odd sort of word, and I thought it absolutely perfect. If I didn't live here I'd live there for sure. There's a village green with white thatched cottages all round it, a pond and, believe it or not, *stocks*. They don't even have street lighting. It's amazing, isn't it? Would you like living in such a countryfied sort of place? I know I would.'

'I think perhaps I would. With you, that is. It sounds idyllic.' He took hold of her hand and kissed it, grateful she was for the moment seeing the future as something they would be sharing.

'Good. I'll bear that in mind then.'

Kate paused for a minute, looking out of the window as though she were thinking about them together in Turnham whatever. Then she turned back to him. 'I met Maggie again this afternoon. Tell me about her.'

Seb sat for a moment contemplating her question, worrying about his answer. Eventually he said, 'We were very close and very happy for a time, but she's twelve years older than me, although she didn't seem like it. She's a very generous person, very loving, and at the time I needed her. Then she got this fabulous offer to play the lead in a TV series, and it was what she'd wanted all her life. But for two pins she'd have turned it down and stayed in Barleybridge. With me.'

Kate couldn't help but show her surprise. 'As serious as that!'

'I wanted her to stay, but not at the price she would have to pay, knowing for the rest of her life that she'd turned down the chance of a lifetime.'

'So you *persuaded* her to go?'

'She didn't need much persuading. I saw there was no alternative. It hurt me to say it, but I said she had to go before we got too serious about each other, and us breaking up had become too painful to bear.'

'Oh, Seb. I guessed there was something there between the two of you. She just left as though . . . she'd no alternative but to go.'

'But from today . . . seeing her . . . it's all very different. She's still a generous person for whom I have the greatest respect, but I've met this other girl, you see, who's stolen me away and I can't escape. I'm positively chained to her, but I don't mind. She fills my heart and my mind and I want her for ever. So there it is.'

He switched on the light over the windscreen.

'But you know that, don't you?'

Kate nodded. 'Yes, I do. But not yet. I'm not ready, you see. I can't commit until I'm absolutely sure. Damn my blasted mother for doing what she did to me. You think you don't care, that it doesn't affect you, then it comes out of the woodwork and ruins everything. What does it make me? Shall I be just as careless of someone I love? That's the worry.'

'Perhaps the difference is she wasn't capable of loving anyone but herself so leaving you didn't break her heart. But it doesn't mean *you* won't ever love someone completely, so . . . when you do, you wouldn't do what she did.'

'I'll think about that.' Then Kate began to laugh, peal after peal of laughter, and simply couldn't stop. Finally she did have to stop because she got a stitch.

'Kate! Kate! What's so funny?'

'You sound just like an agony aunt!'

For a moment Seb felt cross because he'd tried so hard to make sure she didn't feel too badly about herself and here she was . . . then he began to laugh, too, and the two of them laughed together, uproariously, absolutely unable to control themselves.

Then Seb took her in his arms and stopped her laughing with a kiss, and she kissed him back.

We do hope that you have enjoyed reading this large print book.

Did you know that all of our titles are available for purchase?

We publish a wide range of high quality large print books including:
Romances, Mysteries, Classics
General Fiction
Non Fiction and Westerns

Special interest titles available in large print are:
The Little Oxford Dictionary
Music Book
Song Book
Hymn Book
Service Book

Also available from us courtesy of Oxford University Press:
Young Readers' Dictionary
(large print edition)
Young Readers' Thesaurus
(large print edition)

For further information or a free brochure, please contact us at:
Ulverscroft Large Print Books Ltd.,
The Green, Bradgate Road, Anstey,
Leicester, LE7 7FU, England.
Tel: (00 44) 0116 236 4325
Fax: (00 44) 0116 234 0205